PRAISE FOR JULIA GRICE

"Readers will find the story hard to put down. Love, hate, and a mother's determination to save her daughter make for a tense story."

—*The Midwest Book Review* on *The Cutting Hours*

"Even the most jaded suspense fan will keep turning the pages."

—*The West Coast Review of Books* on *Suspicion*

"Nail-biter mater material from first page to last. Julia Grice hooks you with her characters and then takes you along on their dark and dangerous journey. A first-rate suspense novel."

—Ed Gorman, *Mystery Scene* on *The Cutting Hours*

"Julia Grice is a writer of marrow-freezing suspense."

—Loren D. Estleman

"A mystery-romance that approximates, in its final chapters, the tooth-grinding suspense of *The Silence of the Lambs*."

—Atlanta *Journal-Constitution* on *Suspicion*

"This mystery thriller uncoils as a raw and potent story... a chilling and believable climax."

—*Publishers Weekly* on *The Cutting Hours*

Other books by Julia Grice

The Cutting Hours
Jagged Light
Suspicion
Tender Prey

Pretty Babies

Julia Grice

A TOM DOHERTY ASSOCIATES BOOK
NEW YORK

This is a work of fiction. All the characters and events portrayed in this book are fictitious, and any resemblance to real people or events is purely coincidental.

PRETTY BABIES

Copyright © 1994 by Julia Grice

Cover art by Doug Fornuff Studios, Inc.

A Forge Book
Published by Tom Doherty Associates, Inc.
175 Fifth Avenue
New York, NY 10010

Forge® is a registered trademark of Tom Doherty Associates, Inc.

ISBN: 0-812-51935-3
Library of Congress Catalog Card Number: 94-7021

First edition: August 1994
First mass market edition: December 1995

Printed in the United States of America

0 9 8 7 6 5 4 3 2 1

Since this book concerns a reprehensible sort of crime, I would like to emphasize that *all* of the characters in this book are absolutely fictitious. I did not use any parts or portions of any real persons, and Madisonia College, as well as the town of Madisonia, is also completely fictional. If by some coincidence any of the characters do resemble real-life individuals, it was pure accident and not deliberately intended.

I would like to thank my bright, warm, and intelligent editor, Melissa Ann Singer, for all her considerable help and encouragement, and my husband, Richard, for his love. His emotional support was all I could ever want. Thanks also to Margaret Duda, Jean and Will Haughey, Don and Lorraine de Baptiste, Roni Tripodi, the Detroit Women Writers, and, of course, my wonderful sons, Mike and Andy Grice.

IN THE BEGINNING

THE MAN PLACED the videotape in the VCR, grabbed the remote, then went to sit down in the easy chair that faced the TV set. His heart was pounding just a shade fast. This was his most carefully guarded secret. No one knew about this, and of course, that was how it had to be.

The girl who appeared on the screen was young, only eleven years old. Her hips were still narrow, her chest undeveloped. She wore her silky blond hair flowing straight down over her shoulders. Her eyes were huge, starred with feathery lashes, and he'd helped her to put a little mascara on her lashes, along with a little Candy Apple lipstick for her mouth. He liked effects like that.

"No . . . no . . . that's too far, Michele; go back a few feet, so the camcorder can focus." That was his own voice, giving her camera instructions.

They all had to be given instructions. They were too young to know what to do unless he told them. He got around their inhibitions in several ways. First, he showed them pictures of other girls, doing the things he wanted them to do. Once they saw a picture, they would begin to get it, to see that it was all right, and they'd work to please him.

Second, and of course this was very, very important, he always started gradually. He never just— well, he was never rough. He wooed them as cautiously as a woman trying to hand-feed a squirrel.

"Now, honey, I just want to take a few moving shots of you," his own off-camera voice said soothingly. "Just walk around. Move your hips a little. I know the van is small. . . . Yes . . . oh, you're so pretty, so sexy. You're going to make a wonderful model."

The girl smiled at him. Her smile was dazzlingly pretty. Even now, more than a year later, he felt his scrotum tighten.

She had been so beautiful.

1

THE HEAVY MICHIGAN sky had darkened to a nasty shade of pewter, holding in its depths the threat of a pre-Thanksgiving snowstorm. Vivian Clavell accelerated her two-year-old Toyota Camry, turning onto the working-class street in Auburn Hills, a suburb north of Bloomfield Hills, near Pontiac. Fifty-year-old bungalows lined the street, most with two or three older cars parked in the driveway.

Another child, another heartbreaking story, she thought. But today's case, she thought jubilantly, was going to have a happy ending. She'd been working for more than four months, and now she'd located the perfect home, the ideal setting. In fact, a serendipitous setting. Vivian was proud of herself and could hardly wait to see the child's face when she arrived at her new home.

Dani Lynn McVie was a thirteen-year-old girl with a background of stark ugliness. Her cocaine-addicted mother, a hooker in Detroit, had tried to sell Dani into prostitution. Unfortunately, the mother had attempted to make this sale to an undercover police officer. This week, Vivian had completed the paperwork on the adoptive placement. Today she was scheduled to drive the girl to her new parents, two college professors living in Madisonia, a college town about two-and-a-half hours away.

Professors, Vivian congratulated herself again. The father was chairman of the history department, and the mother taught English courses and was a children's book author. *Way to go.*

She slowed her Camry, searching for the house of the temporary foster family. There—there it was. Number 732, a bungalow bigger and neater than the others, with four bicycles, covered with plastic, chained to a pipe alongside the driveway.

Vivian pulled into the driveway behind a gray Chevy van dappled with brown rust spots. In the front window of the house she saw a flash of motion. A second later, a girl came exploding out of the door, skidding across the porch and down the steps.

"Mrs. social worker lady, Mrs. Vivian, is it you? Are you here?"

Vivian couldn't help smiling. She had to admit it; she'd fallen in love with Dani the first time she saw her. Dani McVie was startlingly pretty. Despite her extreme thinness and immature, prepubescent figure, she projected a hoyden beauty. Her hair was an enormous harum-scarum, untidy frizz of red, her freckles a dash of cinnamon. Her blue eyes blazed. She seemed almost lost in a huge, baggy Detroit Pistons sweatshirt and a pair of loose-fitting jeans, both of which emphasized her storky gawkiness.

But most striking of all was the sensation of enormous energy that almost caromed from the girl. "She fills the air with her personality," one poetic welfare worker had recorded in Dani's fat case file. And Vivian had to concur. Dani had such possibilities, which the prospective adoptive parents had also seen.

"Mrs. Vivian, we're not going *yet*, are we? I can say good-bye, can't I?" The plea was urgent, accompanied by begging motions.

"Why, Dani, of course you can say good-bye to Mrs. Zagat, and anyone else you'd like to say good-bye to."

A fat woman of about thirty-five appeared on the porch, carrying a canvas duffel bag. Clinging to the temporary foster mother's leg was a chubby moppet. This was Mrs. Zagat's own adopted two-year-old son, Jimmy, who was the pet of the foster home.

"Oh, Jimbo." Dani squatted down to the child's level. "Jimbo, I got you M&M's. Red and orange and brown. Do you want some?"

The baby boy nodded shyly.

"She really loves Jimmy," said Mrs. Zagat over Dani's shoulder to Vivian. "She just loves that little boy to death. She'd spoil him if I let her. She's gonna miss him."

"I'm gonna miss him," repeated Dani, nuzzling the little boy as she tried to tuck M&M's into his pockets. Her voice had gone quivery. "Gonna miss him so-o-o-o-o much."

Vivian, who had seen hundreds of such partings, sensed the emotional tides about to erupt over them. "I think we'd better get started," she said hastily. "Dani, say good-bye to Mrs. Zagat now, and then we'll get in the car."

Dani rose, her face going white. Her freckles stood out, and even her lips seemed drained of color.

"Dani," said Mrs. Zagat.

Suddenly the girl turned and began running toward Vivian's car. She jerked open the passenger door and hurled herself into the front seat. Slamming the door, she sat staring straight ahead, her profile grim.

"Uh-oh," said Mrs. Zagat, handing Vivian the girl's bag. "Some kids do have trouble leaving. I just hope those new people—I hope they . . ." She gave a rich chuckle. "Well, our Dani will win them over. She can be a charmer when she wants. Oh, when are you retiring, Vivian? Didn't I hear you're going to take early retirement?"

Vivian glanced toward the car. She saw that Dani was still glaring straight ahead. She looked lost and scared.

"I was considering it. But I love these kids so much I don't think I can do it. And I think we'd better be leaving before she—"

Dani reached over and banged on the car horn. The sound blasted through the neighborhood, setting off a chain reaction of dog barks. The girl pumped the horn, BANGBANGBANG, screeching out repeated horn blasts, demanding attention.

The sky had begun to tip out its contents. Snow blew against the windshield, the flakes still tiny and compacted. Vivian didn't think the driving would be too bad for a while yet.

Dani didn't speak for the first eight miles, nor did she cry.

Vivian turned south on Opdyke Road, heading toward southbound Telegraph, which would take her to I-696. The teenager sat huddled in her pink ski jacket, which was too big for her, probably from Mrs. Zagat's closet, and had a soda stain on the hem. Her arms were folded across her chest, her face hidden by a frizz of carrot color. She looked more like an angry eleven-year-old than a girl just turned thirteen.

"I *hate* you," Dani muttered as they merged onto the expressway.

"You really enjoyed living with the Zagats, didn't you?" Vivian said patiently, settling down to the speed limit.

"I *hated* them! I hate you! I hate everybody. And I'm gonna hate this new place. Professors! The people are going to suck eggs. They're low-down dirty turdies and I'm not even going to try to like them."

This was a 180-degree turn from what Dani had said only two weeks previously, when she had spent the day at Greenfield Village with the Lockwoods and had said over and over that she adored them. But given her toxic background, which included sexual abuse, beatings, and whippings, Vivian knew such mood swings were to be expected.

"Dani is terrified of rejection," the psychologist, Dr. Loewe, had written. "She uses her considerable brightness to manipulate others to fulfill her needs. Her tendency to prevaricate and exaggerate may well subside under the security of patient foster parents."

"It takes time to get used to a new home, new people," Vivian said warmly. "Everyone feels a little strange, right at first."

"*I* don't have the time. *I'm* gonna be a dancer, see? I'm gonna write in a letter and be on 'Star Search' and Ed McMahon's gonna see me. I'm gonna be on videos and everything, and I'm gonna make a video, see, and it's gonna be on MTV."

"You'd like to be a dancer sometime?" Vivian asked.

"No, I'm *gonna* be one!"

The exaggerations had been mentioned by nearly every caseworker, psychologist, and teacher who'd recorded entries in Dani's six-inch-thick case file. Some had used crueler words, like "lying" and "compulsive lying." There was a sad pathos to Dani's lies. It was as if, single-handedly, she was trying to create glow and excitement in a life that hitherto had contained little but poverty and hurt.

Dani reached for the car radio and, without permission, switched it on. Rock music jumped into the car, herky-jerking from station to station, punctuated by bursts of static.

Finally Dani found some heavy metal; at least, that was what Vivian thought it was, full of pounding bass rhythms. The girl sat leaning forward, flipping the zipper pull on her jacket to the rhythm. Flip. Flip.

"I wonder what my ma is doing right now," Dani suddenly remarked. "I wonder is she with a trick? You know . . . screwing." She glanced at Vivian as if to register her shock.

Vivian carefully didn't react. "You're thinking of your mother right now?"

"Yeah. . . . She got a pimp, a black pimp named Harley. He has this Harley-Davidson motorcycle he rides sometimes. That's how he got his name, see? I rode on it one time and then he let me drive it, and *I* steered it all alone."

Vivian doubted that very much.

For the next fifteen minutes, Dani regaled Vivian with a long, involved story of being left in their apartment by herself for a week with no food because her mother was vacationing in Vegas with a "trick." Dani had walked to a Coney Island restaurant and gone in and ordered a full meal, then exited with a family group, slipping past the cashier without paying.

"I had to wait for a family that was white, see, 'cause they wouldn'ta believed it if I'd stuck with a black family, know what I mean?"

Dani was a survivor. Vivian hoped the Lockwoods would be patient with her. But they had seemed wonderful people, willing to give Dani the extra time she would need to adjust.

As they left the metro Detroit area, the snowflakes grew fatter. But they only dusted the ground, not really sticking to the surface of the road. Vivian began telling Dani about being adopted herself.

"You mean . . . *you* were adopted?" Dani stared at her.

"That's right. But I didn't find out until I was fourteen years old. Believe me, Dani, I know how it feels because I've been there."

"Did your mother ever come and find you? Your real mother, I mean?"

"No," said Vivian. "But I didn't really mind because my adoptive mother was so lovely, and she cared so much."

Dani seemed to tense as the town of Madisonia came into view. There were some old redbrick factories built next to a river, then a tiny downtown with Victorian boutiques and a big white water tower on which the letters TKE FOREVER had been painted in uneven red spray paint. Then finally the sprawling college buildings, built of gracious old brick and covered with ivy, now brown because it was November.

"Well, this is the campus," said Vivian.

"Campus, like a camp?" inquired Dani, trying to

sound confident. "Ha, ha, I didn't mean that. I know what a campus is; it's where college kids go."

Vivian made her voice very enthusiastic. "That's right, Dani, and you're going to be living within two blocks of the library and the college swimming pool, which you'll be able to use every day if you want. Won't that be fun? This college is over two hundred years old. A former Michigan governor went here."

Dani nodded, sinking back in her seat.

"I hope I'm gonna like them," she muttered. "I mean, I *hope* I'm gonna, I *hope . . .*" Her voice trailed off as they pulled up in front of the Lockwood house, a magnificent three-story Victorian structure with a mansard roof, pale yellow siding, and beautifully crafted white gingerbread. An etched-glass window decorated the front door, scrolled with intricate roses and fleurs-de-lis.

"Isn't the house pretty?" said Vivian. "It's Victorian, Dani. That means it was built over a hundred years ago, when Queen Victoria was still alive."

"Does it have bathrooms?"

Vivian looked at the apprehensive girl beside her. "Of course. In fact, you'll have one all to yourself. Mrs. Lockwood—you'll call her Maureen—said they've even put up new wallpaper, especially for you."

Dani fidgeted with her jacket zipper. Her voice was hollow. "What if these people only keep me for a couple of days and then they decide they don't like me? I mean it takes a long time for the adoption to be final, right? Will they take the wallpaper down then?"

Vivian reached over and gave the girl a sympathetic squeeze. "They'll like you. It's going to be *your* wallpaper, Dani. They like you very, very much.

They've already told me that. Out of all the kids we had available to place, they asked especially for you."

They started up the front walk, Vivian herding a reluctant Dani in front of her, carrying the bag herself. But before they could ring, a woman pulled open the door. Joy crossed her face like a flash of light.

"Dani!"

"Hi," said Dani. Her face was red, too.

Vivian felt a clutch of emotion squeeze her windpipe. She'd watched hundreds of mothers meet their new children; she'd restored kidnapped infants to sobbing mothers; she'd once reunited a family of eight brothers and sisters. But still such scenes choked her up, and she knew it was the reason she continued in the job, and why she probably wouldn't retire until she was seventy.

"Oh, Dani." Maureen Lockwood fluttered her hands, rubbing them down the side seams of a fashionable maternity top sewn with soutache embroidery. She was forty-two years old, tiny and dark-haired. Ordinarily the agency did not place children in homes where there was a pregnancy, but Vivian had pleaded with Melva Bernstein, her superior at the agency, to make an exception. Dani adored babies and the new baby would make her adjustment much easier. Also, families like the Lockwoods were so rare. Bonner, whose Ph.D. had been awarded by a prestigious university, had published several scholarly books and hundreds of articles on his favorite subject, the Korean War. He was frequently called upon to give talks all over the country. Maureen's first book for young readers had been nominated for a Caldecott Award.

"Well!" Maureen said brightly. She rushed forward and gave Dani a hug, pulling the girl against her taut, seven-months stomach. "We wondered if you were going to be delayed in this snow. . . . Well, obviously you haven't been. Are you hungry? I've made you a little snack, just some cheesie squares—those are little sandwiches with the crusts cut off—and some chocolate chip cookies. I'll have to call Bonner. He's upstairs working; he has his office on the attic level. He's writing a book about Korea, you know. Very dull . . . but he doesn't think so."

Maureen's heightened emotion was making her gush. And with every word she blurted, Dani became more silent, more shy. She huddled closer to Vivian.

"Dani," prodded Vivian gently. "Let's go in the house now."

"Oh," said Maureen, red spots appearing in both of her cheeks. "Oh, I'm just so happy today. Good Lord, I forgot to ask to take your jackets."

Maureen took Dani's shabby pink jacket, piled Vivian's coat on top of it, and, carrying both, bustled ahead of them. The pregnancy made her seem a tiny but strangely bulbous figure, the effect intensified by the high heels she wore on her dainty size three feet.

"*She's* got a cake in the oven," whispered Dani, nudging Vivian.

For an instant, Vivian was startled. "You mean she's pregnant. She's expecting a baby. We already knew that," she whispered back, deciding that the proper terms had better be explained, and quickly.

"But she's got a—"

"We'll talk about that later," said Vivian hastily.

"I've got the table all set in the solarium," announced Maureen, hanging the coats in a huge closet that was wallpapered on the interior in huge cabbage roses. At least three umbrellas hung on hooks, one with a handle in the shape of a duck. Dani stared incredulously at the sight.

"Oh, and I forgot to tell you," Maureen went on. "Bonner has bought a new Ski Doo snowmobile."

"A *snow*mobile?" Dani croaked. She seemed stunned by this news.

"He thought you might like to go snowmobiling, if we get any good snow this winter. We've had such weird winters recently, hardly any snow compared to the way it used to be when I was a girl."

Maureen ushered them past rooms furnished in antiques that smelled gently of lemon oil and beeswax and floors that glowed with Oriental rugs. Shelves held collections of porcelain animals, of characters by Beatrix Potter and others. The solarium was suffused with winter light from windows on three sides. Plants were everywhere, on stands, on the floor, and hanging from the ceiling, a jungle of green. It was a beautiful, warm setting, like a magazine illustration.

Dani hung back, plucking at Vivian's sleeve, commenting on the various items they passed.

"Is she for real? This place is rich. Man, is this a dream or something? Fay had a trick once, this guy—"

"Hon, we can talk about that later," said Vivian, afraid that Dani was going to launch into another one of her graphic stories about her mother. Of course, Maureen and Bonner had been fully apprised of Dani's background, but there was no sense emphasizing it now, when the bonding process was still in beginning stages.

The table, spread with spiderwebby antique lace over a green cloth, was undeniably elegant. The

plates, arranged with exquisitely cut finger sandwiches and carrot curls, appeared to be real English
bone china. Vivian almost envied Dani this life. She
was going to have all the advantages. A four-year
education here at Madisonia was virtually guaran-
teed; it was one of the faculty salary perks, the Lockwoods had said on their application. Or Dani might
choose any other college in the country, assuming
her grades were good enough. The Lockwoods were
willing to send her anywhere, even Harvard. How
many girls from the tough Woodward/Eight Mile
area of Detroit ever got this fabulous opportunity?

There was the sound of footsteps on tile, and a
man entered the room. He paused in the doorway,
his eyes riveted on Dani. Bonner Lockwood was
about fifty, with a full head of silvery hair, the type of
ruddy, handsome man who is called a "silver fox."
His slight paunch only made him seem more distin-
guished, and the tweedy sport coat he wore aug-
mented that impression.

"She's here!" cried Maureen.

"I see that." Bonner strode toward them, exuding
energy, like a college president about to meet with
some alumni he wants to woo. In his hands he carried a deck of Bicycle cards.

"Why, hello, beautiful Dani," he said jovially, lifting both hands and flashing the deck of cards open
in a perfect arc.

Through their "snack," which was really a full lunch,
complete with cookies from the campus bakery,
Bonner kept them entertained with stories about his
interest in magic tricks, his new snowmobile, and
various interesting things to do in Madisonia, which

boasted two fudge factories and a Lippizaner horse farm, in addition to the college of three thousand students.

Dani sank down on the base of her spine, squirming in her chair as she tried to copy the exact way that Maureen and Bonner ate their sandwiches, so that she would not make any mistakes. She munched cautiously on her carrot, hoping the noise wasn't too loud. She kept burping up pizza from the lunch Vivian had bought her on the way, at Pizza Hut.

She just couldn't believe it. A snowmobile! She didn't know *anyone* who had one. In fact, people in Detroit where she lived were lucky to have cars. She took tiny bites and told everyone how she'd ridden in a snowmobile race and won. The lie just popped out of her, as effortless as breathing. She wanted so much for them to like her.

Across the table, Bonner Lockwood winked at her and began shuffling the deck of cards again. This was his fifth card trick.

"Okay, okay now. Dani, pick a card, any card, and I'll tell you what it is."

Obediently she reached out. His hand brushed hers as she selected the bottom card from the deck. His fingers were very warm. She gazed at the card, which was a seven of hearts.

"Which one have you got?"

They were all looking at her, expecting her to say the seven of hearts. But no man Dani knew had ever done card tricks. It was all too good here . . . too perfect. It wasn't real.

"Nine of . . . those black things, those spades," she blurted, then immediately was ashamed of her defiance.

Bonner looked surprised, but the warm smile never left his face. "Why, I think you might be fooling me, Dani. I think you might just be holding the seven of hearts." He unfolded her fingers, exposing the card.

Dani looked up. He was staring at her, something hot in his eyes.

"We're very proud of the house," Maureen said, walking ahead of them. Bonner brought up the rear, constantly joking and making comments to catch Dani's attention.

Maureen went on like a tour guide, "When we bought the place it was falling apart, and we've put over seventy-five thousand dollars into fixing it up. You should have seen all the insulation we had to put in, especially up on the third floor where Bonner has his office. The insulation there was practically zero. The wind blew in through the cracks, and last summer we had squirrels. They did some damage."

"Squirrels? I like squirrels," said Dani, but her voice was small, intimidated.

Original cover art from Maureen's two books, *Acrobat Squirrel* and *Dancer Mouse,* hung in a pretty little second parlor. The house had two staircases, one a servants' stairs at the back of the house that was entered from the kitchen utility pantry.

"*Two* stairs?" said Dani, stunned. "Get back."

But it was Dani's room, newly redecorated, of which the Lockwoods seemed proudest. "*I* designed it for her," announced Bonner, smiling his dazzling smile.

As they entered, Dani edged closer to Vivian. It was a room straight out of *Country Living,* or the Spiegel catalog. There was pink and green floral wallpaper with a matching border. Ivy green carpeting. Four charming windows, each with its own cushioned window seat. A canopied bed swagged with floral chintz that matched the walls. Vivian saw a twenty-four-inch TV set on a stand, and a portable CD player with a box of CDs.

"A TV?" Dani said, her voice rising.

An attached bath carried out the floral theme, and a tiny sitting room held bookshelves on which had already been installed a sizable collection of teen girl books.

"*Babysitter's Club. Sweet Valley High.* Judy Blume. All the good ones," said Vivian, reading their spines.

"I bought those," said Maureen, smiling at Dani. "And I've added my own two books, autographed just for you, Dani. I hope you'll enjoy them."

"Is that a lot of books or *what?*" muttered Dani.

Vivian knew Dani was ashamed of her low reading ability. Her mother, Fay, had kept her out of school so much, once for a full year, that she read barely at second-grade level. She would not be able to enter a regular seventh grade but would require special ed for some time.

"You remember, Dani, that the Lockwoods are getting a reading tutor for you, honey. Plus you'll be going to a nice, new school. You'll be zipping through all of these books in no time."

"Not me. I don't like books."

Bonner went to answer the telephone that was ringing upstairs on the third level, and Maureen took them to the end of the second-floor hallway, where a window looked down on a pleasantly treed side garden. Through the bare-branched trees they could see the brick walls of several of the older campus buildings and some students, wrapped in winter gear, on their way to classes.

"It *is* nice here for a young girl," Maureen said. "The swimming pool is just around the corner, and I've already enrolled Dani in lessons. I always wanted a girl. Dani, I hope so much that you'll like it here. I . . . I've looked forward to your coming."

"Well," said Dani, doubt turning the word into a "no."

"Maybe Dani has some questions," suggested Vivian.

"Of course," said Maureen.

Dani stared at the small, pretty Maureen. The girl's eyes were still widened, stunned by all the material possessions she had just seen. "When are you gonna break your waters?" she asked. "Will your baby be all bloody and covered with that cheesy-looking stuff like I saw on TV once?"

Maureen said, "Goodness," and took two steps backward.

"You *said* I could ask a question."

"Yes, but not that graphic," said Vivian hastily. "There will be plenty of time to learn about pregnancy later. I'm sure Maureen will have a good book with interesting pictures."

"Oh, I'll get her a book at the library," said Maureen.

"What's *graphic?*" asked Dani, her eyes filling. "I mean who really has all this stuff for some stupid foster kid? I never had a bathroom to myself in my life. I never had wallpaper. I never had a TV. I never had a snowmobile. This damn place isn't real."

Both Vivian and Maureen rushed to hug Dani, one of them holding each of her shoulders. "Dani . . ."

"Well, it isn't." Tears rolled down Dani's face. "I want Mrs. Zagat. I want Jimbo."

While Dani was in the bathroom, Vivian went into the beautifully decorated living room with Bonner and Maureen and tried to allay their anxieties.

"It's natural for a child to have mood swings during the first few days and even months. They are usually so terrified of rejection. Coming from her background, where she received such minimal attention and love, it must seem almost unreal for Dani to suddenly enter a home with as many material things as yours."

"Of course," said Maureen. "She is so beautiful, isn't she? I can't wait to take her shopping. If she . . ." She stopped. "I hope the adjustment doesn't take too long."

"I'll be back in two weeks to see how things are going," Vivian went on, handing the Lockwoods her card, although they already had it. "Call me tomorrow morning, and let me know how the night went."

"The night?" asked Maureen.

"The first night in a new home is tough, and Dani sometimes has nightmares, as you know," Vivian said. She glanced out the window, where snowflakes still dusted the ground. "And now I think I'd better get back on the road. I still have a staff meeting to attend this afternoon at the agency, if I can make it back in time. But first I need to say good-bye to Dani."

"I don't like these people; I *don't* want to stay here," Dani said, following Vivian out to the car. The girl's face was crinkled with anxiety. "Please, don't make me stay here."

"Dani," began Vivian. "Before we start talking, honey, you haven't even got a jacket on. Go in the house and get your coat, and then we'll sit in my car and talk for a minute."

"*No.* I don't want to go back for my jacket. I don't want to go back in there ever again." Dani opened the Camry's passenger door and slid in. She slumped in the seat, thrusting her worn Adidas as far under the dashboard as she could. Her anxiety filled the car. "I don't like them, is all."

Vivian felt a brief surge of alarm. This was the only couple who had asked for Dani on a permanent basis. The Zagats could not adopt her because they had already adopted three and felt that was enough. Vivian slid her arm around the girl's slim, rigid shoulder blades.

"Dani, you feel very nervous, don't you? Of course you do. We talked about that on the way over. It's very natural—you might even feel sad or mad—but the feeling is going to get less and less in the next few weeks, until finally you'll hardly notice it at all."

"I just don't fit in!" the girl cried. "I mean they got more books in my room than I ever saw in my whole damn life. And *card tricks,* gimme a break, Mrs. Vivian. Does that guy think I'm gonna like baby stuff like that? How old does he think I am, eight years old? I mean I lived on the streets. I got a mother who's a crackhead, for Jesus' sake. I saw her fuckin' guys. *I'm* not no baby."

"I think he just wanted to put you at your ease, Dani. Give him some time and he'll learn to relate to you more where you are."

"He won't. He doesn't like me."

"Of course he does, honey. Both of the Lockwoods want you very much. They were very eager to have you. They think you're beautiful, honey. Trust me; they were very excited."

Vivian fished in her purse for another business card, and underneath the office number she scribbled her home phone number. "This is for you. Keep it in your purse, Dani, and call me any time you want. I mean that, day or night. Don't be afraid to call."

Hardly any of the kids ever really called, but Vivian always gave them her card. She spent a few minutes instructing Dani about her answering machine tape. The car had begun to steam up from both of their breaths, the windshield turning a misted frost color.

Then Vivian gazed into the clear blue eyes of the young girl who sat beside her, eyes that seemed both innocent and as worldly as those of a streetwalker. "Dani, I'm going to be back here again in just two weeks—that's December tenth or eleventh—and I'll be making regular home calls, just to be sure everything is going all right."

"Okay." Dani seemed dubious.

"Dani, I won't desert you. Do you understand me? I'm not abandoning you."

"Oh," choked Dani, looking into her lap.

Then they heard a voice. Bonner, smiling broadly, was standing on the porch, beckoning to Dani to come. "Dani!" he called. "I want to show you the snowmobile. And I bought a snowmobile suit and goggles for you; I hope they're the right size. You'll have to try them on."

Dani wavered. Vivian could sense the decisions going on inside her, the hope.

"I'll show you how to drive it, Dani."

"I've gotta go," mumbled Dani, opening the car door and slipping out. She ran back up the sidewalk, a slim, gawky child with a flame of red hair. Vivian watched her, feeling her throat tighten. The last sight Vivian saw, as she backed her Camry out of the driveway, was Bonner with his arm around Dani, ushering her back into the house.

Vivian drove back the way she had come, again passing through the little Victorian downtown with its bookstores, pizzerias, and Madisonia Four movie theater. She supposed the Lockwoods would be taking Dani to movies here and buying her ice cream at the small, quaint-looking 31 Flavors.

Still, turning onto the main road that led back to I-696, where a tattered HAVE YOU SEEN THIS CHILD poster had been tacked to a telephone pole, Vivian felt a fleeting prick of unease. Dani *had* seemed overwhelmed, scared. Had she done the right thing in placing the girl with the Lockwoods? Perhaps the environment was too dissimilar to what Dani had known before, too intimidating.

But the girl was so bright, Vivian told herself, and had so much potential. It would be tragic if she didn't receive a home that could nurture that potential.

2

BONNER HELPED DANI on with her jacket, then took her out to the garage. She waded through the dusting of cold fluff in her scuffed tennis shoes, which had holes in the toes. There were two shiny clean cars parked in the Lockwoods' garage, a blue Dodge van and a white Mercury Cougar.

Two new cars, Dani thought, feeling the amazement again. Fay's old ghetto cruiser barely held together; she was always complaining about it.

Parked behind the Cougar was a snowmobile so new that it still had a shrink-wrapped instruction booklet taped to its black vinyl seat. Dani stared at the Ski Doo, awed. She'd never been this close to one before.

"Yours. Ours," Bonner told her proudly, removing the booklet. "Get on it, Dani. Go on, test-drive it right here in the garage."

Dani scowled, nervousness and the day's stress making her voice high. "What am I supposed to do, drive it through the wall?"

"Just pretend," Bonner urged, putting an arm around her. "Later, when the snow gets thick, we'll take it out for real."

Attracted by the chrome and shininess, the mus-
cular-looking treads, Dani went to the machine and
threw her leg over it. Bonner stood behind her and
placed her hands on the steering mechanism. "Just
get the feel of it," he urged.

Dani leaned forward and did a few *zooms*, pretending she was a professional racer on a white, snowy
mountain. Gradually, a feeling of power swept over
her. She gripped the cool metal, wishing she had a
snowmobile suit, goggles, gloves, boots, wishing she
were *really* outdoors and *really* steering it.

"That's it," encouraged Bonner. "That's it—you
love to drive, don't you?"

She did. She really did. Even in a garage with only
her imagination. She laughed aloud.

"Great," responded Bonner, laughing, too. "Just
great. You're going to be a super driver; I can tell. Not
to mention the fact that you're so pretty. I think we
got the prettiest girl in Detroit."

At dinner, Bonner talked about the rappers Hammer
and Ice T, saying that he had once seen Hammer
leaving his limousine heading for a concert date.

"Really?" said Dani, excited. "What was he wearing?"

"Oh, something white, with sequins. And he had
three bodyguards."

Later, Maureen and Bonner began to talk between
themselves, something about the dean being sick
and who was going to take over. Some man had
"gone over Bonner's head," whatever that meant,
and Bonner was displeased.

"He can't play politics and he shouldn't try. I've

been around too long," said Bonner sourly. "I can squash him like a bug."

None of it made sense to Dani, and she was tired, exhausted and dazed from the long, stressful day. The room swam around her, and her head drooped over her plate.

"Maybe you'd better go to bed right after dinner, Dani," said Maureen. "Tomorrow I want to take you shopping, and I want you to meet Jill Rudgate, your tutor. She lives right next door, so you can walk to your tutoring, won't that be nice? And the day after that, you'll start school. Special classes, but only for a while, until you catch up."

After Bonner and Maureen disappeared into their bedroom at the far end of the hall, closing the door behind them, Dani's sleepiness immediately vanished. Barefoot, she began to explore. The upstairs hallway, paneled in some burnished wood, seemed big and echoey with its high ceiling. It was lined with doors. A locked door led to the third-floor attic level, where Bonner had his study. Maureen had a writing room; she'd briefly shown Vivian and Dani her computer. There were closet doors, and the door to the servants' staircase. Another door led to the room that would be the baby's.

A baby!

Dani eyed this door with anticipation. Would Maureen decorate the room in pink or blue and put in a pretty crib such as Dani had once seen in a magazine? The baby was the real reason she'd decided to come here. She *loved* babies.

As she was examining an antique mirror that was hung on the wall, its carved edges picked out with gold swirls, a floorboard creaked. Dani jumped, and guiltily moved away. She felt sneaky, wandering around when the Lockwoods didn't know. After all, she didn't really live here yet. Oh, she had a *room* here. She even had part of a snowmobile, she supposed. But that didn't make her belong, did it?

Suddenly she heard Maureen's voice. "*Magic tricks?* Bonner, I didn't even know you knew any card tricks. And talking about some rap group. You never saw really saw Hammer leaving his limousine, did you?"

"I was only trying to make her feel at ease."

"Well, you acted like Soupy Sales."

Bonner's reply was cut off by the sound of a drawer opening and closing. Dani sucked in her breath, listening to the jumble of more argument, which wasn't really angry, just bickering. Finally she retreated, running lightly back on her bare feet.

She slipped into her room, closing the door behind her. Somehow hearing Bonner and Maureen bicker made her feel better. Arguing was what adults did; it was the natural way of life. Fay had yelled and screamed at every boyfriend she ever had. And when she and Harley argued, dishes got thrown.

Feeling an odd surge of relief, Dani walked toward her extravagantly canopied bed. The Lockwoods were real, after all. They shit and fucked and farted and yelled and laughed just like everyone else. Maybe she *could* get used to this house.

"I think she should have the blue dress," said Maureen, standing at the counter that was stacked high with piles of sweaters, pants, leggings, blouses, underwear, and socks. "It will be perfect for Thanksgiving, and she can wear it when we take her to the theater."

"Yes, she certainly looked adorable in it," agreed the saleswoman, overjoyed at the sales she had made.

"Theater? What's that?" asked Dani, gulping as she stared at the huge pile of stuff that was partially spilling off the Formica counter near the cash register.

"*Cats* is coming to Lansing and we have tickets," said Maureen. She put down the dress and strolled over to a rack of knit tops, where she began pulling out button Ts, in blue, cream, and lilac.

"Tickets," repeated Dani, wondering if *Cats* was some new rock group, but she forgot to ask about it because now Maureen was gathering up a group of pretty leather purses and bringing them over for Dani's inspection.

Her cheeks flushed red, Dani picked and chose. Blue. She liked blue. And the reds.

"I ain't never had nothing like this," she muttered as Maureen instructed the saleswoman that they were going to be using package pickup.

"Well, now you do," said Maureen, smiling. "And tomorrow we're going to get you a new haircut, Dani. A good cut will work wonders, and maybe I'll even have the manicurist do your nails."

"Nails?" squeaked Dani. Awkwardly she touched Maureen's arm. "I never had . . ."

"I want you to look pretty," Maureen said. "Thanksgiving's on Thursday, you know, and we've got a houseful of people."

The dark, rich, meaty aroma of turkey permeated the house, mingling with the delicious odor of pumpkin and apple pies. The guests were Bonner's sister and

her husband, their three young daughters, and several elderly relatives of Maureen's. As the adults
chattered, the children milled through the house,
drinking Pepsis, watching TV, and playing board
games. The youngest two girls, Petra and Tessa,
wore party dresses, their hair pulled back with ribbons, but Tracey, the fourteen-year-old, wore a
spandex dress and flats with glitter on them. To
Dani, they all looked like kids in a magazine, their
faces pink and smooth.

"To our growing family," said Bonner, raising a
wineglass to make a toast at the long table that had
been set up with extra leaves in the dining room. "To
our beautiful Dani, our new daughter."

"Hear, hear," several of the adults said, while Dani
flushed hotly and looked down at her plate, embarrassed at being the center of attention, yet proud,
too. Everyone clinked their glasses. She picked up
hers, which held milk, and clanked it against Maureen's glass, then Tracey Hagen's, the oldest niece.
Tracey looked back at Dani sardonically.

"You're the new girl, huh?" said Tracey, as the
children sat in the TV room sprawled in front of one
of the videos Maureen had rented for them to watch,
Radio Flyer.

"Yeah," said Dani.

"You like it here?"

"I guess. Yeah, I like it. We went shopping and
Maureen bought me a whole bunch of clothes. She's
nice."

"Yeah," said Tracey, scowling. "Better not let *him*
take you shopping."

"What do you mean?"

"I mean . . ." But Maureen had come into the room
and was passing out Thanksgiving favors, small

stuffed animals, and Tracey didn't finish whatever it was she had been going to say.

Later, Vivian Clavell called "just to see how your first Thanksgiving with the Lockwoods went."

"Oh, great, great," enthused Dani, sleepy from being curled up on the couch. "We ate turkey and I ate more than anyone, and we took out the wishbone and we watched a movie and then we watched two more movies. And we clinked our glasses."

Later that night, after the guests went home, Dani struggled under the bedcovers, caught in one of her nightmares. It was Tracey's voice that had triggered it: "Better not let *him* take you shopping." Now dark shapes seemed to lean over Dani's bed, hands reaching out to touch her.

"No," she sobbed, her voice thin. "Ma . . . Ma . . . Ma!"

"I told you, I don't want her like this; I want her happy, not blubbering. I thought you told me she was okay," a man said angrily.

"She'll be okay. I already told her all about it; she's just being ornery," said Fay.

"Well, shit, I don't want no ornery kid."

When the hand touched her, Dani twisted and bucked, calling out for her mother. She clawed and fought, sinking her baby teeth into warm skin. . . .

Then she felt the real hand on her shoulder, shaking her. Its temperature felt warm, even through the blanket.

"Dani? Dani, are you all right? What's wrong? I heard you cry out. Are you having a nightmare?"

She sat up. Bonner was perched on the edge of her bed, wearing a striped bathrobe of some thickly sheared, luxurious material. His teeth and eyeballs looked very, very white. The flowery bedroom was aglow with the phosphorescent light that streamed in the windows from the falling snow.

"Honey, are you all right?" he persisted.

"Yes. Yes."

"But what was it? What caused you to cry out like that? Did you eat too much turkey?" He leaned forward, one hand brushing her knees.

"I don't know."

He reached out and brushed her frizzy hair off her forehead. His palm was smooth and warm. "Well, you're here with us now; you're safe. You don't have to have bad dreams anymore. I promise."

"Okay." She sank back on the pillow, waiting for him to go.

Bonner smiled. "Now, is there anything you want? A glass of milk maybe? I can get it for you from the kitchen. I'll even warm it up for you. Would you like hot cocoa?"

Nobody ever made her hot cocoa. She'd seldom even tasted it.

"I'm not a baby," she said proudly. "I don't want any."

"Of course I know that," he responded in a gentle, kind tone. "And it's fine if you don't want cocoa. Dani, I just want you to feel safe here; I want you to feel as if this is really your home, as if I'm really your father."

"And Maureen my mother?"

"Yes, yes, of course," he said, standing up, still smiling.

After he had gone, Dani stared at the doorway, her eyes watering, but then sleep came. This time there

were no voices. She blanked out, falling deeply down
into the blackness.

Bonner left Dani's room and walked down the corridor. He thought about Dani.

Beautiful. She was just so beautiful and sexy. He'd
looked forward so much to her coming . . . to what he
might do. But he shouldn't hurry, he told himself.
Hurrying would ruin it. This was to be savored, step
by tiny step, not gone after like a dog savaging a
bone.

He'd seen a lot of girls, hundreds of them, including his own little nieces, but never one with the
qualities that Dani had, the beautiful, melting inno-
cence coupled with a worldly, seductive air that
drove him wild. She was a beauty who didn't even
know her true, feminine self yet, and who would
have to be taught, little by little, until—

Stop, not so fast, he told himself, using a key from
his ring to open the doorway that led to the third-
floor staircase. He climbed the stairs, his hand gripping the handrail. He could feel it starting again, the
yearly tension. He'd always had so much trouble dis-
sipating it. This year it was much worse, starting
when he learned that Maureen was pregnant. Now,
as she had reached her seventh month, the feeling
seemed to be getting stronger, more dominant.

He reached the slope-roofed study, which was private, and his. The college girl who came twice a
month to clean never touched here. Even Maureen
didn't come upstairs. He'd trained her not to do that,
claiming he couldn't write when there was another
person around, and now he had the lock, for double
surety.

He had several rooms. One was his office, where he corrected term papers and exams and worked on his definitive history of the Korean War. Another room contained his TV, two VCRs, and a collection of two hundred videos he'd purchased last year when a small catalog outlet had gone under. Some were straight movies; others were not.

The attic also held several closets and cubbies and a huge unfinished area that stretched over the floor joists over half the upper rooms, including Dani's bedroom. Which, of course, was why he'd decided she should have *that* room, rather than the guest room at the opposite end of the corridor.

He went around pulling window blinds down. Jill Rudgate, the wimpy thirty-two-year-old history instructor who taught in his department, lived next door, her attic windows on a direct line with his.

Finally, feeling safe, he went into the audiovisual room and switched on the TV set, then powered up the VCR. He thought about Dani. That amazing red hair. He was especially partial to blondes and redheads. Dani had eyebrows like little wings, and her freckles were adorable, the most seductive small dots he had ever seen. But best of all was Dani's immature hipless, breastless body. He loved it that she looked barely eleven. When a girl started growing breasts, she passed beyond his narrow range of interest. The only reason he had been able to marry Maureen was that her natural body shape was childish. Now her pregnancy had spoiled that, of course.

He frowned as he inspected his shelf full of video cases and tried to decide which one to watch tonight. Or should he go and get one of the special ones?

He decided on the special.

Watching it would help him hold off . . . help him not to move too quickly.

Snow tapped Vivian's office window, cold drafts of wind penetrating through the cracks underneath the windowsill that the agency had never bothered to have sealed. On the wall was a quilted Christmas hanging in cheery shades of light and dark green that Vivian had brought from home.

She was dictating a case record about a five-year-old black boy named Andre who was autistic and had a condition called echolalia. Like a tiny living tape player, he kept repeating random phrases from TV or radio, or snippets of conversation. These were his only words. He had never even said "Mama." Vivian had been trying for six months to find adoptive parents for him, but Andre, born to a heroin-addicted mother, was not toilet-trained and the prognosis was that he probably would never learn to convey real ideas. Few people could really cope with that.

The ringing of the telephone gave her a welcome respite from the depression of Andre. She reached over the dictating machine to pick it up.

"Dani on line four," said the receptionist, Angie.

"Dani," said Vivian, pleased. This was Dani's second call. Vivian had begun to look forward to her occasional conversations with Dani, so full of artless chatter and tough cynicism. This morning, when Dani first called, Vivian had been in a meeting, and when she had tried later to return Dani's call, no one had answered the telephone. "Dani, how are you today?"

"I'm going to my new tutor now," chirped Dani. "She's a real dweeb."

Vivian smiled. "A dweeb, Dani?"

"I guess. She wears these clothes, wool pleated skirts and sweaters, and she wears loafers, and her hair just hangs there."

"Long hair?"

"Just loose hair, you know? And I think she has maybe a hearing problem or something, 'cause she told me I have to sit on her right side all the time, and I have to speak up, she said, and not slur my words. We did phonetics," Dani added. "And she let me help bake a cake. And I had a taste of her beer."

"Well, she sounds like a very interesting tutor," Vivian said, amused.

"And guess what! I'm gonna go over to the regular junior high for jazz dancing and science lab; can you believe it? I'm gonna get to dance! I *will* be a video dancer!" cried Dani, wildly excited. "I'll go on TV! I'll dance with Paula Abdul. And . . . I'll write a children's book, too, just like Maureen."

"I think you will," said Vivian, pleased and proud of the way Dani seemed to be adjusting.

"Anyways." There was a pause punctuated with the girl's breathy breathing. It stretched out long enough that Vivian began to wonder if the child had put down the phone. "Anyways, I—I just wanta say . . ."

"Yes?"

"Would you call Mrs. Zagat and ask how Jimbo is? I told you I would miss him and I do." The girl's breath caught. "I . . . miss him a *lot*, Mrs. Vivian. And no new baby is gonna make me forget him."

* * *

Jill Rudgate rushed around her living room, tripping over a stack of books she'd been looking through the previous night, which were still lying on the floor. She snatched up a couple of empty Coors cans. She was no housekeeper. And she'd overslept again—the third time this week. Depression did that to her. She was only thirty-two and stuck here in Madisonia, Nowhere, under the iron thumb of Bonner Lockwood.

It seemed hopeless. For her to get another teaching job, with her hearing disability, with the glut of Ph.D.'s in this rotten economy, was going to require a miracle, or at least some friends in very high places.

Out of her good ear, she heard voices, and moving to the front bay window, she saw Bonner and Dani coming up the walk. Bonner was leaning down in order to hear something that Dani said.

Jill frowned. She liked Dani—in fact, the girl actually was rather fun—but Bonner's interest in his foster daughter seemed overdone to Jill. Maureen had told Jill that Bonner had even bought the girl a snowmobile. The doting daddy bit seemed so out of character for the man, whose students' nickname for him was Bummer.

Jill hurried to her door and opened it just as Bonner and Dani reached the steps.

"Why, hello, Bonner . . . and Dani!"

"Hi," said the girl. "Are we gonna bake again? I want to make chocolate cookies with two kinds of chips. I saw that on TV. I want to use those butterscotch kind of chips—"

"I've brought a few books that you can use to get Dani's reading going," interrupted Bonner, producing a small shopping bag from the local B. Dalton's.

"Something a little more interesting than that dry stuff you've been pushing on her. And I don't think baking is the answer either."

"We were going over vocabulary and I was getting her trust," said Jill, taking the sack. It contained teen paperback fluff, those Sweet Valley romances. She was irritated with herself for accepting six dollars an hour for her tutoring services, but in a burg like Madisonia, extra money was sometimes hard to come by.

Dani strolled into Jill's living room, peeling off her new, expensive green jacket. Remaining by the front door, Bonner fixed Jill with a stern eye.

"As I told you, we're expecting great things from you. This girl isn't any ordinary girl. She's very, very bright, and I expect her to make enormous strides in only a very short time."

Jill knew an order when she heard it.

"Naturally," she said.

"Well, then—I'll leave you to it."

"Yes, fine."

When Bonner had left, Jill turned to the thirteen-year-old now sprawled on her couch. Dani had picked up a copy of *You'll Never Eat Lunch in This Town Again*, a Hollywood exposé by Julia Phillips. Dani's lips moved as she slowly puzzled out the words of the title.

"This is real dumb," said Dani. "Why won't I eat lunch? What does this mean?"

"It means—well, the author of the book told a lot of secrets about people in Hollywood. The title doesn't mean, literally, that she can't eat lunch; it means that they might exclude her from their usual *business* lunches, snub her, so to speak. *Snub* is a word

that means to behave coldly toward, to slight or ig-
nore."

Dani stared at her. "You talk funny," she said. "Do
you always talk like that?"

"Most of the time," admitted Jill. "That's what
comes when you've got two master's degrees and 90
percent of a Ph.D."

"And you don't like *him*, do you? You're afraid of
him."

Jill flushed, her hand unconsciously going up to
her left ear, where the flesh-colored hearing aid was
hidden by her long, straight brown hair. "Of course
not," she lied.

"Hey, it's okay," said Dani. Her eyes met Jill's and
they looked at each other for just a second, just long
enough for something to connect between the two of
them.

Then Jill went to a desk drawer and took out the
stack of flash cards they'd been using two days ago.

"Flash cards?" groaned Dani. "Again? That's baby
stuff. And anyways, I already know them things."

"These things," Jill corrected. "And it's *anyway*,
not *anyways*."

"Yeah. At my last school we did flash cards all the
time and my teacher said I could make my own, and
they had a contest and *I* won first prize."

Bonner had warned Jill about this. "Dani . . . you
were only in school for three months last year. You
didn't make any flash cards. You were truant most of
the time."

"No! I wasn't! Well, I missed a couple weeks, but
that was because I broke my leg. I broke both legs. I
was in traction."

"Dani, you don't have to . . ." Then Jill shut up.
Since Bonner was her employer, with total control

over her career, she could hardly tell his daughter she was lying, and anyway, she didn't want to see Dani's face fall when she confronted her.

Jill backtracked, "Anyway, we'll only do the flash cards for ten minutes, then we'll have a snack; do you like Doritos? And then we'll read whatever book you want, okay? A book out of that bag, maybe."

"Sure," said Dani.

The length of Jill's front sidewalk glistened with a thin slick of ice. Released from the hour of tutoring, Dani aimed herself toward the ice, sliding down it with grand abandon.

Suddenly she felt something hard hit the center of her back. Pieces of icy snow spattered all around her.

"Hey, Bic Head!" called a boy's voice, the tone mocking. "Hey, you got flames comin' out of the top of your hair or something? You look like somebody set you on fire."

Dani whirled. A boy a little older than she was stood a few feet away, his bare hands already fashioning another ice ball.

Indignantly Dani squatted and began scrabbling at the hard-packed snow, scooping up an ice ball of her own. They both finished their balls at the same time, but Dani was faster, and she lobbed hers while she was still on the ground, hitting the boy in the chest.

"Hey!" he cried.

"Hey, yourself!" she yelled, jumping up. "Don't you know it's rude and stupid to hit someone you don't even know? And I *haven't* got a fire on my head; I just have red hair. Can't you see that?"

The boy scowled. He had light brown hair that fell

across his forehead in a floppy forelock, almost obscuring his eyes. His mouth was full and red, curled
with disdain. There was a paper sticker affixed to the
black leather jacket he wore. She couldn't read it
very well.

"You've got the reddest Bic Head I *ever* saw," he
told her. "Is that your snowmobile in the garage
there?"

"Yeah, all *mine*. You're not riding on it."

"I will if I want to."

"No, you won't."

"I will, 'cause my father works with Bonner Lockwood; he's the assistant dean of students. Ha, ha, I
bet you don't even know what that is, do you? You
don't know anything about a college, do you? You're
just that dumb girl who's moved in with the Lockwoods. The girl who tells all the lies. Compulsive
liar-r-r-r," he added, stretching out the words into
an insult.

Dani stared at him, appalled and humiliated. Did
people really know all about her already? Who had
told them?

"I'm not a liar! I'm not; I'm not!" she screamed,
pouncing on the snow again, scooping up another
hard ball. "Damn you! Damn you, ugly butthead!"

The boy threw himself on her, his weight pushing
her to the ground. They struggled for a few minutes,
the boy repeatedly pushing Dani's face into the
snow. Her teeth banged against icy cement. Finally
she lay still, the boy pressing into her. She heard his
panting breath in her ear.

"You give?"

"No!" Dani squirmed onto her side, kicking the boy
in the groin.

"Ouch!" he yelled. He pulled away from her, clutching his privates. "Dammit—!"

Dani sprang to her feet. The boy didn't look tough anymore, and there were angry tears glittering in his eyes. Suddenly she was in a very good mood. "Hey, I'm Dani McVie; who're you?"

The boy mumbled something, backing away from her.

"I said who are you? Or you get another ice ball."

"Ryan Sokol, what's it to you?" he said sullenly.

"How old are you?"

"Fourteen. Well, I will be in May."

"Well, I'll be fourteen in July, so what? What's that stupid sign on your jacket? 'Refuse and . . .' "

"Refuse and Resist," he told her. "I got it from my brother. He's a canvasser for this group, Sane Freeze, see; they're against nuclear war. I'm a rebel," he added. "I'm tough and I'm mean."

"Su-u-ure," drawled Dani, grinning.

Maureen Lockwood was on the phone to Marilyn Rabaul, Dean Rabaul's wife, who was in her writing group. Marilyn was curious about the young girl Maureen and Bonner had taken in.

"Why did you want an older child, especially a . . . well, a disturbed one, when you're already expecting a baby of your own?"

"We have to make up for lost time," Maureen said. "I'm forty-two and the pregnancy was really a fluke; my periods have been very irregular. Both of us decided we'd better start having our family now before it was too late."

"Is she very disturbed?"

"She actually has been fairly well behaved, but she does tell fibs."

"Fibs?"

"Well, small lies. She says she rescued a dog from a river once, she drove a snowmobile in the mountains, she won ten thousand dollars in the Lotto, she's going to be on 'Star Search.' It's almost humorous in a way. But the case record did say she was a compulsive liar."

"Ah," said Marilyn, who had already heard all of this through her husband, who had talked to Bonner. "Well, how is Bonner taking her? I mean he hardly seems the type—"

"Oh, very well. He's enjoying himself. I admit I was a little surprised. He's actually doing all the father-daughter things; it's really quite amazing. We took her to a movie on Sunday. We saw that new Steve Martin picture, and she ate a whole tub of popcorn by herself."

"Well, that's very nice," said Marilyn, immediately losing interest. Conversation turned to the writing group's attempt to get Elmore "Dutch" Leonard, who lived in Birmingham, to come as a speaker.

As they talked, however, Maureen found herself frowning. Actually, she thought, Bonner was being a little selfish about Dani. He had scheduled some of their activities for when Maureen had other plans, or simply not invited her to go along.

But at least he was showing interest, she assured herself. Years ago, when they first married, he'd flatly told her he wanted no children. In fact, he had told her the very idea of parturition repelled him. Now he was proving he had changed.

*   *   *

As Christmas lights began to sparkle on the streets, strung in rows along eaves and encircling windows, a sizable snowfall coated the town with a thick frosting of pristine white. Even the telephone wires bore narrow ribbons of snow.

Bonner took Dani out on the Ski Doo, and she straddled the seat behind him, yelling and screaming in wild delight as they roared across the open center lawn of the campus, which Bonner said was called the "diag" because of its diagonal walk. They were wearing matching black snowmobile suits, with puffy boots, gloves, and yellow wraparound goggles.

"Do you like it?" Bonner shouted.

"Oh, yes!" she screamed back over the engine's roar.

"Do you want to drive?"

He showed her how to steer, and she sped recklessly, caroming along so fast that her breath was torn away by the wind. She was going too fast, but Bonner didn't stop her, and as they sped across a soccer field, Dani suddenly realized that he would do anything she wanted. Anything! That's why he had bought the snowmobile, just for her.

It gave her a strange, sick feeling of power and anxiety.

"I want to go back and take Ryan for a ride," Dani said, finally, when she and Bonner had stopped in a small campus coffee shop for hot chocolate. She was perspiring inside the snowmobile suit, her inner clothing soaked.

"Ryan?" Bonner frowned. "You don't mean Ryan Sokol, from across the street? Bing Sokol's son?"

"Sure. He's neat. We threw ice balls at each other yesterday. I won. He's a real pussy."

"Young lady," said Bonner, fixing his eyes on her. "I want you to stay completely away from that boy. He's a rebel without a cause, if you understand my meaning. He has been in trouble with the police for vandalism. He was caught spray-painting the administration building, and his brother is a hippie. He is no person for you to become involved with."

"But—" began Dani.

"He is *trash,* Dani. I mean it. I want you to stay away from him. Now," said Bonner, reaching for his snow-damp gloves, his hand accidentally brushing across Dani's side. "What do you say we go home again? You can drive all the way if you want to."

After dinner, Dani felt still so excited about the snowmobile, so entranced with the fact that she had *really* driven one, that when Bonner excused himself to go upstairs, she followed him. She just wanted his attention for a few more minutes; she didn't want the day to end.

Halfway up the stairs to the third floor, he realized she was on the steps. He turned, annoyed. "Dani, what are you doing here? Don't you have a TV program to watch?"

"I—yeah, it's time for 'Roseanne,' but—"

"Then go watch it. I have work to do," he said impatiently.

"What kind of work?"

"I'm chairman of a very busy department, young lady. I have twelve professors, instructors, and graduate assistants to supervise. I teach three senior classes myself, and I'm writing a book. That all takes a great deal of time."

Already she was used to having him baby her and

fawn over her. "But Maureen said you have a computer. Could I type on it? I love computers."

"My study is off-limits, Dani." Bonner softened his tone slightly. "I hope you understand that I have to have some place in this house that is personal to me."

Hurt, Dani backed down the stairs. As she exited into the hall, she heard the lock click behind her.

That night, she was nearly asleep when she heard a sound in her bedroom. She awakened to see Bonner approaching her bed. In the light that streamed into the room from the hall, she could see that he was no longer irritated with her.

"I brought you an extra blanket," he explained. "The temperature outside is supposed to go down to five above tonight. I was afraid you might get cold."

He unfolded the blanket and smoothed it over her bed, bending over her to tuck it firmly in on both sides, fastening her into a tight cocoon. Was it her imagination or did his hand brush across her chest, ever so gently?

Dani stared at her foster father's face. He was looking at her again—that way. She lowered her eyes, and when she glanced at him again, the hot look was gone from his eyes.

When Bonner had left, after kissing her lightly on the forehead, Dani turned over in bed. *Was that the way he had looked at Tessa?* she wondered sleepily. *Or had he . . .*

But she fell asleep before she could finish the thought. Almost immediately she was dreaming about the hands again, and Fay's thickened, wheedling commands.

* * *

Ryan and Dani were seated on a rolled-up throw rug that was being stored in plastic on the floor of Ryan's dad's garage, next to Bing Sokol's black '79 Corvette. The 'Vette, as Ryan called it, was Mr. Sokol's obsessive pride, and he drove it only on Sundays, guarding it from scratches, door dimples, and even human fingerprints, especially Ryan's.

A rickety space heater blasted out waves of heat, keeping the garage warm.

Dani and Ryan talked for hours. He told her about an antinuke demonstration he'd been to, and how a policeman had dragged his brother, Brandon, to the police car and frisked him. Brandon had been arrested, and Ryan had visited him in jail. In the visitors' room, Ryan had seen a man who'd been accused of murder.

Dani pretended she thought this was daring. She told Ryan all about Fay and Fay's tricks and the very, very weird guy who had actually asked Fay to pee on his chest.

"No!" cried Ryan, stunned.

"Yeah, they call it a 'golden shower,' something like that," Dani said, pleased that she'd found something to shock her friend.

"Well?" he asked. "Did she really do it?"

"Sure. He didn't hurt her or nothing. She had to. He paid her. She bought some cocaine with the money," Dani added.

Now Ryan's eyes grew really round. "Your mother took *cocaine?*"

"Sure." Dani shrugged. "I did, too, a couple of times. They made me. They had this little mirror, see, and they made me sniff it up through a one-dollar bill." She demonstrated. "It was funny. It made me feel . . . I don't know . . . great. But then she

wouldn't let me have it anymore; she said it cost too
much money."

Ryan sat very still. He seemed impressed, almost
stunned, by what Dani had said, so much so that
Dani began to wonder if she should have told him at
all. Finally he said, "I know where Dad keeps the
keys to his 'Vette, on a hook in the laundry room.
Want to go for a ride?"

"In your dad's *car?*"

Ryan shrugged. "Why not? I'm getting my learner's
permit next summer. It's no big deal; anyone can
drive. You just have to put a cushion under your butt
so you don't look too short behind the wheel. You
know, too much like a kid."

"Can I drive, too?"

"Maybe." They both stood up. "Well, first let me get
the keys," Ryan began fussily. "Then I have to make
sure my dad is still at work, and my mom is still at
work, and then maybe—"

"*I've* driven a snowmobile," Dani interrupted. "Not
just with Bonner, but on my own, too. I drove one all
up and down a mountain, and there was this ski
jump thing. I went over a ski jump. The wind just
flew in my hair."

"In a snowmobile? Can it," snapped Ryan. "You
never did that. Do you think I'm stupid or something? If you want to drive the 'Vette with me, then
you've got to tell me the truth all the time."

"Okay," she agreed humbly.

The Big Boy restaurant near campus was jammed
with students, packed four, five, and six to a booth.
The noise was raucous, and Vivian had to lean

across the table in order to hear what Dani was saying.

". . . so Ryan and me, we went to this video arcade and we played all these games, and I beat him twice; no, I beat him three times. I scored 150,000 points, more than practically anybody."

Vivian couldn't help smiling. Dani's "stories" hadn't changed, but Dani herself certainly had. In a month, the girl had been transformed.

Dani's dense frizz of hair had been thinned, trimmed, glossed, tamed. It was now a pert cap of red silk. She wore a touch of pale pink lipstick. Her clothing was trendy, a chartreuse and fuchsia tunic over chartreuse leggings, and her wrists jangled with the latest fad in teenage bracelets. Vivian felt a swell of pride that she herself had been partly responsible for this.

"So you have a new friend," she drew Dani out.

"Yeah. Ryan is cool; he's my best friend. And Maureen is getting pregnanter and pregnanter," the girl went on. "She let me touch her stomach and I felt this funny wiggling; it was the baby kicking. She's already reading out loud to the baby—she's reading to her own stomach!" reported Dani, laughing gaily. "And there was a baby shower, and Maureen let me help her open the presents!"

Later, sipping a chocolate milk shake through a straw, Dani asked about Jimbo. Vivian gave what news she could, saying she had stopped by Mrs. Zagat's to see another child, and the boy was fine.

Dani grew pensive. "Nobody's touching him, are they?"

"Touching, Dani?"

"I mean—*you* know."

When Vivian tried to draw her out, Dani looked

down at the tabletop, and finally Vivian was forced to
let it drop. After all, Dani *had* been sexually abused
as a child, and it was only natural she would worry
about it.

Vivian drove the girl back to the Lockwoods' and
spent an additional half hour talking with the adoptive parents. Both of the Lockwoods felt that Dani
was getting along well.

"Vivian," Bonner said, gazing at her earnestly, "I
can't tell you how much it means to us to have Dani
with us. She's perfect. The perfect girl for us. Perfect
in every way."

"Mrs. Vivian?" said Dani, again following her as she
walked out to her Camry, as she had done on the
first day Vivian delivered her to the Lockwoods. "Do
you think my mother will ever find me again?"

"Your mother? Why, Dani, Fay's parental rights
have been severed. She hasn't been told where you
are. It's a secret, honey. And, darling, you know she's
waiting for her trial. I don't think you have to worry
about her."

"I called her a couple times, but she didn't answer
the phone. Sometimes she don't answer, like when
she's with a trick or something, or with Harley."

Vivian felt dismay. "Do you want her to find you? If
you talk to her on the phone, she probably will."

"No. Oh, no!" The girl looked so frightened that
Vivian reached out to put her arm around the thirteen-year-old. Underneath the fashionable new
jacket, Dani's shoulder blades were thin. Vivian felt
a sweep of strong affection for the child. Already
she'd become attached to Dani, more so than was
recommended, she supposed. She was making Dani

a pillow for Christmas, as a matter of fact. But Vivian had always put her feelings into her job.

"Well, you don't have to worry about Fay, darling. She's out of your life now. There's every chance she'll go to prison. Fortunately, you aren't being asked to testify; the police officer will do that. So just relax and enjoy your new home, honey. You're very, very lucky to have such nice parents."

"But—" The worried look didn't leave Dani's face. "What about Mr. Watermelon?"

"Who?"

"My mom's old boyfriend. That's the name I called him, because of his funny name, and his stomach. It was all big like a melon." Dani demonstrated with wide gestures. "He made me, you know, do things to him sometimes. He would bring me candy."

A frigid wind was blowing, penetrating through the folds of Vivian's cloth coat. "Dani, why would you mention that now? Is something bothering you?"

"No!" Dani licked her lips. "No."

Christmas came in a glow of holiday lights that Maureen and Dani spent hours stringing all through the house, standing on stepladders to reach the high places. Dani felt sure she would be receiving a lot of gifts—Maureen had told her that one of the guest bedrooms was off-limits because she was using it to wrap presents.

Dani purchased a pair of thin, dangling plastic earrings for Maureen and a pen for Bonner. After a lot of thought, she added an embroidered baby bib for the new baby, and she bought a card for $1.50 that she sent through the mail to Jimbo. She splurged and sent another card to Mrs. Vivian. It said: "From Our House to Yours."

The relatives arrived for Christmas Eve supper, the pretty, blond Hagen girls stamping into the house with wet, snowy, patent-leather shoes. The oldest girl, Tracey, wore a red tunic trimmed with colored stones, and black leggings. She had on full makeup and looked seventeen. She was pouting and sullen, having evidently wanted to go somewhere else for the holidays.

"Maureen rented movies again," offered Dani. "We've got *Home Alone 2* and *The Mighty Ducks.*"

"Oh, *The Mighty Ducks,*" scoffed Tracey. "That movie is dorky. How do you like it here? Do you still like it?" She stared at Dani as if waiting for some strange reaction.

"I like it fine. Why wouldn't I?"

"I just wondered."

After the dinner was over and they'd sung carols, Bonner leading them all in a rich baritone, Bonner took the middle Hagen niece, Tessa, upstairs to the second floor to show her the room where the new baby was going to sleep. Tessa was eleven, with a slim, sturdy, flat-chested body and a dusting of pale freckles. Dani watched them go. Twenty minutes later they returned, Tessa's face puckered up in a scowl, as if she were about to cry.

"I'm getting a baby sister," said Dani, going up to her. She looked sharply at the younger girl.

Tessa tossed her head. "So what. I don't care."

"I'm going to change her diapers and give her her bottle and do everything for her. You can come over sometime, if you want to, and I'll let you hold her."

"Oh, thrill," snapped the girl, turning away.

"What's wrong with you?"

"Nothing, you idiot. I want to go home. Why did we come here anyway? I hate Christmas," declared Tessa. "And most of all I hate *him.*" She glared savagely in the direction of Bonner.

"But why?"

"I won't tell *you.* You're so dumb. You're just dumb," Tessa said, beginning to cry as she ran to sit on the couch next to her mother. She threw herself down, then sat huddled and silent, her mouth clamped tightly shut. Dani stared after her. Suddenly she was getting a very sick, nervous feeling in the pit of her stomach.

The way Tessa acted . . . not just mad but scared. It was the way Dani herself acted when something bad happened, something she was ashamed of and didn't want to tell anyone about. But Tessa had been fine before she went upstairs.

What had Bonner said to her up there? What . . . what had he done? But then Maureen was calling them all to watch the beginning of another movie, and Dani put the puzzling event out of her mind. This was her home now. . . . Bonner loved her. He was her new father. It was wrong to have such thoughts.

3

A *JANUARY WIND* rattled Dani's bedroom window, its icy breath seeping between the cracks of the expensively lined chintz curtains. Somewhere far away boys were setting off firecrackers left over from New Year's Eve, the sounds popping and small.

"I've brought you a nice glass of water," Bonner said softly, pushing open her bedroom door with barely a token knock.

"I'm not thirsty," Dani mumbled, burrowing under the covers.

"Just a half-glass, Dani; it's ice-cold from the tap. You know what they say about drinking water; you're supposed to have eight glasses every single day—that's to help your body cells grow strong so they can transport your wastes."

"I drink tons of Pepsi," she groaned.

"But Pepsi isn't water. There's nothing like water. Please, beautiful Dani, my pretty baby . . . please, for me. I want you to be healthy and strong."

Scowling, she sat up. As if she were a tiny girl, Bonner slid one arm behind her back to support her while she sipped the cold liquid. As he did so, she felt his hand press along the side seams of her oversized pink sleep T-shirt.

She jerked away slightly, pushing the glass so that a few droplets spilled on the bedcovers.

Bonner pulled away, smiling. "Do I make you nervous? I'm just getting you some water, Dani. After all, I am your new father, and I'm your legal guardian. I'm just being affectionate as any father would be."

Dani stared at him. At first she hadn't minded these nighttime visits, but now Bonner's deep, unctuous, perfectly pronounced voice, his babying of her, his slight yet insinuating touches made her feel strangely uneasy.

"I guess I'm pretty sleepy now," she lied.

"Fine, then."

He picked up the water glass and left, snapping the door shut behind him. As the door closed, Dani sat upright, her back rigid. Her heart had begun to pound.

Since Christmas, Dani had come to a startling and uneasy realization. Bonner liked her almost *too much.* The card tricks, the snowmobiling, the CDs he bought her, the money he kept giving her, his deep interest in everything she was interested in. It was all beginning to make her feel uncomfortable. He'd even come to watch her jazz dancing class, not once, but three times. None of the regular fathers had come at all. And more often now, he left Maureen out of the little jaunts he took Dani on. Once he had even walked in on Dani while she was in the shower, saying he was only trying to put some towels in her bathroom.

And oddly, the more interested he became, the more she withdrew. She'd begun to feel an aversion to his touch. She couldn't help it. In her experience, grown men didn't touch unless they wanted something. And she was beginning to worry . . . had Bonner touched Tessa, on Christmas Eve? Was that why Tessa had screwed up her face and made her mouth into a thin, scared line?

Dani got out of bed and flicked on the bedside lamp. Her beautiful pink and ivy green bedroom sprang into life around her, like a picture in one of Maureen's home magazines. She padded into the bathroom, which was too pretty to be real, stocked with towels sheared so thick they were heavy to hold.

She touched a rheostat and the vanity mirror lights began to glow. There was also a beautiful crystal-and-brass fixture on the ceiling.

Suddenly Dani had the odd feeling that Bonner was watching her.

Right here. Right now. *Staring* at her in her big sleep T-shirt. She whirled, wondering if he had walked unannounced into her room again, but when she peeked around the door, there was no one.

Walking over to the toilet, she sat down and flipped up the hem of her shirt, lowering the matching pink bikini panties. The sounds her water made, splashing into the commode below, seemed too loud.

She jumped as she heard a creaking noise that sounded almost as if it were overhead, in the ceiling. But then she remembered that the house was more than a hundred years old, and her nervousness went away. All old houses were noisy, Maureen had told her. They creaked and snapped and popped, especially in cold weather.

*   *   *

In the attic, Bonner Lockwood balanced himself delicately on the wooden plank that extended outward across the floor joists over their sea of pink insulation material. He had drunk several shot glasses of Jack Daniel's and now felt very loose, his skin glowing.

"There, there, there," he whispered to himself. "Let's see; let's see what we've got here."

He reached his destination and hunkered down on the board, reaching out for what appeared to be only another bunch of the insulation material. He lifted it up, revealing a hole cut in the floorboard, into which he had carefully positioned a video camera. He had done the installation before the girl had arrived, working only when Maureen was out of the house.

The sound of a toilet flushing made him jump. She was right underneath him! Bonner waited, still and frozen, as the water soughed in the old pipes, gargled, and finally was silent. God, he'd nearly blown it. He decided to make sure Dani was back in bed and asleep before he attempted to take the videotape out of the camera.

Waiting, Bonner could feel his muscles, already tensed from the adrenaline boost of his secret maneuvering, grow even tighter, bunching up across the back of his neck in waves of low-grade pain.

The memories flashed on him. That morning of his eleventh birthday, when he and Melinda Beson had crawled into her father's garage and started sex-playing. Melinda, although only twelve, skinny and narrow-hipped, was no virgin. She had done it with boys before, fifteen or sixteen times.

They did the whole thing. At least, he had tried to put his thing in her, but it was soft, rubbery, and Melinda took hold of him and tried to stuff him between her legs. He became angry and pushed harder at her, but his dick still didn't get hard.

Then the unthinkable happened. Her father walked into the garage and found them.

Howling with anger, the man had charged savagely at the pair, hurling Bonner against a wall, grabbing Melinda up in one huge, hamlike fist.

And Bonner with his growing erection, so hard, so painfully rigid, he had never been so hard before, he thought he would explode with it. And when he looked, Melinda's father had slammed her onto the floor and she was lying sprawled with her legs wide open and Bonner could see . . .

The memory-fantasy, repeated thousands of times since until it now formed his actual sexual orientation, had its desired effect. Bonner's erection was now huge.

Moving fast, he crawled to the end of the plank and managed to reach down and grab hold of the camcorder. Thanks to his expertise in installation, it came up easily. He was sweating as he extracted the cassette.

He could hardly wait to view it.

Midnight traffic buzzed north-south on Woodward Avenue, its rumble slightly muffled by snow. Horns were honking at a nearby White Castle as customers, many inebriated from the night's festivities, lined up in their cars at the drive-up window, waiting for their miniature burgers flavored with fried onions.

Two blocks away, in an apartment on a side street that she had once shared with Dani, Fay McVie pawed the secret lining of her purse. She was searching for the small plastic Baggie, one corner of which held fifteen grams of cocaine. It was payment for her night's work, entertaining three johns from Urbana, Illinois, in town for a sales convention at Cobo Hall.

"I'm puttin' this on credit, honey," Harley, her pimp, had informed her as he doled it out to her. "You owe me nearly fifteen *thou*, honey, and don't you be forgettin', 'cause I ain't."

Lately, Harley had been telling her she was getting too thin. Looking in the mirror, Fay *was* beginning to worry. Despite her curly California-streaked blond wig, she looked ten years older than her real age of thirty-three. Her cheekbones now had deep hollows, and her nostrils were reddened, with sores inside from where the constant sniffing of cocaine had ulcerated the mucous lining.

Anxiously she raided her billfold, finding a five-dollar bill and rolling it into a tight cylinder. She took an old piece of mirror and spooned a small amount of powder onto the glass. Using a credit card, she began forming it into two lines. Barely enough.

She lifted the mirror and inserted the cylinder of the bill into one nostril. Pinching the other nostril shut, she greedily tilted her head back and sniffed deeply. Then she sucked up the other line.

The miracle happened.

The powder hit the back of her throat and numbed it almost immediately. Within seconds, she began to feel the first overwhelmingly pleasant rush of euphoria. It zinged through her, pounding her pulse and blood pressure up, electrifying every vein and artery, every capillary.

When she was at last high, she jumped up from the mattress and began to pace restlessly around the small apartment. Jesus! What a rat hole. It smelled like a goddamn garbage can from all the stacked-up empty pizza cartons and old White Castle bags. Before she left, Dani used to keep things picked up, and she had cooked most of their meals.

A pile of clothes lay on the floor, some gold and rhinestone four-inch high heels, a black lace cat suit, and various spandex junk Fay wore for the johns, along with a tousled red wig that badly needed washing. When Fay kicked these aside she saw, exposed on the bare floor, a photograph of her daughter.

The Polaroid had been taken five months ago by Carl, one of Fay's regulars. It showed Dani, wearing nothing but a pair of lavender bikini panties, glaring over her shoulder into the camera.

Fay scooped up the picture and tossed it onto her dresser. The little priss. Couldn't even smile for the camera. She wondered where Dani was now. The state had taken her away, put her in a car and driven off with her, and the injustice still rankled. Dani was *her* kid. She had parental rights.

Fay's brief high had already crested, and was starting down the other side, bringing the first symptoms of the savage anger and abysmal depression that were its aftermath. She threw herself back on the bed, sudden hatred pouring through her.

Little smart-ass Miss Dani. If Dani were here, Fay could use her to get some more coke out of Harley, enough to fly on for a while, and she wouldn't have to live like this, in garbage and squalor.

The phone began to ring. Was it Harley, wanting her to turn "just one more trick"? Why should she, when he paid her so poorly? She should be living in some luxury apartment in Farmington Hills or West Bloomfield, not like this.

Fay glared at the phone until finally, on the six-teenth ring, it stopped.

"What about Brittany? I love the name Brittany. It's a cool name."

Maureen was hurrying to get ready to leave to teach her freshman English class. She wore a gray pinstripe maternity suit with white piping, and matching gray high heels. "Brittany is a common name," she told Dani. "Half the little girls today are being named Brittany; the shopping malls are full of Brittanys."

"What about Heather? I think Heather is so-o-o-o glamorous. I wish *I* had a name like Heather; it's really cool, even cooler than Brittany."

Maureen was rushing about, combing her hair, collecting her eyeglasses. The pregnancy hampered her, and now the doctor said they may have made a mistake in her due date. She was also beginning to worry that she wouldn't have any natural mothering skills. After all, she was old, very old, to be giving birth for the first time.

She remembered Dani. "Yes, yes. Or Whitney is a lovely name. Don't you think it's pretty?"

Dani fidgeted with a flake of cereal that had fallen on the linen tablecloth, mushing it with her thumb. "Yeah. Maureen, I, that is, I think Bonner touches me too much."

Maureen was so startled she nearly dropped her glasses. *"Touches* you too much? Oh, come on, Dani!" She gave a short, incredulous laugh and with quick motions began transferring the contents of a brown purse to a gray one.

"I mean really. Really he does. He all the time puts his hands on me, and he tucks me in too hard, and he pretends like it was all an accident. And I think he touched Tessa. And he was watching me last night in the bathroom, only I don't know how he—"

Maureen caught her breath, feeling frozen in a tiny moment, trapped like a fly behind glass. She had an instantaneous choice: either believe Dani and wreck her marriage and the way she thought about her husband, wreck forever the way she thought about the *world*, or. . . . She chose the second choice. It wasn't even a choice really. It was an instinct.

"And you are full of stories this morning, aren't you, young lady? I mean really, Dani! You have more imagination than ten other girls your age."

"It's true," insisted Dani. "He touched me a hundred times, I bet. And Tessa was mad and she wouldn't talk to me, and—"

"I don't know what Tessa has to do with this. Bonner is your father, Dani, and that's what fathers do; they hug their daughters. Now, Dani," she said quickly, as the girl seemed about to interrupt. "Aren't you late for school? You'd better hurry, or you'll get a tardy slip."

Maureen left the house and walked out to the garage, where she got into her Cougar, starting the engine. Her breath was coming rapidly in her throat, and she could feel a sudden pulse pounding in her neck.

Dani's comments—so careless—had set her on edge. *A child brought up with abuse is naturally going to think about abuse*, she told herself. *Read it into the simplest, most common acts.* In fact, hadn't Vivian warned them this might happen?

She certainly wouldn't tell Bonner about it, she decided. He'd be insulted—deeply angry.

Her thoughts went to her husband, with whom she'd had a few words this morning while both were dressing. Nowadays she was forced to step aside to her dressing room to shield her cumbersome body from her husband's gaze. Bonner hadn't said anything directly, but Maureen knew he disliked her bulging abdomen and found it repulsive.

"That new sweater you bought Dani yesterday," she'd started things. "Her birthday isn't until July. Don't you think you're overdoing it a little? She's going to become very materialistic if you keep on indulging her."

"I have to win her trust, Maureen. Besides, I think you're jealous. If you want a new sweater, just go out and buy yourself one."

She pulled on her maternity blouse, buttoning it rapidly. "I can't wear regular sweaters now. Bonner, I hope you realize that a thirteen-year-old doesn't need all the things you shower on her, and material things aren't going to help her to love us more."

"I'll buy her what I want to," Bonner had said coldly. "*You* wanted an infant, didn't you? And I really didn't. Now you're going to have what you want, so why shouldn't I have what I want, too?"

"Which is?" she'd dared to say.

"What?"

"I mean what is it you really want out of fatherhood, Bonner?"

He'd stared at her. "If you have to ask, Maureen, then just don't bother."

Now, pulling into the faculty lot, Maureen found

an empty space. "Bonner touches me too much,"
Dani had insisted. Parking, Maureen had a sudden
vision of Bonner and Dani arriving in from snowmobiling, Bonner helping the girl off with her snowmobile suit. Taking the zipper of the suit and sliding
it downward, his knuckles lightly brushing her
chest.

Instantly she pushed away the image.

Bonner wasn't . . . that way. It was totally ridiculous; it was just impossible. He was a college professor, for God's sake. He had the respect of thousands.
He was in line to become dean.

A sudden thaw that week had warmed the air, creating a suggestion of the spring that would not arrive
for another three months. Over the roofline of the
Sokols' garage, an icy crescent moon tried to peek
out through a mass of swiftly blowing, platinum
clouds.

"Sit on the cushion; make sure you sit tall," Ryan
ordered, turning and making a face as he backed
Bing Sokol's cherished Corvette out of the garage.

"Is this as fast as you can go?" Dani urged.

"I'm backing *up*. Hey, if I scratch anything on this
baby, my dad will murder me. He lives and breathes
for this car; he won't even let my mom touch it. Am
I too close to that garage door? Shit, shit, shit. . . ."

Both of them knew how dangerous this was. Ryan
had a yellowish mark on his lip from where his dad
had hit him during an argument the previous week.

After Ryan had managed the feat of backing out
and had turned onto the street, Dani expelled her
breath with relief. She and Ryan had been driving
the 'Vette almost every week, usually just around the

block, so as not to build up too much mileage on the odometer. She felt sure it was only a matter of time until Ryan was caught. What would Bing Sokol do when he discovered his precious Corvette had been driven? Especially by the son he seemed to be angry with most of the time?

Ryan thought this was all a joke, a rebellious way of getting back at his dad, but Dani had seen what happened when Fay got beat up. . . . Once Fay had actually peed blood.

Tonight they were going to a party given by Brad Stringer, a kid Ryan knew from school. There would be a keg of beer. Nervously Dani touched her hair, which she had combed to one side of her head and anchored with mousse. In it she wore rhinestone clips, and underneath her new down jacket, her black sweatshirt fairly dazzled with more rhinestones and beads. But still she knew she wasn't going to attract much attention. She still looked like such a baby . . . flat-chested. Since she'd arrived in Madisonia, Dani had begun to hate her own late-maturing body.

Something made her flash some of this anger on Ryan.

"Why do you do it? Take the 'Vette, I mean," she asked. "You know he'll do something terrible when he finds out."

"It's there." Ryan laughed harshly. "I don't know why I take it; I guess I just want to do something he would hate, and get away with it. I'd like to piss all over the seats if I could. Anyway, why do *you* lie?"

"I don't lie—not anymore."

"You do, too. You lie all the time. You told Jill Rudgate that your mother is a rock singer and used to sing with a real band."

"Well, she did," said Dani, tightening her mouth. "Once. That's really true. She sang at the Rhinoceros."

"Yeah, and I'm Michael Jackson."

"Well, I don't lie to you," she muttered.

With supreme care, Ryan drove the black Corvette down the street, passing the Lockwoods' house on the right. Several of its windows were lit, including the attic.

"What's that old Bonner Lockwood do up there anyway?" Ryan asked, forgetting they had been sniping at each other.

"Oh, he works on his book," Dani said.

"Yeah, I bet," Ryan sneered. "And something else, too."

"What do you mean?"

"He does dirty things up there, get my meaning? He jerks off up there. Don't you know *anything*?"

Ryan turned right on Observatory Street. The moist air seemed to haze the neighborhood, creating halos around the porch lights. The house where they were going was less than three-quarters of a mile away.

"I don't believe you," she blurted. "I mean . . . how do you know?"

"I know because I saw him one night. I was riding past the house on my bike and I heard somebody's cat in the bushes, and I went back in there to see if I could catch it, and I looked up, and there he was. He watches TV and does it," explained Ryan.

"Oh, gross."

"He probably has a big collection of dirty movies," Ryan explained. "That's what guys do; they play the movies and jerk themselves off, or they buy these magazines. My dad has some of those. *Penthouse*, you know. He keeps them in the basement under his workbench."

As Ryan continued with his monologue, showing off for her a little, Dani sighed. She had told Ryan about her nightmares, the sights she'd seen in her mother's apartment. But she hadn't told him all of it, and she knew Ryan didn't really understand. No one could.

"You think you know *everything!*" she finally exclaimed.

"Sure I do; I'm a guy," Ryan said, pleased. "Yeah, I know everything, huh? I'm King Ryan. I own the world. I own this 'Vette. I'm gonna race it in the Grand Prix. I'm gonna make my dad have a heart attack! I'm supreme!"

Dani couldn't help grinning at him. Ryan thought he was so bad. She knew better.

The party was being held in a garage, heated by a pair of electric space heaters. They entered from the side door and were drawn into a head-pounding cacophony of yells, shouts, and heavy metal. Most of the fifty teenagers jammed into the small space were aged thirteen to fifteen. All were dressed in Madisonia's current idea of "cool," black jeans, black jackets, rhinestones, beads, and tons of clunky steel jewelry. Several of the boys wore Harley-Davidson T-shirts emblazoned with snarling eagles and black boots decorated with boot bracelets.

"Where's the garage punk band?" Dani whispered, nudging Ryan. Despite the fact that she was wearing the right clothes, she felt shy in this group. She was in a special ed class at school, not a real one. If one of them dared to call her a *retard*—that had happened once at school—she was going to fight.

"Oh, they're not coming until eleven," Ryan said. "Come on, Dani, they've got a keg; let's get some beer, huh? Brad gets it from his brother; he buys it for him."

Some kids began calling to Ryan. Terrified he would desert her, Dani clutched his arm. "Hey," she begged. "Ryan . . . I don't know any of these guys."

"You know Megan Berkey from school. Anyway," Ryan said magnanimously, "I'll stick with you. You can be my date; would you like that? You're the prettiest girl here."

Dani tried to smile. "I see girls lots prettier."

"But they haven't got red hair, do they, Bic Head?"

An hour later, the garage had grown stiflingly hot from the combination of the heaters and the warm bodies, periodically blasted by cold air as someone else arrived.

Dani was dizzily drunk. The punk band had not yet arrived, but someone had turned up the boom box to maximum volume, and the bass beat seemed to thump her insides apart.

A group of them was sitting on the cement floor at the back, telling wild stories. The wilder the better. Dani was at the center, telling them all about Fay and Fay's pimp and what the johns did and said. She talked fast, gesturing.

The more she talked, the more they laughed.

She told them about the blood spot that had been in their previous apartment building, where a junkie had been murdered.

Then Megan Berkey, who'd been staring at Dani most of the night, interrupted.

"Hey, did you hear about those missing girls? Six of them, my mom says, all of them within thirty miles of here. None of them has ever been found. This girl, Alexis, she went down to the mall last year out near the highway and bought two pairs of crystal earrings and then disappeared. I mean maybe somebody took her. She's on a milk carton now . . . you know those milk cartons? And I saw her poster at the post office."

Dani didn't want to give up being the center of attention. "Oh, that's nothing. She prob'ly just ran away."

"No, I bet something happened to her, like she got caught by some guy and murdered. Just like in *Red Dragon.*"

"Oo-o-o-oh," said several of the kids.

"Yeah, some guy made her skin into a jacket."

Ryan said, "Yeah, some real weird guy, he's got a *dozen* jackets like that, and he sells 'em in a store at the mall, and *you've* got one on, Megan!"

Everyone roared.

"Oh, ho," said Dani, emboldened by Ryan's protection. "*I* bet she just ran away and now she's workin' in Detroit somewhere; a lot of girls do that. Some pimp is nice to them, and then they work for him. They turn tricks. You'd be amazed."

They all looked at her. "You're really a dirty girl, aren't you," said Megan.

Defiantly Dani stared back. She felt an enormous heave in the center of her stomach and wondered if she was going to throw up.

* * *

The Channel 7 news was finishing a story about two Utica teenagers who had been found dead in their car when Dani walked into the house.

"You're drunk," said Bonner as Dani sauntered in, her jacket slung under her arm.

"I'm not; I didn't," said Dani, swaying toward him and expelling a big gush of beer breath. She'd thrown up at the party, and now all she wanted to do was go upstairs and wash out her mouth.

"You're falling-down drunk. I can't believe it," Bonner said, grabbing her jacket and propelling her farther into the house. As he caught a whiff of her, his face became heavy with disgust. "Where did you go? I thought you were going to watch TV at Jill's house. I'm going to call her right now."

Maureen, looking hugely pregnant and uncomfortable in a dark green bathrobe, had come down the front staircase. "Bonner? What's going on? What's the trouble? Is Dani all right?"

Angrily Bonner picked up the phone. "This girl has just—"

"No," begged Dani, grabbing his hands to stop him. "Don't phone Jill. I didn't go there. I was . . . at a party," she admitted reluctantly.

"So where was this party then, young lady?"

"It was over on Observatory Street; we . . . they had a keg. We were gonna have a punk band, but then the band never showed up."

Bonner put down the telephone and started toward Dani. His eyes blazed with anger. "At thirteen years old, you went to a beer blast. Who accompanied you to this stellar event?"

"Bonner," said Maureen. "Please."

"Was it that little prick Ryan Sokol?" As Dani nodded, Bonner said, "I thought I told you not to talk to that little hellion. Dani, I made it very clear to you my feelings on that matter."

"I didn't do anything," she mumbled. "All we did was talk and dance a little."

"Dance!" Tiny balls of spittle flew out of Bonner's mouth. Dani watched them in drunken fascination. "Ryan Sokol is a juvenile delinquent; can I make myself any clearer than that? He runs with the wrong crowd and he is cruising for a nice, long term in some military school or juvenile facility. I do not, I repeat, I do *not* want you associating with characters like that, Dani."

"But Ryan is nice," she said defiantly. "He's my only friend here. He's my best friend."

A hand flashed in the air, and Dani, accustomed to dodging Fay's hits and slaps, automatically ducked, so that she received only the brush of Bonner's fingertips across her left cheek.

"Bonner, don't!" cried Maureen. "Bonner, please."

"You're grounded, young lady, do you hear me? You are absolutely grounded for *one week.* You'll go only to school and to your tutoring, and you will receive no phone calls, not one, do you understand me?"

"Yeah, sure, right," said Dani sullenly. "Grounding" was something they did here in Madisonia. She'd never even heard the word until she moved here.

But Bonner wasn't finished with her yet. "And you're going to promise never to see Ryan Sokol again. *If* you like living here, you'll do as I order."

If she liked living here? What was that supposed to mean?

"I . . ." Dani was about to begin a torrent of defiance, but then she remembered the new baby on the

way, the baby she was looking forward to so much.
She lowered her head. "Sure," she whispered.

"I *didn't*," muttered Dani, passing Maureen as she
climbed the stairs.

Maureen reached out to hug her, the position awkward because of her bulk. "Don't stir him up, baby.
He means well. He's never been a father; he's new at
it—"

"I said Ryan is *nice*," wept Dani, hurrying past.

Once upstairs, Dani used her bathroom, which
she desperately needed, rinsed out her mouth, and
crawled into bed. Her room, filled with all the new
things the Lockwoods had bought her, seemed big
and dark.

She lay with her eyes open, wondering if Bonner
and Maureen would really send her away. Terror
clutched the pit of her stomach.

Maybe they would. After all, hadn't she been sent
away from Mrs. Zagat's? The thought of not being
able to see the new baby caused tears to stab the
backs of her eyes. Maureen had *promised*. Dani was
going to diaper the baby and give her bottles and put
baby powder on her rear.

Dani drifted off to sleep for a few minutes, but then
the windy scrape of a branch against her window
awoke her. She lay listening to the sounds of the
wind rattling at the house, harrying a downspout. It
was turning cold again, the springlike weather moving on.

Finally she sat up in bed and dialed Ryan's private
line, the one in his bedroom. He picked up on the
first ring, as if he'd been waiting.

"*He* was mad," she whispered into the phone. "He

said I was drunk. I'm not supposed to see you any-more. He called you a little hellion."

Ryan gave a bitter laugh, but she could hear the hurt in it. "I knew this would happen. I guess that means you'll do it, huh? You're afraid of that dick-head, aren't you?"

"I'm not," she replied, stung.

"You are."

"I'm *not.*"

"Then prove it. Do something really bad; do some-thing they won't like."

"I don't know. . . ." Then Dani stopped. She thought about Bonner's study, the place where he kept his computer that he wouldn't show her, the attic rooms that were always kept locked. The way he'd been so reluctant for her to go upstairs.

"Well?" Ryan demanded. "I let you drive my dad's 'Vette; now you have to do something."

"Okay," she whispered. "We'll sneak into his rooms upstairs. But there's just one problem. He has a lock; he usually locks the stairway when he goes upstairs."

"What kind of a lock? It isn't a dead bolt, is it? My dad uses a dead bolt."

"No, it's just a regular lock."

Then Dani paused. She had just remembered something. Sometimes when Bonner took a nap downstairs in front of the TV in the family room, he left his keys and wallet lying on the table beside him.

"Ry," she said, giggling. "Do you know a place where we can get keys made? Somewhere quick and close?"

"Yeah—the hardware store around the corner. I copied some keys for my dad there once."

* * *

Dani put down her bare right foot, so softly her toes seemed barely to brush the carpet. Then, catlike, she took another step, moving noiselessly into the downstairs TV room where Bonner Lockwood lay snoring underneath an opened book, the television blaring out a documentary on World War I.

It looked as if he'd barely moved in the twenty-five minutes since she'd stolen the keys. She had relayed them to Ryan, who waited outside, ready to run them over to the ACO hardware store.

Ryan had kept the copies of the keys. Now all she had to do was put the key ring back down on the table where she'd found it.

She took another cautious step, edging toward the table from which she had taken the keys. Maureen was in her writing room, engrossed in her book, and Dani knew she'd be there for at least another hour. The key ring was slippery with the girl's own perspiration, and it jingled slightly as she started to put it back.

Suddenly Bonner's mouth moved. Dani's heart slammed, her windpipe closing as her adoptive father uttered a snorting mutter and jerked his body, snuffling as he changed positions. The book he'd been reading slid farther down his lap and appeared to be about ready to fall on the floor.

Hastily, conquering her fear, Dani darted her hand out and managed to deposit the keys on the table surface without letting them jingle. When she had done this, she sagged a little with relief. At least if he woke up now, she wouldn't have his keys in her hand.

Now she had to get out. She danced a cautious

step backward, and that was when she felt the hand close on her leg. Dani bit back a scream. The hand was thick, meaty, warm, the fingers gripping her slender thigh with iron strength.

"Muh-muh-melinda . . ." Bonner muttered in his sleep. As Dani stood paralyzed, Bonner's hand tightened, sliding farther up her leg until the fingers dug into her crotch.

"Muh-muh . . ."

Revulsion seized Dani. She twisted backward, shoving Bonner's hand away. To her relief, almost instantly the hand fell loosely, dangling over the arm of Bonner's chair.

Gasping, Dani forgot all caution and darted toward the door, scampering on her bare feet. She heard him moan again as she reached the doorway, but she didn't stop. She raced for the stairs and within seconds was in her own room, closing the door behind her.

Despite the fact that it was still only 3:30 in the afternoon, Dani burrowed her way under the bed quilt. Her body was shaking violently, and hot acid had forced its way up the back of her throat.

He had touched her . . . *there*, Dani thought, gagging. Memories hammered at her mind, searching for a way up to conscious level. Hands. Mouths. Wet tongue kisses. She shuddered, making tiny cries to herself. Then, slowly, her body began to relax. After all, Bonner *had* been asleep. He didn't know what he was doing.

Did he?

It was two days later, a school half-day. Ryan and Dani had the house to themselves. Maureen was out

shopping for a baby crib, and Bonner had left for one
of his committee meetings. Janice, the little college
girl who cleaned, had departed for class.

"There, there, that silver one, that might be it,"
said Ryan, searching through the ring of duplicate
keys. He began trying the keys. On the third try, the
bolt slid open.

The door opened silently, as if the hinges had been
oiled recently. The flight of stairs leading to the attic
stretched upward, covered by a gray carpet runner.
The walls were painted a plain white. A ray of wintry
sunlight slanting in from an upstairs window cast a
bar of light across the upper steps. Floating in its
nimbus were tiny, swirling specks of dust.

Up at the top was Bonner's secret place.

"All *right*," said Ryan, smacking his palm against
Dani's.

"All *right!*" she cried, smacking him back.

They started up the staircase.

The attic had collected an entire afternoon of sunlight and was now giving it back, stiflingly warm.

"Wow!" Ryan exclaimed, almost dancing into the
vestibule that opened onto the office and the room
that held the TV and VCR. "Look, Dani . . . this place
is *huge*; there's rooms and rooms!"

Dani was in a nervous, edgy, teasing mood. "Yeah,
and if there are any ghosts this is exactly where
they'd be. Ghosts are always in attics."

"Okay, let's start looking; he isn't gonna keep
magazines and dirty stuff out in plain sight. Guys
always hide them under beds and in drawers, and
places like that."

They roamed through the attic, poking at the computer, fingering disks, discovering fascinating low doors that opened into slanting crawl spaces, filled with old suitcases and men's suits wrapped in garment bags. One closet held a cache of empty Jack Daniel's bottles. They opened drawers and peered under couches and sat in Bonner's swivel chair and spun themselves around and around.

Ryan sauntered toward the back of the audio-visual room, discovering another low door. "What's this—wow!"

Dani came running, and they both bent over and peered into the crawl space. A breath of stale air came out to envelop them.

This wasn't a small cubbyhole like the two or three others they'd found. This space was huge, covering half the house, lighted only by weak sunlight coming from a couple of tiny windows under the eaves. Stretched out before them was a sea of floor joists marked with rows of fluffy pinkish material. A couple planks had been laid across the flooring, one going to the far left corner, the other branching off toward some pieces of plywood that formed a small island. Stacks of cardboard boxes occupied a third area.

"It smells like dead spiders. What's that pink stuff?" Dani said, swallowing.

"Insulation," said Ryan. "We have that in our attic, too."

A string hung from a bare light bulb overhead, and he pulled it. The forty-watt bulb cast a weedy circle of light.

Ryan said, "I'm gonna walk out on that board. I wanta see what's over there—maybe he keeps his dirty magazines in those boxes and junk."

"Ryan . . . no . . . what if they come back?"

Suddenly Dani's teasing mood was gone. The attic

was old and smelly, and if Bonner came home and discovered them here—she remembered the anger she'd seen in his eyes and shivered.

"Oh, they won't. We've got plenty of time." Ryan started across the plank.

Drawing a deep breath, Dani followed him.

Seen up close, the cardboard boxes looked *old*, their lids coated with a nasty mixture of spiderwebs, dead insects, and dust. But one had only a little dust on it, as if it hadn't been sitting there as long as the others.

"I'm gonna open one," Ryan said.

"No," she protested, but Ryan was already pulling a Swiss army knife out of his pocket. With a flourish he slit the strapping tape. The cardboard flaps came open with a small pop.

Both teenagers stared into the box.

Dani was the first to speak. "Why, this is nothing but a bunch of Barbie dolls."

She reached in and pulled out a doll with long, glistening yellow polyester hair that reached nearly to its ankles. It was wearing a cheap little spandex dress in shades of pink and purple that looked rather like what Fay wore when she went "out."

"Barbies? Aw, disgusting," said Ryan, disappointed. He continued to poke around in the box. "Look, there's about a dozen here, maybe more. And a Ken doll. And some pictures."

Dani sank back on her heels, frowning. She had never owned a Barbie doll and didn't find these appealing. "Why would Bonner and Maureen have Barbie dolls up here? Where no one can play with them?"

"Maybe Bonner plays with them." Smirking, Ryan

picked up two of the dolls and began waving them around, forcing their heads to butt each other.

"Don't do that," Dani begged.

Nervously she reached into the box and pulled out a stack of eight-by-ten glossy photographs. A familiar face grinned up at her. "All my love, Donny Wahlberg," had been printed across the photo. There were several other pictures of New Kids on the Block, each "signed."

It didn't make sense.

New Kids on the Block! Why would Bonner have their pictures in his attic? Why locked up in a *box*, where no one could ever see them? It was definitely weird. The shuddering feeling began in Dani again, sweeping over her. She made an effort to push it back. After all, Bonner hadn't *meant* to touch her between her legs, he'd been asleep, and he was her father now, he was . . .

"What's wrong?" asked Ryan. "Why are you just staring like that, Dani? Don't be a wuss. Come on; I want to find those dirty magazines." He reached for another box.

"No," said Dani anxiously, looking at the new watch Bonner had given her several weeks ago. "We'd better get out of here."

But Ryan had already slit open the second box. As the flaps sprang open, they smelled the staleness at the same time they saw the clothes, neatly folded. White cotton with tiny printed flowers on it. Scraps of pink and blue, trimmed with lace.

Young girls' underwear.

"This is *weird*," Ryan whispered, glancing over his shoulder toward the doorway where they'd entered the crawl space. "I mean this is really, *really* weird.

Underpants?" Gingerly he held up a pair of small yellow seersucker panties. There were a few dark brown stains along its elastic waistband. "God, and they aren't even clean."

When Dani breathed in, her breath seemed to whistle all the way down her throat to the pit of her stomach. Suddenly this wasn't an adventure, it was getting scary, and all she wanted to do was get out of here.

"What if that's . . . blood?"

"Don't be dumb. Blood is red, not brown."

"But—"

"Look, I gotta get out of here anyway," Ryan said. "I've gotta clean up my room or my dad is gonna go into orbit." Ryan was already edging along the board, the way they had come in. With alacrity, Dani followed him.

"Ry," she said when they had reached the door. "Ry, do you think—I mean what if Bonner is some kind of awful kidnapper or something?"

"Get back," Ryan said.

"No, really. What if *he* stole that girl, Alexis, the one who went to the mall to buy the crystal earrings? And then h—"

"For Jesus' sake," Ryan snapped, cutting off her flight of imagination. "What's wrong with you, Dani? The man is your father. He's just a jerk, that's all. Anyway, maybe this is Maureen's old junk, ever think of that? Or it belongs to those girls, those nieces you told me about. We only came up here for a game, and now I've gotta go and clean my room."

"But, Ry—"

"Chill *out*, Dani. You're always thinking these

weird things. Hey, this isn't Detroit; this is Madisonia. Boring old Madisonia. If we had a kidnapper living here, he'd move away because this place is too dorky and stupid."

4

DANI FELT THE hands on her and woke up so fast that her heart seemed to leap and wriggle like a live thing. She had been dreaming about that stained underwear in the attic, and the secret Barbie dolls.

She stared at the figure that was bent over her bed, arms cradled protectively around the abdomen. Delight exploded in her. "Our . . . our baby is coming?"

"Yes," groaned Maureen. "I think my pains are about five minutes apart, and I want to drive to the hospital. I don't want Bonner to drive me. He's—he drank a little too much last night and I'm afraid he'll have an accident. Will you ride in the car with me?"

Shaking away sleep, Dani looked at her foster mother. Maureen wore a pair of blue sweatpants and a matching maternity sweatshirt that was stretched to bursting over her abdomen. A layer of perspiration coated her upper lip. She looked very frightened, yet deeply elated.

Dani felt a jolt of pleasure and pride that Maureen had actually called on her for help.

"Yeah, sure, oh, cool! Yeah!"

Dani flew around her bedroom, pulling on a pair of

jeans and her favorite rhinestone tunic top, so excited she nearly put on two different shoes. While she was doing this, Maureen wrote Bonner a note and took it to their bedroom.

"Hurry," Maureen urged, when she returned. "This is it; this is real. God . . . the baby is really coming."

Five minutes later they were walking across the stiff winter grass toward the garage. Dani had to hold onto her adoptive mother's arm to help her. Despite her tininess, Maureen was heavy as she leaned on Dani's arm. A chilly wind buffeted them, full of tiny, hard snowflakes, pushing Maureen's sweatpants against her legs.

"God," moaned Maureen, as they struggled along. When they reached the detached garage, Maureen flicked the automatic door opener and then stood still, her legs braced, her eyes fixed on space as if concentrating on some inner message.

"Maybe you'd better get Bonner. Dani, I can't—"

"I'll drive," Dani said quickly.

"You?"

"I can drive. My ma taught me," Dani lied, realizing that she couldn't betray Ryan. "Get in the backseat," she improvised. "You can lie down back there. Here, I'll show you."

She helped Maureen to get in, feeling both terrified and important. The only car she'd ever driven was the Corvette, which had something that Ryan called a "four-speed," with a clutch pedal on the floor. Already she could see that the Cougar didn't have that.

Maureen moaned again, the sound small and animal-terrified. "Start the car, Dani!"

Dani felt a rush of panic. But she managed to insert the key in the ignition and switch on the motor.

"Lights," said Maureen. "Push that button—to your left! Oh, Dani, are you sure you can do this? God . . ."

The dashboard lighted up. Dani looked anxiously at all the meters and gauges, which suddenly were outlined in a garish green glow.

"Start it! Start the car, Dani. Use the gearshift . . . put the lever on *R;* that's reverse. And *D* is drive, Dani! Oh . . . God . . ."

Dani slammed the car into reverse.

When Bonner's alarm clock went off at its usual hour of 6:30 A.M., he had been dreaming that he was caught in a crowd just leaving a movie theater. He looked around him and saw that all the people leaving the theater were beautiful young girls, walking in twos and threes, their laughter like sweet, high bells. Some he even recognized as *his* girls. One was Melinda Beson, his first.

"Bonner!" called Melinda, and Bonner happily turned. But his eagerness turned to terror as he saw that the girl wore the head of a rotting, desiccated corpse. Her slitted eyes were crusted with white ooze, her lipless mouth opened in a howl. . . .

He awakened himself with his own cry, jerking upright in bed. He could smell himself, fumes from the whiskey he'd drunk last night, along with the sourness of fear-sweat.

Glancing around, he saw the note Maureen had left on her pillow, printed neatly. "I left for the hospital; come as soon as you can. Love, Maureen."

She was at the hospital.

Giving birth.

"Oh, holy shit," he kept repeating as the waves of

faintness rushed over him again and again. He had to grip the edge of the bedside table to keep himself from falling over. What should he do? She knew he had a weak stomach. She couldn't possibly expect him to go to the hospital, put on a mask and gown, and stand there in the delivery room, watching her expel it? He'd read enough about childbirth to know it would be full of blood and grunts and screams.

No, he thought, panting. She *couldn't* expect him to look at birth. He'd told her he wouldn't. Well, actually, they had not talked about it, but Maureen knew him; she knew how he felt about things like this. Having the baby had been her idea. In fact, the thought rushed into his brain, maybe the baby wasn't even his. He would almost rather it wasn't.

Quickly he got dressed, pulling on the same pair of gray dress slacks and heather-tweed sports jacket he had worn yesterday to class. Bile threatening to mount up in his throat, he hurried out of the bedroom.

Briefly he paused in the second-floor hallway. He could hear the wheezy bong as the grandfather clock in the downstairs entry hall chimed the hour, thirty minutes late.

Maybe he could say that he hadn't seen the note right away. Yes. Yes, that was an excellent solution. When he finally went up to the hospital to visit, all would be cleaned and sanitized and presentable.

The relief that spread over him was like getting a shot of vitamin B_{12}. Suddenly he felt wonderful. In command again, not helpless anymore, all of his dizziness and nausea gone as if they had never occurred.

He found his keys in his pocket and unlocked the door to his attic sanctuary. He had no classes to teach today and only a few student appointments scheduled for the afternoon. He would work on his Korea book for a while, he decided. Maybe look at a few things in his collection, just to calm his nerves.

As Bonner walked slowly up the stairs, he remembered that Maureen had had amniocentesis. Their baby would be a girl. He'd blanked the knowledge from his mind for months, but now it came flooding back. He would have another girl in the house, a baby he could mold and teach.

A baby who—

Sweat had begun to pour down his face.

He could feel the tension, generating itself, growing exponentially.

Dani leaned on the window that separated the baby nursery from the hospital hallway, both of her hands resting on the glass. Her eyes anxiously searched the row of isolettes.

The third isolette from the end contained a pretty, chubby infant who was trying to scrunch her small fist, whole, into her mouth. A squiggle of light hair formed a point at the top of her head. Her nose was a perfect button, her eyes already looking around as if she could see. She had kicked off her blanket and both tiny, bare legs kicked vigorously. Her coloration was milky pink.

Dani felt a rush of something so pure, so happy, that she could not find a name for it.

"There! There she is! That's *my* baby!" she burst out loudly. Her voice carried down the corridor to a nurse who was walking briskly, carrying a tray of medications.

The woman smiled at the girl's enthusiasm. "Your baby brother or sister?"

"My sister. She's called Whitney Maureen. An' she weighed nine pounds! I drove Maureen to the hospital, and *I'm* gonna change Whitney's diapers every day, and give her *all* her bottles."

"That's wonderful, honey, but visiting hours are over now, dear. You'd better go downstairs to the lobby with your father, and turn in your pass."

Dani sagged in disappointment. Bonner had finally arrived at the hospital—after the baby was already born—but had only stayed five minutes, saying he had a meeting to go to. He'd given Dani money and told her to take a cab home when she was ready.

Dani rode down in the elevator, still on a high. She was unable to resist telling several other visitors all about Whitney, magnifying the baby's weight to ten pounds. When Dani reached the lobby, she was attracted to the row of phone booths along one wall.

Dani hurried to the nearest one, stopping to fish inside her purse for the business card that Vivian Clavell had given her three months ago.

Vivian was coughing as she answered the phone.

"Just a little spring cold," she explained. "It's hung on a little. So Maureen had the baby? And it was a girl? Oh, Dani, that's wonderful," the social worker said warmly. "And I think Whitney is a beautiful name."

"Yeah, and she weighs eleven pounds."

"Eleven, Dani?"

"Or twelve. She's huge, the nurses said she was very, very big, and she's already sucking on her hands, and she's got her eyes open. She waves her arms around and tells people, 'Get outta my face, bro.'"

Vivian laughed. "Oh, Dani, Dani. I'm sure she's just a delightful baby. You're going to love her a lot." She paused. "As a matter of fact, I was thinking of driving over to Madisonia this weekend. The agency has just bought three new computers and I was able to bring one of the old ones home. It's still in good condition. I thought you might like it, if Maureen and Bonner think it's okay."

"A *computer?*" Dani nearly screamed. *"You're bringing me a computer?"*

"It's not an IBM, it's just a clone, but it works very, very nicely and I've put a word processing program on it for you, and a flight simulator game. There's a dot matrix printer, too. I'm giving you my old one."

Dani was ecstatic. "Oh, great, oh, it's so great. I never had a computer before, or a baby either."

Bonner hunched over the desk in his office, staring blearily into the glass that held several inches of dark golden liquid. He hadn't been able to dissipate the tension that had seized him in its quivering grip. A strange feeling was rippling up and down his arms, the lights in the room throbbing in and out of his brain. He was drunk. Royally drunk. And he was going to get even drunker.

He was a father now; he was legal guardian in any court of law. Yes, every bite of food Whitney ate would be due to him. He would control every aspect of her existence, from selecting the style of diapers she would wear to picking out her college.

Lifting the bottle, Bonner sloppily poured another golden shot of whiskey into the glass. He had never wanted a baby in his house, he thought savagely; he had told Maureen this before they were married. Maureen had forced this on him, claiming she had "miscalculated" and thought she was going through early change of life. Saying this was her last chance . . . a lot of bullshit about her biological clock.

He realized that he was crying. Startled, he put a hand to his right eye, scooping up a tear on the pad of his right index finger. He brought the finger down and stared at the small globule of liquid.

Then he put it in his mouth and tasted it.

The tear was tiny, salty, exquisite. It spread along his tongue like a miniature explosion. He felt a strange thrill of excitement. He had tasted other tears before, tears of his pretty girls, his beautiful girls, but never his own.

That was something he had never done before.

He realized that he was pushing up out of his chair, walking out of the door.

He drove aimlessly along the country roads that fanned out from Madisonia, populated by small farms, farm implement dealerships, apple orchards, and an occasional cider mill. It was late afternoon and he didn't really know where he was going yet, but he always felt this way at first. He knew the decisions would make themselves, one by one.

This is not my fault, he told himself as he drove. *I didn't ask for this. This time I won't hurt her. I swear it. I'll just hold her and love her and let her seduce me. Then I'll let her go.*

There was a town called Nellis Lake about fifteen miles away from Madisonia, situated near Highway 37, which headed south through Hastings, then Bat-

tle Creek. He pulled the van into the little town,
which featured a tiny Main Street populated with
some down-at-the-heels stores. A few shoppers were
out walking from store to store, country-type people.

Two blocks from downtown, he spotted a small,
shabby grocery store next to a closed restaurant
called Eddie's Country Inn. A girl of about eleven was
just walking in the door, letting it swing behind her.
She wore a short pink parka, stone-washed jeans,
and purple sneakers, cheaper versions of the clothes
he and Maureen had bought for Dani.

Driving the van around to the side, Bonner
parked, noting that there were no other cars in the
lot. He waited patiently for the girl to come out, tapping lightly on the wheel of the van. Beside him in the
front seat was a box containing six or seven of the
Barbie dolls, carefully arranged in compartments.

Gradually his patience waned. Her stay inside the
small family store seemed to take forever. What was
she doing, picking out the week's groceries? He
shifted nervously, thinking about driving on. Vans
were common as dirt here in the country, but he
didn't want his remembered.

Shit . . . but then he saw the door bang again and
the girl came out. This time he was able to see her
face, not as pretty as he would have liked, her nose
a bit wider than he usually preferred. But she had a
beautiful mouth, full, pouty, and red.

As she started across the small parking lot, Bonner opened the van door and stepped out, smiling. In
his hands he held the box of Barbie dolls. Concealed
in his pocket was a bottle, and a folded square of
cloth already saturated with chloroform.

"Pardon me," he said. "Do you know the way to
Janet's Doll Hospital? I think I've gotten turned

around somehow on these roads. Is this Main Street?"

"What?" She had stopped, as alert as a young white-tailed deer, and then she giggled. "Main Street. We're *on* Main Street. But I don't know about any doll hospital."

"*Janet's* Doll Hospital? I was told it was here in town." Bonner lifted up one of the Barbies. She was wearing a pink net evening dress trimmed with lace and a few sequins, her yellow hair streaming down her back. "I sell these, you know. By the bulk."

"Really?" The girl approached a few steps closer.

"Could you possibly give me your opinion about something?" Bonner said. "As a customer of dolls, I mean. Do you like your dolls to have really long hair, down to their feet, or would you prefer the hair at shoulder length? And do you want to be able to comb it yourself? Is the doll grooming an important part of the picture for you?"

She giggled. "I guess."

She was standing right beside him now, her small figure blocked from view by the bulk of the big blue van. Bonner didn't wait any longer. He dropped the doll and gripped the girl, his left hand cupping her small head, the right one stuffing the chloroform-saturated cloth over her mouth.

Its smell was sweetish, yet sickening. She struggled against it for a few seconds, then abruptly sagged, her knees going out from under her. She was tinier than she'd appeared; barely sixty pounds was his guess. Bonner tossed her into the back of the van and slid the door shut.

A minute later, he drove the van out of the lot, proceeding at a normal, safe speed designed not to attract the attention of any passersby. He had rigged the back of the van so it could not be unlocked from the inside. But he didn't hear any sounds from back there.

He drove outside of town to a wooded area he'd seen before and parked the van underneath a stand of bare trees. It would take her a few minutes to wake up. He could feel his tension peaking, blood tremoring through his veins, beginning to mass in his groin, hardening him to iron.

Already he knew he was not going to let her go.

Vivian pulled into Madisonia. The February thaw had melted the snow from the campus grounds, and clean-cut students in down jackets rode bikes, book bags slung across their backs. A sign advertised a poetry festival. She felt a lift of her spirits at the thought of seeing Dani. And she had to admit it; she was dying to see the baby Dani was so excited about.

Dani rushed to the door to greet her.

"Mrs. Vivian, Mrs. Vivian! I gave Whitney two bottles today and I changed her diapers, and I can get her to burp. She makes a noise like this . . . eerrrg."

Vivian laughed. "I guess she must be a champion belcher."

"Do you want to see her? Do you?"

"Of course, but first we'd better tell Maureen I'm here, don't you think, Dani?"

Dani rushed off to get Maureen, who obviously had been awakened from a nap. Her hair was tousled and she was still yawning.

"I'm sorry," Vivian apologized. "I'll just stay for a few minutes. Dani wants me to see the baby, and I want to bring the computer into the house and help her set it up."

"Of course." Maureen yawned. "Bonner isn't here.
. . . He's out driving around, I think. Sorry I sound so
sleepy, but Whitney does have a way of keeping us
up." A reedy infant's cry interrupted her. "Oh, there
she is now. I'll go get her."

"She's the prettiest baby in the whole *world,*"
gloated Dani as Maureen returned with the infant
cradled in her arms, several layers of flannel blankets wrapped around her.

"Oh . . ." said Vivian, who loved babies. "Oh . . . she
is."

"She's our girl," said Maureen.

"She can see everything. She looks right at me!
And she bubbles spit," volunteered the proud Dani.

Vivian admired everything about Whitney and was
permitted to hold her for a few minutes, and then she
excused herself, saying that she wanted to carry the
computer up to Dani's bedroom.

"Of course," said Maureen. "I'll put this punkin
back down again."

Vivian decided to set up the computer on a table
near Dani's front window. With Dani practically
dancing around her, providing a dozen suggestions,
Vivian managed to connect all the cables to the
proper outlets. She had brought a six-outlet wall
adapter and plugged in the cords, admonishing Dani
as to proper safety.

"Can we turn it on? Can I type?"

"I don't see why not."

They sat together at the screen, Vivian showing the
girl how to position her fingers on the keyboard, how
to scroll up and down with the arrow keys, and how
to erase. Seated so close to Dani, Vivian felt a sensation of emotional warmth. Why hadn't she herself
ever had a child? But her husband, Carl, had had a

low sperm count and found adoption repugnant. Then she was too old, and he had died, ending the possibility forever.

"This is fun," Dani said, bouncing a little. "This is real fun. We never had any computers in Detroit. I'm gonna type twenty letters. I'm gonna write a book here, a kids' book just like Maureen. Only mine's gonna be for little babies."

Finally Vivian left Dani still sitting, enthralled, in front of the screen, and went downstairs to say good-bye to Maureen.

"It has been a bit exhausting." The foster mother looked tired as she warmed up a bottle of formula on top of the stove. "I lost a fair amount of blood, and my hemoglobin is low. The baby wakes up every night about 2:00 A.M., and my husband is absolutely no assistance at all. He does a very good job of ignoring Whitney entirely. And he spent all of five minutes visiting me in the hospital. Natural functions upset him."

"I suppose Dani is a great help."

Maureen sighed. "Oh, yes. It gets tiring some-times, her enthusiasm. But at least she's willing. Oh," she added, apparently remembering that Vivian was a social worker. "I'm sorry for sounding like such a complainer, Mrs. Clavell. It's just post-partum depression, I guess. The doctor says it's very normal."

Antoine "Harley" Jones walked around Fay's un-made bed, where she was seated, taking off her panty hose, trying not to snag them with the rings she wore on four fingers.

With disgust he bent to pick something up off the

floor. "Shit, Fay, your place looks like a dog's dinner. Pizza boxes growin' penicillin on them. Don't you never clean it up?" He handed the object to Fay, and she saw that it was the Polaroid photo of Dani.

"This here is your little girl, right? She some pretty piece of ass."

"Yes, yes. . . ."

"Virgin?"

Fay threw the hosiery on the floor and licked her tongue over her mouth. "You know, Harley, you know she isn't; you know what we—"

"Well, she gonna *be* a virgin. She's young, right, she's a pretty piece of candy, and I got a guy that's willing to pay good money for her. An important man, big in the city of Detroit, know what I mean? He wants her, and if you get her for me, I'm gonna do you a nice, big favor."

Fay was exhausted from a long night dealing with johns who had tried to cheat her. One had given her no tip, and another fool had balked at wearing a condom. Now she was waiting for Harley to give her her night's supply of coke, so she could get high and forget all of this, just be herself for a little while.

She said suspiciously, "What favor?"

"I'm gonna declare your debt to me partly paid, girl. I'm gonna write off five thousand dollars of it. What do you think about that, huh?" Harley stood with his hands akimbo on his leather-clad hips, grinning at her.

Fay swallowed. The way they were positioned, her seated, him standing, his midsection was close to her eyes. She could see his gold-inlaid belt buckle, an object that had been used on her more than once. She hated him, and yet she really did love him, too, because he gave her the coke, and he provided a way for her to live, and she depended on him.

"Sure, Harley," she whispered. "Now, baby, I really, really need something. I—"

"Can you get the kid?"

"I don't know where she is. Please, Harl. . . ."

"Bullshit. She went through Social Services, right? Or some fucking agency? They got things written down; they got it all in their folders somewheres."

"Yeah, but . . ." Fay shrugged. She wasn't interested in Dani right now. She needed something to bring her up.

"Do it," snapped Harley. "I got a man waiting, he likes pale white pussy, and I don't want to disappoint him."

"Aw, Harl. . . ."

Suddenly a pair of black hands were clamped around her neck, closing off Fay's air. She gasped, trying to pull away the thick, dark, spatulate fingers, but Harley's fingers were the thickness of Ball Park franks, immovable.

"Do it, cunt," he whispered as she gasped and grunted and kicked her feet. "Baby, don't you get it? You mine, so she's mine, too."

A week had passed since Bonner had made love to the pretty blonde in the pink jacket, and already he had put the Barbie dolls back in the attic and relegated the girl to the dimness of memory, something best forgotten.

That Saturday noon, Bonner came downstairs, locking the attic staircase behind him. An irritating sound greeted him. Whitney was squalling for her bottle.

"Maureen!" he called down the stairs to the living area. "Maureen!" he called again. "Dani!"

But no one responded, and the baby's wails continued. Bonner sighed with aggrieved annoyance. He hadn't been able to work because the cries had penetrated upstairs, disturbing his concentration. Now, glancing out of the window, he saw Maureen standing on the front porch steps, accompanied by Dani, both of them having a nice, long chat with the mail lady.

Grunting in disgust, Bonner strode into the large, sunny room that Maureen had decorated in pink and sea foam green for the baby.

Cautiously he approached the white crib that had been set up at the far end of the room. Reaching it, he stared down at the sobbing infant. The baby lay on her back, wearing only a newborn-sized pair of Pampers. Her legs kicked energetically, her fists waving. Her crying mouth was wide open and pink, exposing toothless gums.

Stepping closer, he placed his forefinger on the baby's cheek. Instantly the cries stopped. Whitney turned her face toward him and began to suckle, her greedy lips fastening on his finger as if it were a nipple.

Shocked, Bonner felt a quivering sensation run up his finger and up his arm, then somehow down to his groin. My God, what was she doing? What did she want? Did she think that his finger was the bottle? For the first time he noticed the tiny, exquisitely perfect, winglike eyebrows, the small button nose.

"Whitney," he whispered.

He stood for a very long time letting her suck, and allowing the strange feelings to drop over him, the warmth, and yet the feeling of power, too. That something so small, so little, so helpless, should be turning to *him.*

"Whitney? You're pretty, aren't you? You're a very pretty baby."

It was a revelation.

Carefully, so as not to disturb the sucking, he reached down with his left hand and touched the baby's full, distended stomach, bare above the diaper. Her skin was satiny, so incredibly soft that he felt as if his fingertip was scratchy and might hurt her.

Delicately, working with only his left hand, he managed to get a tab of her diaper loose. Then the other tab.

He stared down. She lay naked before him, frankly open to him. Tears flooded to his eyes as he realized that all his fears about what a newborn baby looked like had been foolish, ridiculous, a product of his horror dreams, not reality.

This baby was truly beautiful. Every inch of her skin, from the cunningly wrought protrusion of her belly button to the beautifully enfolded crevices between her legs, was perfect. And yet, as he stared, another feeling, much more dark and guilty, began to grow in him.

Angrily he pulled his finger out of the baby's mouth. It emerged with a wet pop. Interrupted, she started to cry again. It was the same high-pitched, nerve-screeching wail.

Bonner slammed out of the room, fed up. Why the hell was Maureen talking to the mail carrier anyway? Why didn't she come up here and do her job? It was *her* baby, not his.

Walking downstairs, he saw an old Toyota drive slowly past the house, its muffler slightly rackety.

The neighborhood was getting scruffy, he thought.
Why didn't people work hard and save their money
and buy decent cars, instead of old cruisers that pol-
luted the environment?

Fay McVie grimaced as the old, rusted Toyota gave a
cough, its engine making a threatening rattle. She
pulled to a stop at the corner near the Lockwoods'
house, careful to observe the sign, just like a regular
citizen. She'd heard that in these small towns they
were hell on traffic violators.

She was wearing one of her wigs, a black number
that streamed in dozens of tight curls to the center of
her back, just as good as the hairstyles she saw in
the Victoria's Secret catalog. She'd pulled it back
with a ribbon, in order to pass as a housewife or
secretary.

She was angry and pissed because of Harley, and
the only reason she was here was because he had
forced her into it.

*"Bring back the kid; she's mine, and I got a use for
her. Or . . ."* The thick, dark fingers had flexed. *"Get
the picture, girl? We got money hanging on this one.
Big money. And I never turn my back on money."*

Fay had assumed it would take weeks to weasel
out Dani's address, but the receptionist at the social
service agency, probably new on the job, had been
dumb enough to believe Fay's story about being a
court-appointed child psychologist. Shit, she could
talk the talk; hadn't she gone to therapy for two
months once? Of course she'd walked out when they
started talking about why she continued to hook.

She drove around the block, taking in the huge
Victorian houses, painted in shades of sunshine yel-

low, Williamsburg blue, warm gray, and country cream. Front porches were decorated with pillars and that pretty, gingerbready wood. There were wooden decks and stained-glass windows and winter wreaths on doors. One house even had a huge structure built onto the deck that Fay thought was called a gazebo.

Some fancy place Dani had fallen into, Fay thought dully.

Well, she was going to fall out of it pretty quick, just as soon as Fay figured out how best to lift her. These rich bastards that had adopted her would probably get their asses in a sling, and Fay had no intention of going to jail over this. She'd been to jail a couple times before, and one of the male guards had raped her.

She cruised past the house a couple of times but didn't see any sign of life, and finally she turned the car and began driving aimlessly. School . . . on TV didn't they show people waiting outside schoolyards, kidnapping their kids as they came across the playground? But when she found the redbrick junior high, she saw that it was empty of students. Dismayed, she realized that it was Saturday.

"Shit," she said, laughing harshly, then gripped the steering wheel until her rings cut into her skin. "Am I dumb or what?"

Driving past a party store, she saw a phone booth, and she actually drove up to the booth and parked, thinking that she would call Harley and tell him she couldn't get Dani today. But then her mind clicked into gear and she said to herself again, *"Dumb."*

Harley didn't have to know she'd found Dani yet. Jesus, she didn't have to tell him her every move, did she? That would give her time to come over here a

*couple times, go past the house at night, find out
whether little Dani ever left the house with her girlfriends . . . find out when would be the best time to
snatch her.*

5

R_AIN SWEPT GRAY_ sheets over College Street, rattling the windows as bursts of wind drove it against the house. Dani wore a big, roomy lavender T-shirt with a dancing unicorn on it that Bonner had given her.

Sitting in the rocking chair in Whitney's room, Dani could hear the April rain gushing along the gutters, then flowing to the ground, spattering the bed of daffodils beneath.

"Aaah," crowed the baby.

"Rocky baby, rocky baby," Dani crooned. She cradled the ten-week-old infant in her arms. "Oh, rocky baby."

"Guh," responded Whitney, her bright eyes focused directly on Dani. She made cooing, smacking noises.

Dani sighed with pleasure. Babies were wonderful, especially Whitney. She adored the way Whitney snuggled, the way she grinned and laughed when Dani sang rock-and-roll songs to her. Holding Whitney gave Dani the warmest, softest, sweetest feeling she had ever known.

Finally, when the baby's eyelids fluttered shut, Dani regretfully put her back in her crib, positioning the infant on her stomach, so that her small rump protruded upward. Dani called it her "frog" position.

Dani had some spelling work sheets to complete, and she left the baby's room, intending to go to her room and get them. That was when she saw the door to Bonner's stairs, opened a full four inches.

He must have forgotten to lock it.

She paused, drawn by a burst of compelling curiosity. Since she and Ryan had sneaked into the attic, she had not been able to stop thinking about the odd things they had found up there. Ryan had told her to stop thinking about it, that everyone kept old junk somewhere, but Dani had become obsessed with wanting to know more.

The gaping door continued to tempt her. She glanced around, making sure that she had the upstairs hallway to herself. Finally, stealthily, she pulled the door a few inches wider and slipped between the space. The carpet runners hid her noise as she crept up the steps toward Bonner's domain.

Bonner sat in his "audiovisual center," staring at the running red lights on his VCR as he rewound the tape he had just been playing. It was one of his "specials," a video he had made using two VCRs, transferring onto a master tape the scenes he liked best.

It had rained four days out of the past six, and the lack of sunlight was beginning to wear away at his nerves, making him irritable. Dean Rabaul was waiting to be admitted to the hospital for a double bypass. Talk was that Bonner was a shoo-in for the post of temporary dean, and possibly the permanent dean if Rabaul should decide to retire this spring, following his surgery. Bonner had waited years for just such a chance, and now he couldn't shake this persistent unease, this *tension.*

The girl in the pink jacket hadn't lasted long, and now she might as well have not happened at all. Already Maureen had asked him what he'd been dreaming about that was so bad he'd woken up and cried out.

The VCR completed its task. Bonner reached down to punch the eject button and caught the emerging tape, cradling it in both of his hands.

He consulted the stack of videos he'd selected, chose another one, and inserted it. Settling back in his chair again, he began to watch as Dani appeared on the screen, a pink, pretty Dani all naked and shivering after her bath. He narrowed his eyes, beginning to get excited as he inspected the lissome purity of her body. Dani. His homegrown girl, the one he was saving.

He had not been able to rig a satisfactory sound system, so there was no sound, just the bare essence of Dani as she walked to the vanity sink, turned on the tap, and ran water into her cupped palm. Lifting her dripping palm, she gulped water. Bonner watched, fascinated. The bathroom was supplied with a pink plastic drinking cup, but to his knowledge Dani never used it, always preferring to drink out of her own hand. Maybe in her previous home there had been no cups. Those ghetto types lived like animals, he thought.

Dani drank three handfuls of water, then wandered over to the toilet, where she sat down, leaning forward, her legs spread. Her feet on tiptoe, she began to urinate. The act made her seem unbearably vulnerable. It tore at Bonner's heart. How much longer could the girl remain at this level of perfection? They always grew older . . . faster than you believed possible.

In fact . . . wasn't Dani getting breast buds?

In a few short months she was going to be too old for him. In a few months he was going to find her repellent. He would have to make his move before then.

Dani reached the top of the stairs. She was excited now, with the prospect of uncovering a secret. Light bathed the top treads of the staircase. She could smell dust, mildew, and the musty chemical odor of attic insulation.

She heard the sound of a chair creaking, then the familiar whir of a VCR. Dani felt a spasm of disappointment. Was that all he was doing, just watching some movie? That didn't seem interesting to her, not worth the risk of getting caught. She was about to turn and slip back downstairs again when she heard Bonner laugh.

It wasn't his regular laugh but seemed to come from low in his throat, strange, almost caressing. Then she realized something even stranger. This movie that Bonner was watching and laughing at—it had no sound.

Drawn now by intense curiosity, she crept up the final few feet into the hallway. The wide room that served as a sort of foyer for the attic area had a wall hung with a clutter of old photographs and framed diplomas and awards. The floor was covered with a large rag rug. A light shone from the room where Bonner was watching TV.

Dani moved catlike across the rug, reaching the half-opened door. Positioning herself low, she peered into the room.

What she saw was terrifying.

She jumped violently, her hand accidentally scraping the wall.

Bonner jumped as he heard the small, scrabbling noise.

Automatically, his hand darted out for the remote and he punched "stop," swiftly removing the incriminating videocassette.

He felt sick to his stomach as he rose from his chair, but when he walked into the vestibule, he saw nothing out of the ordinary. Everything was as it had been. Rain still spattered against the window, making clacking noises as it hurried along the gutters toward the new downspouts he'd installed last year.

Probably that was what he had heard.

Or maybe it had been a squirrel running along the roofline. Last fall they'd had problems with squirrels and he'd gone to a lot of trouble blocking up an access hole in the crawl space.

But just to be on the safe side, Bonner walked down the staircase to check the lower door. It was still locked exactly as he had left it. Yet he thought he smelled the drift of Dani's candy-flavored perfume. He could still feel the tension in his neck and shoulders, the rigidity in his stomach. If anyone ever saw those videos—

He needed a drink.

*　*　*

By the time Dani reached her bedroom, she was shaking all over. Underneath her unicorn T-shirt, shivers multiplied over the surface of her skin, until her goose bumps merged into one quivering ache.

Bonner had been watching her naked.

Videos he'd taken of her in her bathroom. Videos of her peeing!

She threw herself toward her bed, grabbing the top of her quilt and burrowing inside, unable to find warmth even when she doubled up her knees and formed a tightly clenched ball. How had he done it? And why?

There was something wrong with her! she thought, choking. She clamped her knees up toward her face, clutching her thighs with her hands. She remembered the way Bonner had grabbed her when he was sleeping, all the other times he'd touched her "accidentally." Bonner was acting . . . dirty . . . just like Fay's tricks had done, the sickening boyfriends who wanted to touch her and have her rub them through their pants.

And this house was supposed to be safe! This house was going to be a family! Dani choked back sobs. *Why had this happened to her again?*

After about an hour, she heard a soft knock on her door. She stiffened, her body going rigid.

"Dani? Pretty girl? My pretty? I've popped you some popcorn."

"Thanks, I . . . don't want any," she managed to say. She tried to make her voice sound sleepy.

She heard the door creak open. Bonner walked across the leaf green carpet toward her bed. She could smell his spicy aftershave, the laundered smell of his white shirt. "It's all nice and fresh popped and I've put lots of good melted butter on it," he tempted, his voice fulsome, the way it got when he was feeling jovial and had his arm around her.

"I don't want any," she mumbled, her mind searching for a lie. "I—I just threw up."

She could sense it had been exactly the right thing to say. Bonner hated body things; he hated it when Whitney made a mess in her diapers. Repelled, he took a couple of steps backward. "You're coming down with something?"

"I just lost my whole dinner," Dani said, gaining courage.

"While I was working upstairs, I heard a funny noise. That wasn't you, was it?"

Dani felt sweat pop out on her upper lip. "How could it be? I was in the bathroom, and—and I had corn for dinner tonight, and it was so gross—"

He made a small disgusted sound. "I guess you don't want any popcorn then. Not a sick girl like you." She thought he was going to leave the room, but instead he was staring down at her with laser-beam eyes. "And another thing," he went on harshly. "You're not used to living among ordinary people, and if you were to say things about being here, tell lies about us—"

"I don't tell lies!" Dani burst out.

"—especially to that Mrs. Vivian of yours, then she might just decide to come here and take you away. They'll put you in a group home next, I'd imagine. Down in Detroit somewhere, and you'll go to one of those ghetto high schools where the kids carry guns and girls get raped in the school yard. Would you like that?"

Dani knew all about schools like that—she'd heard the horror stories about fights, drugs, gangs, even drive-by shootings after school let out. Fay's brother had gone to Cody High School and been beaten and robbed of his jacket.

"No . . ." she choked.

Bonner's finger inserted itself under her chin, lifting her face so that she was forced to look into his eyes. "No one will believe your lies," he told her. *"If you tell them. Ever."*

He was gone.

Dani drifted into and out of sleep, fighting a succession of nightmares. Herself on the TV screen, naked. Being hit with a belt . . . held down on someone's lap . . . hands reaching. *"No one will believe your lies. . . . Ever."*

When the first light began to turn the room pearl-colored, Dani opened her eyes and sat up, tossing aside the quilt. She was still wearing the leggings and T-shirt that she'd had on last night when all of this had begun.

She went to the window. A car was rolling past that made her think of Fay's old junker, but then she saw that it was the wrong color. Across the street she could see the dark shape of the Sokols' house, another, smaller Victorian in poorer condition than the Lockwoods'. Even as she watched, a light flicked on, followed by another one.

For a long time Dani watched Ryan's room, wishing she could talk to him. The need to talk overwhelmed her. Ry was her best friend. But how could she tell him this? What would she say? *"Bonner watched movies of me naked. He put his finger under my chin. His eyes were terrible. He told me no one would ever believe me."*

In the grayish light of morning, last night seemed

like a bad dream, not really real. Maybe she'd misinterpreted things. Men like Bonner Lockwood, important men, did not make videotapes of girls going to the bathroom. Maybe it was all a—

Suddenly Dani heard a familiar cry that gradually gathered volume. Whitney was demanding her morning bottle. With relief, Dani expelled the breath from her lungs. It was a normal morning after all; the nightmare was gone.

Without pausing to run a comb through her tousle of hair, she hurried downstairs to warm the bottle.

Rain washed against the Lockwoods' yellow Victorian, which had its porch light on against the spring dusk. Water droplets danced in front of its glow. Vivian could not help admiring the beautiful, gingerbreaded porch, spattered with moisture, as she walked up onto the porch.

Vivian had attended a conference in East Lansing, on the topic of hard-to-place children. Now, tired from sitting in six sessions and enduring a chicken breast with wild rice lunch, she was driving back to Rochester but had decided to stop and see Dani on her way. She'd cleared it with a call to Maureen.

Maureen Lockwood answered the door. "I hope you haven't driven over here for nothing. Dani has a little stomach bug and she's a bit under the weather."

"Oh, dear."

"You'll pardon me, won't you, if I just show you up to her room and then run? I have a sitter here, the girl who usually cleans our house. There's a meeting of my writers' group and I'm tonight's speaker."

Vivian followed Maureen upstairs to Dani's room,

where she rapped on the closed door. "Dani, Mrs. Clavell is here to see you."

There was a pause, and then the door was flung open.

"Mrs. Vivian?" cried Dani. "Mrs. *Vivian?*"

"Why, yes, Dani. I hope I'm not surprising you too much."

"You're here," said Dani, her voice quivering.

Vivian's eyes swept into the room behind Dani, noticing the usual untidy teenage litter, the expensive sweaters and CDs flung about. Then she gazed down at the slight, slender thirteen-year-old. Dani wore stone-washed jeans and a red sweater that pointed up the paleness of her skin. Her hair was frizzy and uncontrolled, sticking up in small corkscrews as if she'd been sleeping on it. There was something flat about her eyes, Vivian thought.

"Dani, are you all right?"

The girl's eyes avoided Vivian's. "I was sick; I threw up."

"It started last night. She's thrown up twice more this morning, so we had to keep her home from school," Maureen explained.

After Maureen excused herself, Vivian lingered, chatting to Dani. "Let's play with the computer," Vivian suggested. "I'll show you how to use the spell checker and the thesaurus. There are lots of fun gizmos we haven't tried yet."

They sat side by side, and Dani moodily called up one of her documents, so they could spell-check it.

"I was going to show Ryan the flight simulator game, it's so-o-o cool, but Bonner won't let me talk to him," the girl muttered.

"Oh? Why not?"

"He says Ry's a juvenile delinquent. But he isn't!

He's nice! He's just kinda, well, he thinks he's bad, but he really isn't."

Vivian nodded. She had a strong feeling that there was more wrong than just this. "Is everything all right?" she asked Dani gently. "Are you happy here?"

Dani did not respond. Her eyes became opaque, evasive, bringing down the shuttered wall that teen-agers erected between themselves and adults.

"You can talk to me at any time, you know," Vivian said. "You haven't called me a lot recently, but you know you can. That's why I'm your social worker, to be there if you do have any problems. And, Dani . . . I'm your friend, too. I care about you a lot."

Dani seemed frightened. She looked down at the rows of keys. "I know."

"And you haven't sent me a letter that you've typed on your computer. I'd love to get one. Here, I think I have a few stamps in my purse."

"I will. I'll write a letter," Dani promised, taking the stamps.

But there was no light in her eyes. Dani's sparkle, the vibrant energy that usually surrounded her like a force field, was gone. Something had happened, Vivian thought, alarmed. But what?

"We missed talking the last time I was here," Vivian said to Bonner, who had arrived home in a flurry of stamping feet and water-spattered umbrella, explaining that he had walked from his campus office after working late.

He greeted her jovially, suggesting they have coffee in the solarium. He was attired in another of his tweedy sports jackets, complete with suede elbow patches, and looked ruddy, hearty, and handsome, almost the cliché college professor.

"It's a rat race at the college right now," he explained to her. "They're going to appoint me acting dean of students, and I am almost positive I will be getting the permanent appointment before very long."

"How nice," Vivian said, following him as they entered the large, plant-filled solarium where she and Dani had had lunch with the Lockwoods the day Dani had arrived here. Rain was sluicing down the slanted greenhouse windows, its grayness against all that glass curiously overpowering.

"There," said Bonner, pointing to a wicker conversation group with chintz cushions. "We can sit here, Mrs. Clavell. I *am* glad that you stopped by."

"Yes. I'm concerned about Dani. She seems upset, disturbed about something."

Bonner nodded. "We've had, well, we're having a few problems with Dani."

"What sort of problems?"

"I'll give you an example. She sneaked out of the house a while back and went to a party some kids were having in a garage and she got smashing drunk. Threw up all over herself. She went with Ryan Sokol. The boy isn't vicious, but he's a bit wild and he plays up to the weaknesses in Dani's personality. It's unfortunate that he lives across the street."

Bonner continued with a litany of Dani's fibs, which included boasting about several school awards she hadn't won and even telling Maureen that she'd seen Fay's pimp, Harley, drive past in his car.

"What?" said Vivian, alarmed.

"Oh, we got it out of her later—she didn't see him

at all. It was just a lie, something she dreamed up to shake us up a little. I think she said it because I grounded her over Ryan."

"I see. We knew going in that Dani had problems," Vivian finally said. "Her lies are wishes . . . bids for attention."

"Of course, and we're dealing with it," Bonner said. "Very well, we think. We are firm with her. We took on the responsibility, and we aren't complaining. I'm sure she'll improve with time."

"It's a matter of trust," said Vivian finally. "These young people have been hurt, and they test their limits; they test the love they are offered. It's very natural, and to be expected, but it does require a lot of patience."

"Yes, well, we're going to pass the test," Bonner said. "Patience, that we have."

Vivian drove home, heading her car into a damp rain, uneasily replaying her visit in her mind. Dani *had* seemed so withdrawn . . . was it because of the inevitable testing? Or was there something else? She decided to return again soon, and meanwhile, she'd call Dani's school to see if she was having any problems there.

By 10:00 P.M., the rain had thinned to a grayish, moisture-ridden mist. Kneeling on the dusty floorboards of her attic, surrounded by the mildewing smells of old books, Jill Rudgate reached for the cold can of Coors she had brought upstairs with her.

She took a long swallow, then put the can down.

She was looking for a copy of her old résumé, which she intended to rewrite and take to a word processing place, hopefully one that didn't know

Bonner Lockwood and wouldn't spread gossip about her wanting to leave Madisonia.

Angrily she shifted a heavy box that contained her notes for her master's thesis. Underneath this was a box that held all of her old high school yearbooks and assorted junk, including a pair of old binoculars her father had given her.

Wait—here it was.

Jill lifted out the stack of professionally printed résumés and carried it to where the light was better. To her left, outside the small, dusty window, something flickered, causing Jill to glance toward the Lockwood house.

A light had gone on in the attic.

Curious, she paused to look. It was Bonner's bailiwick, she knew. She'd seen him before, watching TV up there, but usually he had the blinds pulled. Tonight, however, one of the shades was halfway up.

Impulsively Jill reached for the binoculars and quickly adjusted the focus, aiming the lenses at Bonner's window. He jumped into clear view, seeming as close as if she were actually in the room.

She stared, transfixed. Bonner had sunk into a chair facing the TV set, his hand fumbling at the front of his pants. To Jill's astonishment, he pulled out his penis and began rubbing it with energetic urgency.

She was so startled that she jerked the binoculars, pulling the focus away. Blank walls loomed in the lenses. She struggled with it, but now the focus swung wildly toward a picture on the wall, and finally the TV set.

On the TV screen was a naked girl. A girl who looked *familiar*.

Oh, but it couldn't be.

Shaken, Jill lowered the binoculars, her revulsion warring with her delight at having caught Bonner at such a disgusting occupation. Pornography . . . masturbation. . . . She hadn't expected this of a man as old as Bonner, as . . . *respected*. Jesus, the man had published hundreds of articles in professional magazines and had won various awards, some exceedingly prestigious. He ruled the history department like a petty king.

She fled the attic, not bothering to switch off the light, for fear he would notice the light going off and realize she had been spying on him.

Bonner Lockwood! It was pretty hysterical, actually. Too bad she couldn't tell anybody. She stifled a nervous giggle. Surely it had to be just a coincidence that the girl on the screen resembled Dani.

Her computer screen still glowing green, a letter to Vivian Clavell half-begun, Dani had finally fallen asleep.

In her dreams, she was back in Detroit, in the abandoned apartment building she and Fay had lived in when she was eight, before Fay hooked up with Harley. Broken windows let in sharp gusts of winter air, and because the plumbing didn't work, Fay kept old cooking pots for their bathroom use. At the back of the apartment there was a dark spot that Fay said was blood.

"Baby," said Fay's voice, bright, chipper, and happy. "Baby, look who just blew into town; it's Bill. Remember Bill? Bill has brought us some presents, and he wants to get us out of this dump, okay? All we have to do is be nice to him. Ma has to be very, very nice to him, and so do you. . . ."

Dani moaned, unconsciously drawing her knees up toward her chest.

Maureen, seated at the desk in her writing room, was bent over her book manuscript, lost in a world of talking rabbits and fuzzy moles wearing eyeglasses.

The three-note chime of the doorbell disturbed her concentration. Annoyed, she glanced at her watch. It was well past 10:30 P.M. Who would be at the door at this hour?

She hurried downstairs to the door and was surprised to see, silhouetted through the etched Victorian window, the form of a woman.

Good Lord, Maureen thought. The woman looked like one of the whores Maureen and Bonner had once seen strutting along West Grand Boulevard in Detroit. Tall, almost anorexic in her thinness, the visitor wore a huge, tousled blond wig that overpowered her small face, making her cheekbones seem hollow, her eyes recessed. Despite the foggy April damp of the evening, she wore no jacket and was clad in a black spandex dress so tight that it suggested not only her pubic mound, but both hipbones. On her feet were three-and-a-half-inch spike heels with ankle straps.

Maureen hesitated, unwilling to open the door.

Please, the woman mouthed. She rapped again on the beautifully scrolled glass that had been hand-crafted at a shop in Traverse City. Then she began to pound. If she banged on the glass any harder she was going to break it.

Reluctantly Maureen pulled the door open.

"I'm Fay," the woman announced. "Dani McVie's mother."

* * *

Fay leaned against the door, enjoying the look on the small woman's face as she realized just who Fay was. She'd driven around the neighborhood several times in the past few weeks, but somehow she hadn't managed to catch Dani alone.

So, what the hell, she'd thought. She *was* the kid's mother. Why not just be bold about it? She rubbed her neck, which still hurt from the imprint of Harley's fingers.

"Why you been jerking me around, bitch? You know where the kid is, don't you? You been holding back on me. Nobody does that to me, babe. Not no cheap, whitebread cokehead whore. I want that girl, I got big money waiting for her, and you're gonna get her, hear? Or I'm gonna stick my knife up inside that hot, wet pussy of yours and twist it around until it comes out your mouth."

"Oh," said Maureen, so surprised that she took a step backward.

Fay, taking this as invitation, pushed the door open and stepped inside. "So this is where my baby girl lives." Shifting her weight on the spike heels, Fay gazed around her at the entry hall with its expensive Bukhara rug that Maureen and Bonner had bought three years ago at auction, the stunning grandfather clock, the half-moon table decorated with an expensive arrangement of silk roses and statice.

"This house is what you call it, it's real old, isn't it?"

"Yes, the house was built in 1883," Maureen said, her mouth getting all tight and prissy.

"These rugs," Fay said. "God, I love rugs like this. Did you get this at New York Carpet World? I seen one like this there, only it was redder than this one."

"This rug is Turkish, nineteenth-century," Maureen snapped. There were footsteps in the upstairs hall. "Bonner!" she called. "Here is my husband," she told Fay.

Bonner came downstairs, looking every inch the college department head, his silver hair glinting in the bright light cast by the overhead chandelier. Even Fay was impressed by him. He looked like one of those movie professors, like Donald Sutherland or . . . William Holden or someone.

"This woman is Dani's mother," Maureen began.

"Ah," Bonner said in his most unctuous voice.

Their unexpected caller looked at him, tightening her grip on her cheap knockoff Yves St. Laurent purse. "I want her."

"Pardon?" said Bonner.

"I said I want Dani. I'm taking her, I got her suitcase in the car, I got her clothes in it, and she's coming with me. I'm takin' her to a very good place. I got a new apartment, it's very, very nice, and she'll have her own room."

"Now wait just a minute," began Bonner in a blustering tone. "I have received no notification from the court about this. Dani is my ward. She was placed here by the children's agency, and I was specifically instructed that you have no legal right to her."

"Now *you* wait, fuckhead," spat Fay, narrowing her eyes. "*I* didn't sign nothing. She's *my* kid, get it?"

Bonner drew himself up to his full six feet, puffing up his chest so that his 210 pounds seemed even bulkier. "You are taking her nowhere," he snapped. "And if you don't leave my house now, immediately, I will have to dial 911."

"Oh, 911," Fay sneered. "Oh, aren't you brave? Oh, shit. *I want the kid.*"

Bonner jerked his chin toward Maureen. "Go in the dining room, will you, and dial the—"

Frightened, Maureen started to move, and Fay suddenly lifted her purse and swung it in a big arc. Imitation leather hit the etched window, shattering handcrafted glass.

"My God, you broke it!" Maureen cried.

"She's my daughter, mine!"

"No, she isn't," said Bonner, grasping Fay's arm and propelling her toward the door. Glass crunched under her spike heels as she stamped toward the porch.

She turned to snarl at him. "*You* think you're so great, don't you? Mr. Rich Man, with your shit-ass big house and your fancy, shit-ass rugs. Well, let me tell you something. *I'm* gonna be back."

"No, you aren't, you—"

"She's my kid, get it? I got rights to her! *I'm coming back for her!*"

Dani lay rigidly in bed, listening to the ruckus that was coming from downstairs. Sounds of crashing glass and Fay's bloodcurdling shouts. Terror swept through her as she heard Bonner yelling at her mother. This was followed by deep shame.

Her mother was a prostitute—a pross, a hooker. What must Bonner think of Fay, with her cheap, ugly wigs and her face smeared with makeup, her tight spandex skirts and smell of cheap drugstore perfume? But even more to the point, *Fay had come back.*

Dani pressed both fists to her mouth, remember-

ing the man Fay had tried to sell her to . . . the police
officer. The look of disgust on his face as Fay said,
"She's worth a hundred; she's pure, sweet, virgin."

Please, she prayed, curling herself into a ball.
*Please, make her go away. Make her go back to De-
troit and forget about me.*

Garish blue and red lights flashed, then finally were
doused, as the Madisonia Police Department squad
car backed out of the driveway. However, by the time
they'd arrived, Fay was gone and, to the disgust of
the patrol officer, neither Bonner nor Maureen had
gotten a clear look at her car.

"Call us, sir, if she shows up again," the officer had
told Bonner.

"I want protection!" blustered Bonner.

"We'll cruise past here a couple of times a night,
but that's all we have the manpower for. You could
call one of those security services, sir, maybe get one
with a panic button."

"You people can't do a damn thing, can you?
That's the real problem. All kinds of crimes go on in
this town and you can't get organized. That break-in
at the history department was a total farce and you
know it. Five computers missing and you idiots
couldn't do a thing."

After the squad car left, Bonner went up to the
attic to look for a square of cardboard big enough to
temporarily cover the broken window, while Maureen soothed the baby, who had started to whimper.

"Bonner, can she really take Dani?"

"I'll go to a judge here; I'll get an injunction," said
Bonner. "I'll stop her in her tracks."

"What good will an injunction do?" said Maureen.

Her blood was still pounding from the shock of their unexpected visitor and her threats. "Bonner, she's a whore. She's the dregs of Detroit. And she's *Dani's mother.*"

They were in the kitchen.

"We knew that when we got Dani."

"But . . . Bonner . . . the woman really *is* a whore. You could tell; she just had that look. She smelled terrible, and she had fingernails like claws, and her dress was so tight you could see her pubis."

Bonner got a faraway look. "Dani's not like that. She is as pure as her mother is corrupted."

Maureen stared at her husband. "Bonner . . . how are we going to live with that woman wanting to take Dani?"

"Well," said Bonner. "I will tell you one thing. We're *not* reporting this to that agency."

"But why—"

"Because I don't want them messing their noses in this any more than they already have. That Vivian Clavell woman is already too nosy, and what if they decide we aren't protecting Dani enough, that she'd be better off somewhere else?"

Maureen said it in a very low voice. "Have you ever considered . . . not adopting Dani?"

"Not adopting her?"

"I mean—maybe she isn't good for us. We've changed since she's arrived here. You and I. You're very distant and secretive, Bonner, and you devote yourself to her with . . . with a way that doesn't seem healthy sometimes."

"Not healthy?" Bonner's voice rose. "What are you talking about? What are you accusing me of?"

At the harshness in his tone, Maureen bit her lip. "Nothing, Bonner," she said.

* * *

After Maureen had gone upstairs to bed, Bonner busied himself sweeping up the shards of broken glass. He didn't run the vacuum—he didn't want to wake either Dani or the baby—but he used a broom and dustpan so efficiently that he was sure he managed to get nearly every speck.

Maureen's words had struck a little spark of horror in the pit of his stomach. *"A way that doesn't seem healthy sometimes."* Did Maureen suspect? What had she been referring to? How much did his wife know?

He was afraid Maureen might really persist in her notion of sending Dani back, and the very thought caused him to panic. He couldn't give Dani up now. Not yet. He'd been building up to her, fantasizing constantly ever since she'd arrived.

He put the dustpan away in the utility closet under the kitchen stairs, his thoughts lingering on Fay McVie, the musky, animalistic stench of her. Thinking of the things she must do to men made Bonner feel nauseous.

On his way upstairs to bed, he stopped at Dani's door. Slowly Bonner pushed the door open, and looked inside. His foster daughter was lying still. The quilt had fallen away, and she lay in the fetal position, her creamy, bare arms tightly braced around her thighs. Her breathing was so shallow that Bonner frowned.

Then he saw her stir, emitting a tiny sigh, and he relaxed, moving closer to the bed. As if sensing his presence, the girl stirred slightly. Her skin had the purity of a camellia petal, her eyebrows were like pale wings, and her hair was so magnificent that he trembled as his hand reached out to touch a few silken strands.

He stared down at her, overwhelmed. He had never aspired to or imagined a girl more perfect than this. And here she was in his home, at his disposal. No farther away from him at night than a few walls.

His hand reached out and hovered above her, only a half-inch away from her breathing, living flesh. For a tiny pulse beat he felt a surge of sick guilt. If anyone knew, if anyone at the college found out about this . . . a snake of fear twisted its body in the center of his abdomen.

But then the moment passed, and he smiled down at his sleeping foster daughter.

"I love you," he whispered.

He saw a tiny stir of movement. Had she heard him?

He moved away, leaving the room.

"You mean you were there, you were right at the goddamn *door* and you didn't get her?" said Harley, touching the golden watchband of his Rolex. Except for the watch, he was naked. The room reeked of the juices of their lovemaking, mixed with Fay's strong Coty perfume.

But as soon as he'd come, he'd gone cold on her, asking about Dani again.

"Harl, I . . . I couldn't. They were right there; they were gonna call the cops on me." Fay was strung out, waiting for the cocaine, nervous and anxious because Harley hadn't given it to her yet and she was afraid to push him and ask. He'd been so cool to her recently, even vicious, and the stress had pumped her blood pressure up through the ceiling. She needed him, or someone like him. She couldn't make it on her own.

"So? She's your kid, isn't she? *Isn't she?*" snapped Harley. He shifted his bulk on the bed and knelt on top of her, straddling her so that her face was trapped between his massive naked brown thighs. From this position his genitals, framed by whorls of kinky black hair, seemed frighteningly huge.

"Yeah . . . yeah . . . Harley . . ."

"Isn't she?"

"Yeah, she's my kid. I'll get her; I told you I would. I was just looking around; I wanted to see what kind of security devices they got and all that."

"I don't give a shit; they can have a goddamn pit bull and a junkyard dog for all I care. I want the kid; can I make myself any clearer, babe? You knew I wanted her and you been farting around about it. Nobody farts around with Harley."

With each word, Harley was pressing his iron-thick knees closer together, locking Fay's face in a vise. *"Nobody,"* he emphasized.

Fay tried to speak. The pressure was shutting off the blood flow to her face. "I . . . I'll get her!"

"Damn right you will, baby . . . and here's how I know." There was a flash of movement, a glint of light. Suddenly Fay felt a sharp pain cutting into the skin at the hollow of her throat. Terrified, she looked down the end of her nose.

It was a knife.

"I want the little pussy. This guy, I tried to interest him in other girls, know what I mean? I tried to switch him. But he don't want no other little girls; he wants this one; he thinks she's real, real pretty. He likes fucking red hair. So you're gonna get her for him, Fay, or this knife . . . see this knife?"

"Yes, yes!" she gasped.

"I'm gonna run this knife right across your throat
. . . like this." Harley demonstrated, digging into
Fay's skin. An elongated needlelike pain traveled
across the circumference of her throat.

"Harley! Harl!" He hadn't cut her deeply enough to
kill her—not yet. He was just trying to scare her,
wasn't he? She felt the warm trickle of blood rolling
down her neck onto the pillow. She remembered,
with a horrid clenching of her breath, that Harley
was reputed to have stabbed one of his girls last
year, leaving her body cut and mutilated in the parking lot outside a Southfield hotel.

"I'm gonna cut you, Fay. I'm gonna cut you bad if
you don't do this. See," explained Harley, "I don't like
to have me no whores that can't follow orders. You're
getting pretty skinny, babe, the tricks aren't gonna
go for you much longer, and if I can't find any use out
of you . . ."

He lifted the knife and inserted the tip of the blade,
small and lethally sharp, up inside Fay's right nostril. Pain exploded up through her head, searing into
her brain, and she uttered a sharp, tormented
scream.

"Do what I say, cokehead whore."

"Okay, okay, okay," she sobbed.

6

MAY AIR BILLOWED through the opened window, bringing with it the scent of grass clippings and the roars of suburban lawn mowers in the neighborhood in West Bloomfield where Vivian's sister, Judy, lived.

"Vivian? Viv?" It was Melva Bernstein, the head of the agency. She peered around the corner of Vivian's sickroom door, carrying a sack from Barnes & Noble. "Are you decent?"

Groggily Vivian sat up in bed. She had been dreaming of herself walking on the beach on Lake Michigan as a child.

"Mel, come on in."

"Just a goodie or two I picked up for you. Torey Hayden has a new book out, and I found a really juicy mystery. I hope you like serial killers. Oh, yes, and your mail. That little girl of yours, Dani, has written you two letters."

Vivian got out of bed, fighting a wave of dizziness. The case of bronchitis complicated with viral pneumonia, coming on suddenly, had left her weakened. Fortunately, her sister Judy had charged to the rescue, bringing Vivian to her house for a week of chicken soup and cluck-clucking.

"You're starting to look like a human being again," observed Melva, "instead of death warmed over. Your face actually has some pink in it. Here, read these letters from your favorite kid. I'm sorry, I opened one of them by mistake."

Vivian took the letters, both addressed to "Mrs. Vivian," opened one, and began skimming.

"The baby she smiles. And talks baby talk," Dani had typed on the computer, the entire composition squeezed onto the top five inches of paper. *"She is very smart. Ryan an me went swimming at the lake and I swam underwater 100 feet and I didn't breathe till I came up. I thought I might drown."*

Vivian laughed. "Oh, Melva, this is so sweet; she used the spell checker just like I showed her. The only mistake is the word *an* for *and.* She's such a doll."

"You really have an attachment to her, don't you?"

"She is so alive, Mel. She's really a special kid. With that terrible background of hers, she still came out so warm." Vivian went on, "Do you mind if I get dressed while we're talking? My teeth feel like they've got fuzz on them."

While Vivian moved slowly about, brushing her teeth in the adjoining bathroom, taking her medication, combing her hair, and adding touches of lipstick and powder, she and Melva caught up on the agency gossip. A young social worker named Kelly Mandar was temporarily handling Vivian's caseload. According to her ("a glowing report," said Melva), everything was fine with Dani and the Lockwoods. In fact, Dani had actually danced in a dance recital at the junior high.

"Oh, and there's one more piece of news," said Melva. "The permanent separation has come through from the judge, so Dani's adoption is now free and clear as soon as the waiting period is over. I think you can call this one of your successes, Vivian."

Vivian looked out of the window at the pale turquoise May sky, remembering the last time she'd seen Dani. That *wall* Dani had erected. But obviously, whatever had been bothering her couldn't have been too serious; otherwise Kelly's report wouldn't have been so glowing.

Vivian closed her eyes. "Mel . . . don't you think that Kelly tends to let her enthusiasms get away from her?"

"What do you mean?"

Vivian said, "She's only two years out of the U. of M. She tends to enthuse about things; she sees the world through rose-colored glasses. Sometimes her reports just glow too damn much."

"What are you trying to say?"

"I have this feeling about Dani. I can't put a finger on it, really." She began to cough, each hacking cough creating bands of pain across her pleura. "Sorry," she gasped.

There was a pause. "Viv, as I said, you've become too attached to that little girl," said Melva. "You've lost your objectivity. That happens to all of us sometimes, and isn't anything to be particularly ashamed of, only—"

"No, I haven't! All right, maybe a little. Mel, I'll admit I . . ." But Vivian began coughing again, and the rest of her confession didn't get said.

"I don't want you to worry about Dani McVie anymore," said Melva as she was leaving. "Kelly has the case now, and we're working with the attorney on the legal end of it. You just concentrate on getting better.

We need you back, Vivian. Everybody's been bitch-
ing about the workload, not that I'd ever pressure
you."

After Melva left, Vivian went into her sister's
kitchen and poured herself a large glass of freshly
squeezed orange juice. She positioned her chair so
that it sat in a large golden beam of sunshine that
shone in through the sliding door. She could see
Dani in her mind, as clearly as a Kodak photograph.

Maureen bent over her ironing board, gloomily pushing the steam iron across the collar of one of her
blouses. It was 9:30 A.M., and she was tired from
sleeping in an unfamiliar bed. Last night Bonner had
been muttering in his sleep again, and he'd thrashed
in the bed so violently that Maureen finally had to get
up and sleep in one of the guest rooms. Was their
marriage falling apart? Was that what this was
about? Dani had created too much stress on their
already fragile relationship, and now who knew what
might happen?

Nearby, Dani sat fidgeting over some work sheets
she'd brought home from school. She had another
half-day off for teachers' conferences, and had been
getting on Maureen's nerves all morning.

Maureen shot a glance in her adoptive daughter's
direction. The girl had been acting odd for weeks
now, too. Quiet, almost secretive, *broody*. Once she'd
tried to broach the topic of touching again, but Maureen got the subject right out in the open. "Dani,"
she'd told the girl. "You've had problems with men in
the past and you're projecting that now onto Bonner.
Which of course is very mistaken. Now, please don't
mention this again. We love you and we're doing the

very best we can for you, dear. But we need some cooperation from you, too."

"Do you think I should get a perm?" asked Dani now, for the fourth time.

Maureen shook her head. "Dani, your hair is curly enough already, and a permanent would damage your hair. Didn't Jill have some work sheets for you to do today?"

Whitney began to cry, her wails picked up on the intercom that Maureen had recently had installed in the baby's room.

"I'll go change her!" cried Dani, jumping up.

"No, I will," said Maureen, shutting off her steam iron and walking out of the kitchen fast, before Dani could dart ahead of her. It seemed as if she always had to leap if she wanted to care for her baby herself.

In Whitney's room, she found her baby daughter lying in her crib squalling furiously. Picking up the wriggling baby, Maureen felt her tension recede. She'd felt awkward at first with the baby, fearing her motherly attachment wasn't going to kick in, but then it had, and now the baby felt like part of herself.

"My punkin," she said. "Is my feisty little punkin wet? Is she?"

She carried the child over to her changing table. As she reached it, she noticed that there were spills of white baby powder all over the changing pad. A pair of damp Pampers had been carelessly laid on the edge of the table, rather than being deposited in the nearby diaper pail.

Balancing the infant, Maureen dropped the diaper in the pail and swept off the powder with her free hand. Pulling the unfastened romper up over the baby's stomach, Maureen noticed a white crust on the child's abdomen. It looked like dried milk, perhaps, the stain extending down the baby's stomach and well into the genital area.

Annoyed, she picked up a Baby Wipe and began sponging. The stain had a faint stickiness. Had Dani spilled the baby's bottle on her? Now Whitney was going to need a bath, and Maureen didn't have time; she was supposed to be on campus in exactly half an hour.

Maureen walked into the kitchen, carrying Whitney on one hip. "Dani, what did you spill on the baby?"

"Nothing."

"Well, you must have spilled something because she was all covered with white stuff. And there was a filthy pair of Pampers lying on the changing table. Wet and soaked. Dani, I can't believe you could be so careless."

"I didn't."

Maureen kept her voice even. "I found the wet diaper right there, and powder all over everything. Babies shouldn't breathe in talc; it hurts their lungs."

"I *didn't*. I haven't even changed her today."

"Dani, don't fib to me!" The heels of Maureen's flats clicked on the tiled flooring as she crossed the kitchen to the refrigerator. She took out a bottle and handed it to Dani. "Please warm this and feed her, and then put her in her playpen if you would. And please, don't spill anything on the baby."

"Okay," said Dani, tousling her fingers nervously through her hair. "But, honest, I really didn't—"

"It's all right," said Maureen evenly. "Just, please, Dani, be careful; that's all I ask."

"I will," said Dani, moving to the stove to begin warming the bottle.

* * *

That night Bonner and Maureen had another of their increasingly frequent Dani disagreements.

"You wouldn't believe what happened today," Maureen began. "When I went to change Whitney I found a mess on her changing table, and the baby was a mess, too. Dani spilled something on her, something white, like milk."

Bonner was going through his closet, pulling out some sports jackets that he wanted to have altered, and seemed to pause briefly as she said this.

"Oh, you're always on Dani's case," he told her.

"Am I? Maybe that's because you *never* are. You hardly ever discipline her, Bonner. You act like she's a little princess, and you devote much more time to her than you do to Whitney. Dani hasn't been good for us, Bonner. You—"

Bonner emerged from the closet, his eyes glittering. "What are you saying, Maureen?"

"I . . . I don't know." Maureen noticed that her husband's jowls had reddened. "When her mother came, that Fay, we shouldn't have lied to everyone," she added. "We should have told the agency that she came around here."

"Well, we didn't. I don't want to get tangled in a lot of bureaucratic red tape. I don't like being under the scrutiny of social workers. It's very demeaning and smacks of a police state kind of atmosphere. I don't want to hear any more about this." Bonner gathered up the pile of jackets and fixed her with a cold look. "I mean it, Maureen. I won't listen to any more of your pettiness, and that's final. Anyway," he went on, "I do have a nice piece of news."

"What's that?"

"I'm definitely going to be dean. It's in the works. Dr. Rabaul has decided to retire. The doctors say his ticker can't stand the pressure."

"Really?" Maureen drew in a shocked breath. Dean Rabaul, now sixty-six, had been around forever, strong and feisty, a benevolent despot who'd brought the college out of obscurity to the point where they'd recently received a national mention in *Newsweek.*

"Yes, *really,*" Bonner sneered. "What's the matter, Maureen, don't you realize how respected I am? Everyone on this campus looks up to me; they treat me deferentially. I've had three books published, and I'm an authority on the Korean War. Even the President's Commission has come to me for information. I'm much more solid than Rabaul with his silly cocktail parties and politics."

Bonner himself played ten times more politics than anyone else on the faculty, and had stepped up his politicking considerably since Rabaul's illness, which was why he had gotten the appointment.

"Congratulations, Bonner," she said, staring him in the eye. "I'm sure you'll put Dean Rabaul in the dust. Now I've got to go downstairs and make sure Dani leaves for her tutoring. Then I'm going out to my writers' club. You can baby-sit for a change."

Maureen left their bedroom and walked downstairs, her heart hammering. If it weren't for her baby girl, her writing, and the members of her writing group who offered her emotional support and admiration, sometimes Maureen thought she would go mad.

*   *   *

The tutoring session was halfway over when Jill received a phone call. After listening for a moment, her face went bright red.

"Oh, I haven't been doing too much. . . . You know, the usual. Stuck here teaching freshman courses. . . . Yeah. . . . yeah, I saw the mention in *Newsweek;* we're finally getting famous. . . . Sure. . . . Sure. . . ."

Bored, Dani began to pace the room. Jill's house was a clutter of books, many of them still in cardboard boxes, never unpacked. Jill usually read two or three at once, marking the places with scraps of paper.

Dani flipped open the cover of a book called *Anne of Green Gables* that Jill wanted her to try to read. "You have to push yourself a little, Dani," Jill insisted. But Dani wasn't in the mood to read. Bonner was on her mind. All the things that had happened. And Maureen kept changing the subject when she tried to talk about it.

No one will believe your lies. If you tell them. Ever.

"Dani," said Jill, seeming embarrassed. "This is a personal call, so I'm going to dismiss you early if you don't mind."

Dani didn't need any more urging. She grabbed her work sheets, jumped up, and started toward the utility room exit she usually used. The keys to Jill's '89 Ford Tempo lay in their usual position, flung on top of the dryer. Dani fingered them, jingling the keys, as she loped past.

At home, she used the downstairs powder room bathroom, where she was sure Bonner didn't have a camera, and was about to skid out of the house for an hour of freedom, when she heard Bonner's cough on the intercom connected to Whitney's room. The cough was followed by what sounded like a deep, ragged groan.

Dani felt a deep chill.

She'd heard sounds like that before.

She crept upstairs, moving stealthily so as not to disturb the old floorboards that often creaked. Reaching Whitney's door, she leaned around the jamb, peering into the baby's bedroom.

Bonner was standing at Whitney's changing table, bent over the baby. Whitney lay on her back, naked, her small, pink, chubby legs kicking energetically. But Bonner wasn't changing Whitney's diapers. In fact, he wasn't even touching the baby. His right hand was centered at his groin.

And then—

Gasping, Dani ran away.

Dani scrambled down the stairs, frantic to get out of there, get away, before Bonner came out and saw her. Horror filled her as she realized just what he'd been doing.

Come on, little girl, what's the matter with you? Don't you want to play with a nice big dick? Uh . . . uh . . . I'll show you what it can do, yes, yes, I'll show you and you'll like it, won't you? Uh. . . . Let's see how far you can get your mouth open, little girl. . . .

By the time Dani reached the kitchen, she was nauseated. She lunged for the kitchen sink. Bending over its gleaming double stainless steel, she vomited into the garbage disposer.

When the last heaves were finished, Dani let go of the sink edge and turned on the water. Hurriedly she used a paper towel to wash the sink clean. Two of Whitney's baby bottles had been left on the counter to dry, the designer glass printed with colorful patterns of dancing rabbits.

She stared at the bottles, transfixed.

A little baby.

Bonner had done . . . that . . . in front of a little, tiny baby.

The telltale creak of the overhead floorboards brought her back to reality. Her foster father was coming downstairs.

Dani spun across the kitchen, slipping out the side door. She ran around the side of the house toward the front, feeling as if her entire world had collapsed. She'd loved having Whitney as her real baby sister, and having Ryan as her best friend, and having pretty clothes to wear, and being away from Fay. She'd even liked Maureen and wanted to be like her. *She'd loved it here.*

Now what was she going to do? If she told anyone about Bonner, it would be horrible. Bonner would say she was lying, and Maureen would agree, and Mrs. Vivian would come and take her away. She'd end up in Detroit again, going to some terrible school with the gangs, and Fay would find her again, and sell her body. Force her to fuck some horrible men, and do terrible things. . . .

But how could she not tell?

He had put his white stuff on Whitney . . . a little baby . . . a little baby.

She had to tell.

"Hey, Bic Head, what're you doing?" Ryan had seen her from his front window, and he pushed open his front door to let her in. He had more black-and-blue marks on his jaw, Dani noticed, and his lower lip was swollen.

"Hi," said Dani, her voice coming out too small.

"What's wrong with you?" he greeted her. "You look like someone squeezed all your juice out of you."

Dani forced a smile that immediately faded. Should she tell him what had happened?

"What's wrong with your mouth, Ry?"

Her friend shrugged. "Nothing."

"You got bruises."

Ryan's jaw tightened. "My dad found out I've been driving the 'Vette. He wrote down the mileage on the odometer and then he checked it again in a week. He really hit the roof. He went flying into orbit, way out into hyperspace."

"Oh, Ryan."

The house smelled of pizza. The spitfire rhythms of a female rapper, a girl called Yo Yo, were bouncing through the rooms, the volume turned up to a deafening level. Ryan's father, Bing Sokol, was at work, and his mother was working a double shift at the Madisonia Osteopathic Hospital.

"You got any Ice Cube?" said Dani, referring to a popular rap group.

"Yeah, I just got their new album. And I got a cool one by Enuff Z'Nuff. I got it yesterday."

They walked up to Ryan's room, the rapper's voice following them. His father disliked heavy metal and hated rap music, considering both inflammatory and obscene, which was why Ryan played them with such persistence.

"So," he said over the music, when they had reached his room, strewn with fallen clothes, Pepsi cans, and comic books, along with an extensive baseball card collection that Ryan had now lost interest in. Rock posters covered the walls.

Ryan said, "I hope you're gonna miss me."

"What?" Dani looked at the bruises along Ryan's mouth. "What do you mean, I'm gonna miss you?"

Ryan's mouth tightened. "They sent for these catalogs, see? From this military school. It's a really gross place where they make you wear uniforms and you have to join ROTC, just like boot camp."

"Oh," said Dani.

"I mean a *military school,*" Ryan said angrily. "Can you fucking believe it? Why don't they just put me in a reform school or something? It's the exact same thing."

Dani swallowed, trying to assimilate this additional shock. "Where . . . where is this school, Ryan?"

"Would you believe in the Smoky Mountains? Tennessee or someplace. I'm gonna be a hillbilly."

"*Tennessee?*" she said over the music. "Did you say—"

"I said Tennessee, I don't know where the fucking hell the fucking shitass place is, and who fucking cares?" Ryan shouted.

Dani wanted to cry. She went to the window and stared out. Her own bedroom window looked back at her, the room with the wallpaper that was supposed to be hers.

"I *hate* him," Ryan muttered.

Neither of them said anything, and she could hear the boy's roughened breathing.

"Anyway," she said after a moment. "I got a problem, too. I saw Bonner, he was, you know, screwing on the baby, and he—"

"Screwing?"

"Yeah."

"Don't talk dirty, Dani," Ryan snapped, throwing himself on his bed.

"I'm *not* talking dirty. It really happened! I really saw it! He was upstairs in her room, and he was pretending to change her diapers, but he was really, you know . . ." Dani's voice sank in shame, and she began to cry. "It was so sick and gross."

"Are you *sure*?"

"I saw it."

"Dani, are you really, *really* sure?"

"I'm not lying, if that's what you mean. I never lied to you since you told me not to."

Ryan nodded bitterly. "Yeah, Bonner's a total creep. But, Dani, how can you do anything about it? He's your father. He's the new dean, and you're just a kid. Adults don't listen to kids; they think kids haven't got any feelings or opinions."

"They'll listen; they have to. Somebody has to."

"Don't be too sure," said Ryan, rubbing his swollen lower lip. "Besides, Dani, they'll send you away if you aren't careful. That's what they do. Look at what my dad's doing to me."

Maureen left the activity center where her writers' group met and walked out to her car, adrenaline still rushing through her system. The group had spent over thirty minutes discussing her latest book, several of the women raving over her "lyrical prose." Of course, Jim Dover, the maverick sci-fi writer of the group, had insisted that too much lyricism made an author's work dense.

"I don't care what Jim said; you were great," said Marilyn Rabaul, catching up to her. Dean Rabaul's sixty-five-year-old wife was trying her hand, rather unsuccessfully, at a Silhouette romance. "Some of those people can be bitchy, but you handled the critiquing so well, Maureen. You always do."

Maureen said crossly, "Jim Dover doesn't know what he's talking about. *His* work is so dense it can't even get published."

"As I said, you handled it," Marilyn said, bending to unlock her Lincoln Town Car.

"How is Charles?" asked Maureen belatedly.

"Oh, he's weak but already working on notes for an article." Marilyn hesitated. "I assume you're giving a big party to celebrate Bonner's appointment."

"Oh," said Maureen. Actually, she had made no such plans. It hadn't even occurred to her, she'd been so wrapped up in her worries about her marriage and the oppressive feeling of impending doom that had been bothering her recently.

"That's not a problem for you, is it? Entertaining is just part of the job. I'm sure Bonner made that clear when he told you about the promotion."

"Of course. . . . I love to entertain."

"Well, think it over; talk it over with your hubby," said Marilyn briskly. "I have a wonderful caterer I use; he used to be a chef at the London Chop House before they closed. You know the college picks up your expenses, so you can't beat the price, can you? Save all your receipts."

At last Marilyn waved good-bye and Maureen got into her Cougar and started its engine, her good mood of the evening rapidly plummeting.

A party? God, she'd forgotten how much work Bonner's appointment would be for her. Lately she'd been fantasizing about taking Whitney and booking a seat on a flight for Brunswick, Maine, near Portland, where her sister had a second home Maureen was sure she would loan her for a few months. She had to get away from these pressures . . . Bonner . . . Dani . . . and more things that she really didn't delineate to herself.

As Maureen drove home, her mood of melancholy continued.

Whatever had made her stay married to Bonner Lockwood for so many years? Fear of the unknown, she supposed. She was a small-town girl who had grown up in a suburb of Kalamazoo. She had gone straight from the apartment she'd shared with two roommates to him. She'd been shy, not exactly pretty, and he'd exuded the sexiness of many intellectual men. She'd thought, *If I don't marry him, who will I marry?* But their marriage had always been a cool one, Bonner a distant, perfunctory husband. Now she was afraid of reentering the singles world. With a baby now, who would want her?

Pulling into their driveway, she noticed that Bonner's attic lights were on. She walked into the kitchen, finding Dani glaring at the window of the microwave with gloomy ferocity. The girl's face seemed white, bleached of color. The room was becoming saturated with the odor of microwave popcorn.

"You aren't going to make a big mess, I hope," said Maureen, putting her purse on the kitchen desk.

"Mm-m-m, no," said Dani.

"Where's Whitney?" asked Maureen.

"Oh, Bonner put her to bed." Dani licked her lips, looking uneasy. "He . . . Maureen, he . . . he did something, Maureen."

Maureen was only half-listening as she rummaged in the cupboard for a couple of Tylenol to assuage the sudden headache that pounded in her temples and along the top of her skull. *At least I have my beautiful baby,* she was thinking.

"What did he do, Dani?"

"He . . . he . . . I don't know. I can't say it."

"Try, Dani. You usually say everything else. You certainly don't hold back," said Maureen, finding the pill bottle and beginning to jiggle the childproof cap.

"He did a thing with the baby," said Dani after a long pause.

Maureen turned her eyes to gaze at her thirteen-year-old adoptive daughter. "A thing?"

"I mean . . . he did this thing, see. He . . . he played with his dick," Dani blurted. *"On her."*

Shock flooded Maureen, nausea choking her, becoming outrage. She stared, stunned, at the girl. "Dani! I just can't believe you! How could you say such a filthy thing!"

"I'm telling you the—"

"You are telling *lies!"* exploded Maureen, grabbing Dani by the arm. The pressure of the past months erupted like lava, spewing out of her. Her husband wasn't; he couldn't; no—

"This is just some more dirt out of your past, isn't it? Like what you told me about that pimp. How dare you dirty our house with your filthy untruths?"

Dani had started to cry, her face twisting. "I don't want it to happen to Whitney, to my baby," she whimpered.

Maureen dragged the girl across the kitchen. "You're going up to your room right now and you are not coming out until morning. I don't want to hear any more dirty talk from you in this house, is that clear? Not one more word."

"It's not dirty talk," sobbed Dani. "I was just—"

"Enough," snapped Maureen. She was close to tears herself. "Jesus, please."

Maureen shut Dani's bedroom door behind her and stood breathing heavily in the upstairs hallway. Was there some small grain of truth in Dani's accusation? But no, her mind insisted. How could there be? This wasn't the first time the girl had used her sleazy background to get attention. She had a case record six inches thick, Maureen reminded herself. She was a *problem girl.* To a girl like that, molestation and unspeakable acts must be a way of life. She'd projected, that was all. Put her background on Bonner, painted him with her brush.

Shaking, Maureen walked down the hall toward the baby's room, opening Whitney's door to peek inside. In the dim light from the hallway, the pretty room seemed neat and fresh. The changing table was immaculate. A rabbit night-light burned in a wall socket. A colorful mobile of chickens and ducks danced over the crib.

Maureen moved to the edge of the crib and stared down at her daughter. The baby girl lay cocooned in sleep, her round, diapered rump sticking up in the air. One tiny fist clutched a wrinkle in the crib sheet.

Maureen bent closer to the infant, until she could smell the scent of talc mingled with the sweet, milky odor of the baby's own skin and hair. Nothing sour. Nothing sexual here, only clean baby. The odor tore at her heart.

A savage protectiveness came over her.

If he really did anything—

Oh, but he hadn't. Of course he had not. It was monstrous and unthinkable. It was totally outside

Bonner's character. My God, he was an educator! He had two master's degrees and a Ph.D. He had published three books and uncounted numbers of professional articles; he had given hundreds of speeches; he received letters from all over the world from colleagues and former students. He wasn't a . . . She couldn't even think the word. People like that weren't handsome and respected; they were dirty old men in stained raincoats.

She tiptoed out of the room, going down the hall to the bedroom she had converted into an office for herself.

Flicking on the light, she flung herself into the swivel chair that faced her computer, and stared at its blank screen.

Bonner was deep in a chapter on his Korea book, dealing with the American Marines' landing at Walmi, a short distance from Inchon, Seoul's port city.

His personal phone line rang, disturbing his concentration.

Annoyed at the interruption, he snatched it up. "Yes?"

"Bonner . . . it's me," said his wife's voice. "Can I come up for a few minutes? I'd like to talk."

Bonner hesitated. He disliked having his wife visit his private space, even under his close supervision. Especially now when things seemed to be changing in his life, growing closer to some sort of peak, the nature of which he did not yet know.

Maureen's voice rose. "Bonner? Are you still there? I just want to talk, not violate your precious sanctuary."

"I'm almost finished here," he told her reluctantly. "I'll come down."

They sat in Maureen's office, surrounded by the clutter of her papers, a long computer printout hanging from a clothespin. The room smelled of her perfume and gave Bonner a cloying sensation. He felt a twinge of unease as he watched his wife fiddling with a ballpoint pen. Her makeup had worn off, giving her delicate features a scraped-bare, stern look, like the painting *American Gothic*.

"Will you stop fussing with that damn pen?" he said. "I was working; I was really into the chapter. I was bringing out some very interesting points that haven't been made before."

Maureen gazed at him. "Are you happy, Bonner?"

He was surprised, slightly alarmed. "What kind of a question is that? I haven't had time to be happy. I've got a thousand things on my mind. I'm a new father, I've got a foster daughter with emotional problems, and I've been busting my balls to be dean so that we can have some real financial security around here, and a decent retirement and maybe the hope of even more."

"I mean are you happy? For instance, take Whitney. Are you glad we had her?"

"Of course I am."

"What do you want out of fatherhood, Bonner?"

It was the second time she had asked him that. He didn't like the penetrating way his wife's eyes drilled him as if she saw through to the soiled edges of his very soul. "And what's that supposed to mean? You called me out of my office for this, Maureen?"

"Do you enjoy all the things you do for Whitney, Bonner? The little jobs you perform . . . like changing her diapers and so forth?"

"No, I don't," he said quietly, getting to his feet. "Frankly, the whole thing disgusts me. I have somewhat of a queasy stomach, but I do it because I have to, because you're busy and need the help and I want to do my share. I don't want to leave all the responsibility to you."

He watched her react to this. First there was surprise; then the acceptance spread over her face, becoming relief. She wanted to buy it. She wanted to believe in him because if she didn't, her world blew apart. She would believe the most incredible things, if he said them to her in the right tone of voice, because she *had* to believe them.

"Anyway," he said softly, clinching it. "I love you, Maureen. . . . I don't deserve to have a wife like you."

"I . . . love you, too," she said in a low, almost pleading voice. "Bonner . . . we have to try harder . . . we have to try . . ."

"Of course." He gently hugged her, trying to avoid burying his face in her perfume-scented hair, patting her back. "Molly Mo," he whispered in her ear, the nickname he had used when they were first married. "My beautiful Molly Mo."

She seemed to relax. Finally, he made his excuses and left the room, keeping his steps even, confident. His heart was hammering, and his scrotum had tightened, crawling up into his body cavity. *Jesus, Jesus*, he was thinking.

But still his eyes could not resist sliding to the right, where the baby's bedroom door was, and then moving farther down the hall, to Dani's room. His babies. His pretty, pretty babies. They were right here in the house with him, his curse and his temptation.

* * *

Dani raged through her room in a whirlwind of grief and weeping anger. Crying, she attacked her bookshelf, knocking all the books that Maureen and Bonner had given her onto the floor. She grabbed up the copy of *Acrobat Squirrel*, Maureen's own book, and ripped its cover off, tearing off brightly colored pages and flinging them wildly. She hadn't been able to read it anyway, not without stumbling. The words were too big. Why had they made her come here anyway? She hated this place! She hated them! She hated everything!

Sinking onto the floor in the middle of the tattered pages, she bent her head over her knees and sobbed.

She *had* told the truth. Why wouldn't Maureen believe her?

Out in the hallway, she heard footsteps. They neared her door, then paused. Dani waited, barely breathing, and then the steps moved on.

She moved to her telephone and punched in the numbers of Ryan's private line.

"Ry?" she whispered when he answered.

"Yeah." His voice sounded husky. "Look, my dad just told me—I mean they got the acceptance letter today. I'm really going. They're taking me down there in two more days. I'm gonna finish out the spring session and stay for the whole summer and then fall and winter."

"No," Dani whispered, shocked.

"The school is right near the Great Smoky Mountains National Park," he told her. "They go hiking there all the time, and they have a climbing club. And a rifle range. All the cadets can shoot rifles any time they want."

Dani could not picture the school at all. It seemed impossibly blurry to her, like a movie on TV, full of things she could never really do or be part of, something that totally rejected her.

"No," she repeated, her voice rising.

"And I'm getting a dress uniform; they have to tailor it to me, and I'm getting fitted when we go down there. You can get ribbons for it, and the shoulders have these things on them, with gold on them. And I'll wear fatigues, too; those are—"

"Shut up!" snapped Dani.

To his credit, Ryan seemed to realize how hurt she was, and he quickly added, "Anyway, that doesn't make me stop hating it. I'll always hate it. I told my dad once I'm eighteen I'm gone, I'm history, I'm never seeing him again."

"Good," Dani said. She was too full of her own dilemma to hold back. "Ry . . . I told Maureen and she didn't believe me. She said I was talking dirty."

Ryan gave a short laugh. "You just don't get it, do you? I believe you, but I'm a kid. *They* run the world, and they won't listen to anything they don't like."

"I've gotta go," she choked, hanging up the phone.

More upset than ever, she began to pace her bedroom.

Finally she went to her purse, where she began searching in the various pockets until she found the business card that Vivian Clavell had given her. She *had* to talk to Vivian now. Maybe Vivian could help her.

Vivian Clavell put down the Torey Hayden book and reached for the telephone that sat on her sister Judy's coffee table. She dialed her own phone number, punching in her remote code so she could pick up her messages.

Frowning, she listened as the machine played back two clicks, which meant hang-ups. She hated hang-ups, with their aura of anxious mystery. Someone had wanted to talk to her; what had they wanted to say? Had it been important? Too important to trust to a tape?

For some reason Dani came into her mind, but she was sure she had carefully instructed Dani to leave a message on the tape, and after a while she returned to her book.

Up in his room, Bonner was plotting how to make Dani his. It was time. Something in his body clock was ticking, and he felt the new flood of urgency. The hue and cry about that little girl in Nellis Lake had finally faded from the newspapers, and he had Maureen on his side now. . . . There was no way she'd ever believe he would do something like that.

He switched on his VCR and slid in one of the tapes, trying to figure out how to make it happen. Should Dani just "disappear"? Yes, he speculated, that would be best. He would blame it on the frowsy prostitute mother, he decided in a burst of inspiration. Fortunately, he had filed a court injunction here in Madisonia against Fay McVie, so it would be believed if Dani suddenly vanished. Fay would get all the blame, while he would act the distraught father, raging at the police for not doing more.

Ah, but what would he do with Dani? He owned a secret three-acre piece of property near Hastings, an old house trailer parked on the lot. He had taken girls there before. . . . He had installed a metal bar in the master bedroom to which handcuffs could be attached. There were a few places on the property that he would hate to see dug up, but that would come later, after he was saturated with all the pleasure he could devise.

He'd savor her. It wouldn't be a hasty experience, as it had been with the Nellis Lake girl, but he would draw it out to long, exquisite perfection.

His Dani. His pretty.

7

THE CLOUDLESS MORNING, hazy with humidity, already felt like August instead of mid-May. A bleached bowl of sky arched overhead, cracked apart by the line of a jet trail.

"Ryan!" called Dani, standing below Ryan's window near a huge-trunked maple. "Ryan!"

He didn't answer. Wasn't he going to say good-bye to her? Helplessly she turned to look at his father's blue Aerostar van, parked in the driveway. Earlier, she'd seen Bing Sokol loading suitcases in the back, along with a small TV set and Ryan's stereo system.

"Ryan!" she called desperately. "Ry!"

"Hey, Bic Head," he said, coming out of the detached garage. He was carrying a tennis racket and several containers of balls and wore dark slacks, a narrow-striped shirt, and black leather shoes rather than his usual Reebok high-tops. His brown hair had been trimmed much shorter and was barely a quarter-inch over his ears.

"Ry . . . are you going to play tennis at that school?" was the only thing she could think of to say.

"I guess so. They have five tennis courts and an

outdoor basketball court." Ryan wouldn't look at her but began to poke at the grass with the head of the racket, digging up bits of sod. His face was flushed and his eyes were reddened and puffy. Dani knew he'd been crying.

"Oh. I never played tennis," she said.

"If you did play, you'd probably chase balls a lot. All beginners have to do that. It's boring to chase balls."

"Oh."

A silence dropped between them, broken only by the sound of an ice cream truck with its merry calliope music, rounding the corner at the end of the block. Its relentless cheer made Dani feel even worse. Ryan was leaving, and then she'd have no one. She'd be all alone, stranded here in Madisonia where she didn't belong.

"Ry," she said desperately.

"Yeah?"

"I don't know what to do . . . about Bonner, I mean."

His eyes met hers. "Look, Dani, maybe you should—"

A male voice from the house interrupted them. "Ryan, I told you to come in the house and check your room, make sure you haven't left anything. Don't you listen? I mean right now. Step to it."

"Yeah, yeah, yeah!" Ryan called sullenly, barely glancing toward the porch.

A door slammed.

"Dani," Ryan said. "Hey, you've gotta find someone. Someone you can tell this to, maybe Jill Rudgate."

"Jill?"

"Yeah, she's all right. Hey, I gotta go now. My dad's

in a shitty mood and we gotta drive all the way to Tennessee with him, I mean, what a stupid drag."

He moved away awkwardly and then stopped. They both looked at each other, and she saw the tears shining in the boy's eyes.

"Ry," she choked.

"I don't wanta go," he blurted. "But I have to. That prick is making me. I want you to go in that garage and key the 'Vette, do you hear me? Take a big fucking house key and run it all along the finish. Will you? Will you promise?"

"Sure," she managed to say.

"I *mean* it, Dani."

"I will. I will. And . . . and I'll throw eggs on their windows, and I'll throw a brick through their windows, and I'll take spray paint and write 'fuck' all over their garage. And on the house, too."

Ryan gave a bitter laugh. "Write 'Dickhead.' That's what I want you to write. And I guess you could write me a letter on your computer, too, huh? And tell me—"

Ryan's mother appeared on the front porch, wearing jeans and a Guatemalan blouse. She was a stocky woman with a harassed look. "Say good-bye to your friend. We're already late, Ryan, and if you're not in the house in two seconds, I'm going to put your father on you. Do you really want that today?"

Ryan thrust something into Dani's hand. When she looked down she saw that it was his Swiss army knife.

"Ryan!" called his mother.

Reluctantly Ryan turned and began loping toward the porch. Within five minutes he would be in the car with his two angry parents, being taken away and dumped like unwanted garbage.

"Ryan!" Dani called desperately. "Ry . . ."

But he had gone inside the house.

Slowly she walked back across the street. The ice cream truck had stopped only a few doors away. A crowd of neighborhood children was clustered around the driver, some of them about Dani's age. She felt in her pocket, but she had no money, and anyway, she didn't think ice cream would ease the terrible scratchy, explosive tightness of her throat.

As she started toward the Lockwood house, Bonner came out on the porch. Despite the humid weather, he was wearing gray flannel pants and a conservatively striped business shirt. His silvery hair gleamed in the sun.

"Well, I see that boy across the street is finally getting what he deserves," he remarked. "Military school is just right for delinquents like him. Some boys need strong discipline. Oh, I see the ice cream truck; do you want something? Here—come and get some money. My pretty little girl deserves something good on a hot morning like this." His eyes rested hotly on her.

Dani forced herself to take the five-dollar bill from her adoptive father's hands.

"Do you want something, too?" she asked politely.

"Oh, no, thank you, honey." His eyes inspected her sharply.

She kept smiling.

She couldn't let him know how scared she was.

"Now, Dani, for God's sake do a thorough job," ordered Maureen, her voice thin with stress. "That silver belonged to my grandmother, and I don't want little tarnishy spots on it."

"Okay," said Dani.

She stood at the kitchen counter, rubbing a pol-
ish-impregnated cloth over sterling silver spoons
and forks, watching as the darkened silver sprang to
life under the cloth. The big party was going to be two
days from now, on Friday night. There would be
more than two hundred guests, including three college presidents, one senator, and several media per-
sonalities.

An electric carpet-cleaning machine whined from
the living room, wielded by a college student, Brent,
who had been hired from the campus employment
office. Brent would also tend bar at the party. Even
Dani was going to help pass hors d'oeuvres.

Maureen was now on the phone to the caterer, in-
sisting that she wanted two different kinds of caviar,
three if they could locate it. She planned to have a
separate caviar table, hot and cold hors d'oeuvres,
and a huge shrimp bowl.

Glumly Dani dug the cloth in between the tines of
a big serving fork. Everything felt so wrong. Bonner
had done something awful and Maureen wouldn't
listen, and now there was going to be a big party, and
everyone would think Bonner was so great. Now that
he was going to be dean, no one would ever listen to
her.

Ryan was the only one who had listened, and he
was gone.

A cry drifted into the kitchen from the intercom,
which Maureen had left switched on in Whitney's
bedroom.

Maureen waved impatiently at Dani. "Go see about
that, will you, please? Take her a bottle."

Eagerly Dani hurried upstairs, the bottle of milk
warm and comforting between her fingers. She was

looking forward to the respite. She loved holding the baby and always felt warm and comforted after she had done so.

She stepped into the room and stopped short. Bonner had taken Whitney out of her crib and was standing with her at the changing table. As before, his penis was out and hugely erect, only this time he was in the act of thrusting it toward the baby's opened, crying mouth. *He was going to make her suck on it.*

Shock slammed through Dani. The baby bottle fell out of her fingers, crashing onto the floor.

Bonner jumped, instinctively grabbing a blanket off the changing table to hold in front of himself.

"What are you doing here?" he snapped.

"I . . . Maureen told me . . . I have to give her a bottle—"

"Well, clean up this damn spilled milk you dropped." As if nothing had happened, Bonner stalked past her, leaving the wriggling baby lying unattended on the changing table.

Dani stepped over the puddle of milk and rushed toward Whitney. She scooped the baby up, cradling her protectively, and carried her to the rocking chair. She sat heavily down. Anxiously she inspected the smooth, pink cheeks, the opened mouth. She even peeled away the baby's diapers but could find nothing unusual, not even any diaper rash. Whatever he had done, Bonner had not actually touched Whitney.

But he would have if she'd walked in even in a minute later.

He had . . . molested Whitney.

Dani knew what the word was, and she knew what it meant.

Vomit rose up in the back of her throat. Grimly she choked it down, cradling Whitney to her, breathing in the soft, milky infant smells. The baby's sobs gradually quieted. What was she going to do? She *had* to make someone listen.

"Dani, what in the name of God is going on up there?" came Maureen's irritated voice through the intercom. "Did you spill the bottle?"

"I . . . I dropped it," Dani said miserably.

"Then come down and get another one. Please, Dani. This is such a hectic day."

Dani rose, carrying Whitney, and went downstairs.

"Maureen," she said pleadingly as she reached the kitchen. "I dropped the bottle, but it was because I got scared. Bonner was—"

Her foster mother whirled on her. "Dani, I haven't got time for your stories right now. I had the intercom on; I heard it all. You dropped the bottle and now you're trying to avoid the blame. Well, just get a clean one, all right? I'm too busy."

"But—"

"Do it, Dani."

Dani did as she was ordered, feeding Whitney the bottle. The baby sucked earnestly, little bubbles of milk streaming out of the corners of her mouth. Whitney seemed to have forgotten all about what Bonner had done. Only Dani remembered.

When she was finished, she hurried upstairs to her private telephone line, and hunched over the phone, dialing Vivian's office number.

"Good afternoon, Children's Agency," came the chirpy voice of a receptionist.

"I want to talk to Mrs. Vivian."

"Do you mean Vivian Clavell?"

"Yes."

"She isn't in the office; she's off sick," said the receptionist.

"But I *have* to talk to her."

"Honey, she's been ill and hasn't been in the office in several weeks. Can I transfer you to another social worker? I'm sure that—"

Dani hung up.

Dani went to her window, where she stood staring out at the street. The streetlight had come on, and in its silvery light the old Victorian houses looked storybook pretty. There were no black kids playing basketball, as there had been in Dani's old neighborhood, no screeching car brakes, no heavy traffic sounds, no drunks wandering around, no gang kids running past with beepers on their belts, no police sirens, no junker cars, no wandering stray dogs. Before coming here, she'd never known such a wonderful street existed.

She'd been right that first day when she said it wasn't real.

It wasn't. At least, not for girls like her.

Across the way, Ryan's house had the front porch light burning. Already she missed her friend with a deep, aching sense of loss. Ryan thought he was so bad, but he wasn't, and Dani had enjoyed the feeling of being much, much badder. Her heart sank as she remembered promising him that she would spray-paint "Dickhead" all over his dad's garage.

Had she really promised such a silly thing? Now it seemed stupid and useless. Mr. Sokol would simply blame the damage on neighborhood vandals and re-paint his garage. Maureen had enrolled her in summer school, and her tutoring with Jill would continue over the summer. By fall, she might be ready for real seventh grade. Life was going to go on without Ryan.

A car pulled up, turning into Jill's driveway next door, and Dani watched Jill get out of her blue Ford Tempo.

Jill, she thought suddenly, remembering what Ryan had said. *Maybe I could talk to her.*

Jill Rudgate let herself into her house, balancing the vegetarian pizza she had picked up from Pasquale's, a campus pizzeria.

She had spent the evening at the college swimming pool, doing her usual thirty-six laps, and she felt shaky with a sudden drop in blood sugar. Still, she was in a cheerful mood. Bonner Lockwood had been appointed dean and would no longer be directly supervising her. That was cause for celebration, and she intended to pour herself a cold Coors to go along with the pizza, and follow it up with several more.

She moved into her kitchen, switched on the lights, and lifted the box lid, stealing a thick slice of cheese-dripping pizza to munch on while she was hanging up her wet bathing suit and putting away her gym bag. She decided to finish reading *The Road Less Traveled* tonight if she had time.

The knock at the kitchen door surprised her, and she was even more surprised to discover that her caller was Dani McVie.

"Dani? Honey, your tutoring isn't tonight; it's tomorrow night."

"I know . . . I have to talk to you. It's important."

Jill let Dani in. The girl was wearing shorts and a New Kids on the Block T-shirt. Her freckles were blotches of cinnamon on her pale skin, and she looked worried.

"Have a slice," offered Jill, pointing to the pizza box.

Dani opened the lid, inspecting it curiously. "No pepperoni? You don't like pepperoni?"

"All that fat. Dani, what is it? I've got some phone calls to make and my—some things to type."

Dani put down the pizza box. "It's something bad," she said in a low voice. "You're gonna think I'm awful if I tell you, but I have to. It's really bad."

Jill busied herself getting out two plates, some napkins and forks, a can of Coors for herself, Diet Pepsi for the girl. "I know you feel terrible about Ryan leaving," she began.

"No, it's . . . it's Bonner," Dani whispered.

"Bonner?"

"Yes. He . . . he did something to Whitney."

Jill looked sharply at the thirteen-year-old. "Dani McVie. What are you talking about? What did Bonner do to the baby?"

"He . . . he . . ." Dani's eyes seemed saucer huge. "He . . . put his thing near her mouth. He was gonna put it in, but I walked into the room."

"Dani," Jill managed to say. "You must never say such things. Maybe you don't know how they sound."

"It's true," Dani insisted. "It is! It is!"

"Your language . . . your terminology. Dani, sometimes our eyes play tricks on us, or we relate something very innocent to our past experiences—"

"He *was!*"

Jill pushed away the pizza box. Uncomfortably, she remembered having seen Bonner upstairs in his attic when he thought he was alone. Masturbating. Her throat went suddenly dry. At her previous university job, there had been a campus scandal when a woman graduate assistant sued her department head for sexual harassment. He had countered that she was lying, slandering him. The cases were still pending, but the money amounts were for well over $5 million.

"Please," begged Dani, edging close to Jill. "Please, you've *gotta* help. Maureen won't listen, and I don't know what to do. When he changes her, he does things to her. He . . . touches her with his dick. It's really, really true."

Perhaps if Dani hadn't added the "really, really true," Jill might have taken it more seriously. But Dani had prefaced several of her whoppers in the past with that exact same phrase, and Jill knew she couldn't listen to this any longer. She couldn't afford to. She liked Dani, but Bonner was still her boss. She had no money to defend herself against possible $5 million slander suits.

"Now, Dani," she said gently. "You can't go around talking about Bonner like this. It's called slander. It damages his reputation. Bonner is a good man, a great and respected man, and he's just been named dean of the college. Do you realize what an honor that is? His name is even going to be in the Detroit papers."

"I don't care," Dani said sullenly.

"Well, you'd better care, because you're living in the man's house, young lady. He supports you. He paid for those clothes you're wearing; he's your *father*. Now, I think you'd better run along home now.

I gave you six work sheets to do last time, and I imagine you still have some of them to finish."

Shaken, Jill closed and locked the side door behind Dani's pleading look, and returned to her now cooling pizza. Was it possible that the girl was telling the *truth*? Oh, Jesus, what if she was? But then Jill remembered Dani's unpleasant background—Bonner had given her a good outline of it—and relaxed a little. She herself had listened to Dani's falsehoods, and many caseworkers and social workers had concurred that she was a compulsive liar.

Still, Jill told herself, it would not hurt to check this out with Maureen Lockwood, in a subtle manner, of course.

Jill slowly moved across the kitchen toward the wall phone, which was equipped with a sound amplifier to compensate for her deaf ear, and dialed the Lockwoods' number.

Maureen was in her writing room, scowling at the computer screen as she debated whether to use the word *danced* or *spun*. When the phone rang, she picked it up with a sigh.

"Yes?" she said impatiently, hoping to signal by her voice that she didn't want to be interrupted for more than a few minutes. She wanted to finish this draft so she could read it to her writers' group next week.

"It's me: Jill. Dani was just over here; she's got some sort of weird bee in her bonnet. Did she and Bonner have an argument or something?"

"Who knows?" said Maureen. "If they have, I haven't heard about it."

Jill hesitated. "I mean—well, Dani was talking kind of strangely."

"In what way?"

"Well . . ."

"What is it, Jill?" Maureen asked impatiently.

"Something to do with diaper changing, I suppose," said Jill after a long pause.

Maureen stiffened. She knew exactly what Jill was talking about. Rage filled her. Now the lies had spread! This was terrifying. How dare Dani do this to them.

"I admit my husband's not very eager to do diaper duty, but he does try, and I suppose we have to give him credit," she said carefully. "You know how men are. They bumble around, they dump a ton of talcum powder on a kid, and think they're doing it right."

"But that wasn't what Dani said. It sounded different than that, Maureen. In fact—"

"Jill. Didn't Bonner brief you about Dani's case record? She sounds so believable, doesn't she? But that's the way these children are. They're pathological; they believe their own lies. Take it from me, Jill, the girl has a problem. Remember, her background is full of sexual abuse. She thinks in those terms. That's all she knows."

Jill sounded only too ready to believe her, and they stayed on the phone for a few more minutes, discussing Dani, her summer school session, and some essays Jill wanted Dani to write. Maureen finished the conversation and hung up, more furious than ever at Dani. Her loose talk, her sick ideas, were getting dangerous.

* * *

In the hall, Bonner paused, then moved on, his heart pounding thickly. He'd overheard most of the conversation and it reverberated unpleasantly in his head. *"Remember, her background is full of sexual abuse. She thinks in those terms."*

Maureen had actually said the words *sexual abuse.* Oh, Jesus, now what? How could he contain this disaster?

At least Maureen had the good sense not to believe the girl, thanks to all the hard work he'd done since Dani arrived in planting the idea that Dani was a pathological, compulsive liar. No matter what Dani said, it would be the statement of an acknowledged liar. But Dani was a clever little thing. What if she somehow convinced someone to listen to her anyway? Like Jill, or that nosy social worker, Vivian Clavell.

It was time he had a talk with Dani.

He walked down the hall and knocked briefly on the door of Dani's room, before pushing it open.

The girl was sitting at her computer, typing something. As soon as he walked in, she pushed a couple of keys, erasing the words on the screen.

He thought he had seen the word *Ryan.*

"You're not writing a letter to that delinquent?" he said.

"Just typing."

They stared at each other, assessing each other. Bonner saw her narrowed eyes, and the way her mouth had tightened. *She knew.* For a second he could not speak, terror thunking into his heart like an arrow hitting home. *The bitch,* he thought. She had power over his whole life if she only knew it. He had to defuse her . . . terrify the hell out of her. Otherwise not only would he not be dean, but he would lose his entire career, and probably end up in Jackson Prison. The thought caused sweat to break out in the follicles of his scalp.

"Well, now, Dani," he began heartily. "I understand you might have some misconceptions. A misconception is when you think something looks like something else, but it really isn't."

The girl said nothing, merely looking at him.

"That day you saw me in Whitney's room, for instance," he pressed on. "I was only trying to massage her stomach to help her to sleep. I would never do anything to hurt a little baby, and anyone who says I would is a liar. An abject, *criminal* liar."

"I *wasn't* lying," Dani burst out. "I was telling the—"

"You were telling stories and you know you were. Your case record is as thick as a phone book, and every caseworker who's ever talked to you has mentioned the *chronic lying*." Bonner moved forward, taking Dani's forearm in his fingers. He squeezed her tender flesh, taking satisfaction in the way her breath caught in pain.

"Now, you listen to me, and you listen very carefully. Your sick lies are not going to contaminate my household. Am I making myself very clear?"

"I'm not lying!" Dani squirmed to get loose.

"You misinterpreted. Well, no one believes your 'misinterpretations' anymore. Did you ever hear the story of the boy who cried wolf, Dani? You're like that boy. You cry wolf and no one will listen. You tell lies and everyone turns away. Well, if you become too annoying, I have a nice little alternative I can invoke. Do you want to know what that alternative is?"

"What?" she asked sullenly.

"Well, it's this. I can send you back to your mother.

I'm certain she wants you back. In fact, I know she does. She told me she does."

Dani's face paled.

"I almost forgot to tell you. She came here one night when you were asleep, in all her glory, blond wig, tight dress, and all. She said she had your suitcase in the car, Dani. I think she was really serious about it. She said you were going to have a room of your own."

The girl didn't say anything.

"We didn't want to tell you," Bonner pressed on, "because we thought it might upset you, but now I feel you have a right to know, hm-m-m-m? In fact, if you aren't good, I might even *drive you back to Detroit to her apartment."*

This was almost fun. Bonner was pleased to see the terror that spread itself across the girl's face, distorting her features.

"Don't. Please don't," Dani whispered.

"Why shouldn't I? The final papers haven't been signed yet, and I don't have to accept you. Your fate is in my hands. I won't tolerate liars around here. Ever. *Ever,* do you hear, Dani?"

"Y-yes. . . ."

Satisfied, he released the girl's upper arm. "I'm glad we understand each other, Dani. Maybe in a day or two I'll take you for a nice ride in the country. Right now, my wife is a little worried about putting on such a large party. Two hundred people *is* a pretty big number, and it will strain our resources. It means we're going to need all the help we can get. Of course you will be available to offer your assistance, won't you?"

"Yes."

Bonner turned to go. "And remember what we

talked about, dear. I don't want to hear any more of
your *misinterpretations*, or you go back to your
mother. I'll drive you myself. You have my word on
that, Dani. And *I* always tell the truth."

This had better work, he told himself as he left her
room and went back upstairs to work some more on
the Korea book. Because if it didn't—

He'd have to engineer her "disappearance" very,
very soon.

Dani closed the door behind Bonner and stood
pressing her entire body against it, wishing she had
a lock, wishing she could lock Bonner out forever
and ever. She hated him! She hated him! But he was
right. He did have control of her fate and he could
take her back to Detroit, where her mother would
sell her to men.

Waves of fear rolled over her, and she slumped
against the door, dropping to the floor to sit with her
face in her hands.

Fay . . .

8

*D*ANI CRIED FOR a long time, until all the tears seemed drained out of her and there was only her despair. Finally, desperate for some shred of comfort, she got up and walked over to the window to look out at Ryan's house again.

Looking at his house gave her just a little bit of comfort. Even if he was far away, he was still her best friend. If he were here, he'd help her. He'd know what to do.

A car came around the corner, its headlights flashing on the branches that nearly met over the old, collegiate street. It had a bad, rattling muffler that sounded terrifyingly familiar.

Could it be Fay?

Dani leaned closer to the window, panic tearing her throat. She narrowed her eyes, trying to see into the darkness, to find out whether the car was an old, rusty Toyota with a crumple on the right fender.

But the car disappeared around the block, and gradually her tension relaxed. If Bonner said he was taking her to Detroit, she'd fight. She'd run and hide; she'd—but then Whitney would be alone, she remembered. Alone with *him.*

Again she picked up the phone, swiftly dialing Vivian's home number, which she now had by memory.

"Hi, you have reached Vivian Clavell. I'm busy now, and unable to—"

Why didn't she answer? Where was she? Dani hung up, tears springing to her eyes. Helplessly she let them roll out, and then her chest began to heave. She lay back on the floor and sobbed silently. She felt alone—so alone.

Mrs. Vivian, where are you? Why didn't you answer my phone call? Don't you care anymore?

In her car, Fay McVie gripped the steering wheel, cursing aloud. "Bitch!" she muttered. "Little shit-fucking bitch!"

She'd seen Dani's face briefly in the window, staring down at the street. The little creep didn't even know or care that her own mother was out here, needing her. It was because of Dani that she was now awaiting trial—her court date, postponed twice, was only two weeks off now. Shit, she could end up sitting in prison because of Dani. If Harley didn't kill her first.

She swerved around a corner, narrowly missing a black dog that wandered out just as she approached. She'd been living in her car for three days, keeping herself going on an eighth of an ounce of coke she'd managed to score off a trick who'd had the bad luck to fall asleep. Her nose, raw and sore, was killing her. She smelled, and she was tired, and she hated the whole fucking world, especially Dani.

How was she going to get into that damn big fancy

house to take Dani? Rich people like that had security systems and panic buttons, she felt sure.

She circled the block again. Maybe she would just park her car down the block a few houses and just sit for a while and watch the Lockwoods' house. Just in case an idea occurred to her.

Pulling up to the curb, she shut off the motor and unconsciously rubbed at the lining of her nose as she leaned back in the seat. It hadn't healed right after Harley cut it. It hurt—it hurt like hell.

And if she didn't bring Dani back home to him, she knew he would ream it out with his knife, stabbing her again and again until she was nothing but a sodden pile of blood and skin.

You bitch, Dani, she thought savagely, staring at the Lockwood house.

A thin morning sun lightened the sky as Vivian and Judy lugged Vivian's suitcase and a shopping bag that contained her lap quilting project into Vivian's condo. Vivian was overjoyed to be home again. Her wall quilts, sunbursts of jewel colors, were a part of her.

"God!" she exclaimed. "This place looks just so great. But just coming in from the car made my heart pound."

"If you feel that weak, then you shouldn't be moving back home yet," said her sister, setting the bag down on Vivian's kitchen floor.

"Look," Vivian said, smiling pleasantly. "I'm too old to have a roommate, and I want to start piecing this project. In fact, I might even work a little after I take a shower."

She went upstairs to her bedroom while, downstairs, Judy Dodara fussed in the kitchen, putting fresh groceries in her sister's refrigerator.

When the phone rang, Judy picked it up on the first ring.

"Is this . . . I want to talk to Mrs. Vivian," came a young girl's voice, high-pitched and anxious.

"My sister is in the shower right now," said Judy, still a little annoyed that Vivian was rejecting her help. "Who's calling, and I'll give her the message later."

"It's Dani."

"Dani? Oh, yes." Judy had heard all about her sister's pet client, the little girl who had captured Vivian's imagination and occupied many of their conversations over the past few weeks. "Well, Dani, I'll give her the message."

"Please," begged Dani, her voice frantic. "Please—"

Judy Dodara thought Vivian gave far too many of her thoughts to this girl. It had been cases like Dani's that had sapped Vivian's strength in the first place, causing her illness. "I told you, young lady, I'll tell her about your call as soon as she gets out of the shower."

But almost immediately after Judy hung up, the phone rang again, one of Vivian's many friends calling to see if she was home, and Judy forgot.

Vivian sewed at her Bernina for two hours, then took a long nap, dreaming about a case she had had more than ten years ago, an eleven-year-old girl whose stepfather had burned her more than 180 times with lighted cigarette butts and tortured her with a charcoal lighting device.

She awoke feeling stronger. In the afternoon several widowed neighbors, alerted by Judy's car in the driveway, paid calls and lingered until the dinner hour. By 8:30 P.M., Vivian was sitting in front of the TV set, quilting while she watched a rerun of "L.A. Law." Judy had fallen asleep in Vivian's La-Z-Boy chair, her opened mouth emitting puffing snores.

The sound of a ringing telephone on the TV set woke Judy from her nap. She jerked upright in her chair, rubbing her eyes. "Is that the phone?"

"It's just the TV."

"Oh," Judy said, sitting up. "It sounded so real. Did I tell you—oh, God, I forgot all about it—you had a phone call this morning from that Dani girl. The one you talk about all the time."

"She called this morning? And you're just now telling me about it?"

"Yes, well, you were in the shower and I forgot. She sounded upset, too. In fact, I thought she was going to burst out crying."

Vivian felt a wave of fury. "And you didn't *tell* me? Judy, I don't know what's wrong with you. I gave that girl my phone number; I told her she could call anytime. Dammit!"

She reached for the phone and punched in the Lockwoods' home phone number.

Bonner Lockwood answered her call. "Hello?"

"This is Vivian Clavell. Is Dani home?"

She felt sure that Bonner hesitated. "She's at her tutoring session and won't be back for at least another hour. Could I help you?"

He was lying. She didn't know how she knew, but she did. A chill rippled over Vivian. She decided not to tell him that Dani had called her.

"Well, I do need to talk to her. But as long as I have

you on the line, Mr. Lockwood, maybe you could fill
me in on Dani's progress. How is she doing these
days? Is everything all right with her?"

Bonner Lockwood's voice was full and resonant,
exuding a powerful ring of authority. "Her school-
work is fine—that's no problem—she's progressing
nicely. She might be ready to be mainstreamed into
seventh grade by fall, which is what we'd hoped. But
the falsehoods . . . well, she has annoyed both my
wife and myself with more of the wild stories about
her background."

"Oh? What kind of stories?"

"Her unpleasant past. The molestation and so
forth."

Molestation? Vivian drew air through her nostrils,
remembering Dani's questions, several months ago,
about touching.

"I see," she said. "Well, Dani's prevarication does
seem to emerge more when she's under stress. Are
there any stressors in the home right now? Anything
unusual happening that might trigger Dani's in-
securities?"

Bonner laughed jovially. "Just the fact that I've
been made dean. It's quite an honor for me. We're
giving a little celebration tonight; actually, it's a big
party. Dani has been helping my wife. I suppose she
and Maureen have been bickering a little bit about
the preparations. You know how women are," Bonner said, chuckling. "Two girls in the kitchen."

Vivian couldn't help grimacing.

He went on for several minutes about preparations
for the party, which apparently was going to include
not only the college faculty and staff, but also various local dignitaries and press. Vivian listened to

him talk, or was the word *boast?* She realized that
he'd skillfully led the conversation away from Dani.

"Well, good luck with your party," she finally said,
cutting him off. "And will you please give the message to Dani that I called? I'm moving back to my
own house—I was staying with my sister for a
week—but I'll try to reach her again tomorrow."

"Is it important?"

"No . . . it's just a routine call."

"Fine. I'll tell her," Bonner promised.

Thoughtfully Vivian hung up. She thought of Dani
as she'd seen her last, the girl's energy oddly
squelched, the shuttered look that had come down
over her eyes. And now Dani had nearly cried on the
phone to Judy. An uneasy feeling was pressing at
her. Could Dani have been the one creating those
hang-ups on her answering tape? Actually, by the
repeated number of hang-ups, she could have been
trying to call Vivian for a week.

Vivian closed her eyes, uncomfortably remembering that even on the day she had first dropped Dani
off at the Lockwoods', the girl had pulled back, in-
sisting she didn't want to stay there. Had she sensed
something? Children sometimes had stronger, surer
instincts than adults, Vivian believed. Especially a
girl like Dani, who'd grown up on the street.

Vivian thought about the dream she'd had today,
the eleven-year-old who'd been tortured by her stepfather. Had her mind been trying to tell her something? Of course, Bonner Lockwood wasn't that kind
of violent person. He was respected, a published author, a college dean.

Still . . . what if . . . ?

"Molestation," Bonner had said.

Her heart had begun to pump faster. As Vivian well

knew, child abusers didn't automatically come from poor homes. They came from every stratum of life, including the very wealthy. Abused children often vacillated about telling, racked with fear that their abusers, who might have threatened them, would hurt them or even stop loving them. One day, they might want to talk, need to talk. The next day, the situation would feel different to them. The "window" of disclosure would have passed, and it might never appear again.

"Are you okay?" Judy said.

"I . . . I don't know," Vivian said.

"That Dani case has been a real annoyance, hasn't it," her sister began.

"Not an annoyance," Vivian snapped, getting to her feet. "She's a wonderful girl. I feel strange about her . . . very uneasy. I think I might have made a mistake, Judy. At least I'm afraid I have."

"Mistake?"

Vivian's anxiety expressed itself in movement, as she walked toward her purse, which she had set on the floor beside the couch. She picked it up and slung the strap over her shoulder.

"What are you doing?" demanded Judy.

Vivian steadied herself. "I don't know. . . . Yes, I do know. I'm driving to Madisonia. I want to talk to Dani myself, make sure everything is all right. I'm sure it will be, I hope it will, but . . . I have to be sure. That placement is my responsibility."

Judy glanced at her watch. "Viv, don't be a fool. It's past nine at night. It's at least a two-hour drive; Madisonia is way past Lansing. You're in no condition."

"I slept three hours today; I feel great. I have the constitution of a horse. And you have nothing to say about it," snapped Vivian, swiftly checking her billfold for money and credit cards. She had $150—that was good—and two Visas. She would stay at the College Inn in Madisonia, she decided. Or failing that, there were several mom-and-pop motels on the road into town.

She went upstairs to her bedroom to pack a small overnight bag. She changed into twill slacks and a cotton sweater, threw a change of clothing into the bag, and added a nightgown and, at the last minute, a pair of jeans and her Reeboks.

She hurried into the bathroom to pack her cosmetics. Staring in the mirror at her face, she noticed the bluish shadows under her eyes, souvenirs of her illness. *Screw it,* Vivian thought. Defiantly she added a dash of pink lipstick.

She was ready.

Maureen was in her bedroom, dressing for the party. She had carried Whitney, in her infant seat, into the bedroom with her, and the baby lay alertly, drooling and sucking on her chubby fists. Succulent smells drifted upward from the kitchen, where the caterer was already at work.

In half an hour the first of their guests would start arriving, and in two hours the house would be packed to the seams with warm bodies. Why wasn't she looking forward to this more? She'd been having fantasies all day of taking Whitney and going up to Maine. Walking along the Androscoggin. Forgetting Bonner ever existed.

She pulled her dress off its hanger, an ice green silk sheath with a long, filmy jacket embroidered in bugle beads. With it she planned to wear a pair of diamond earrings that Bonner had recently given her.

"Guh, guh," said Whitney. Then she began to grunt, stiffening her body and arching her legs.

"Have you got a messy, Punkin?"

"Gah."

"Dani!" Maureen called, going to the bedroom intercom.

"Yeah?" The girl's voice came from somewhere in the house, amplified and made reedy by the transmission.

"Dani, will you please come up here and take Whitney? I think she needs changing. I want you to be in charge of her tonight—make sure she doesn't cry. I don't want the guests disturbed."

"Sure."

A minute later Dani appeared. Maureen noted with annoyance that her foster daughter had not yet dressed for the party. She was still wearing shorts and a T-shirt, and her red hair glowed around her face in a frizzy corona.

"Please change her diapers," she repeated. "And, Dani, comb your hair; it's standing straight up. Why aren't you changed yet? I want you to wear that pretty blue dress you wore at Thanksgiving. You can put on some lipstick if you want, and I'll loan you a pair of earrings."

"I . . ." The girl's lips moved. There was pleading in her eyes. "Maureen . . ."

"Maybe pearl earrings," said Maureen, pulling a pair out of her jewelry box. "These would look nice on you, Dani."

* * *

Dani tried not to cry as she carried Whitney to her bedroom and laid her on the changing table. She hadn't put on the earrings. She didn't want them. No one would listen to her. No one wanted to. They all thought she was lying.

And now there was going to be a big party and Bonner would walk around the house so proud of himself because he was going to be dean.

It made Dani sick.

She unfastened the baby's shortie jumpsuit and peeled it up, then began undoing the tabs of her Pampers. A ripe odor drifted up from the diapers, permeating the air.

"Ugh, ugh, ugh," Dani said, deftly cleaning. "Whitney, don't you know how to be clean? You're so messy. You're just a messy, messy baby."

The baby cooed adorably.

"But I love you," Dani added, dropping the used diaper into the nearby covered pail.

She finished with the baby and put her back in her crib, giving the crib mobile a push that sent it dangling and twirling. "There. Play with those, Whitney. I'll come up and say good night in a little while. Actually, I'll come up a couple of times."

To guard you, she thought.

Then, as she stood staring down at the cooing baby, a horrible thought occurred to her.

She couldn't guard Whitney every minute.

Wearing a gray chiffon dress with a blouson effect and silver earrings she had bought in Mexico, Jill Rudgate walked across the lawn that separated her house from the Lockwoods'. The Lockwoods' driveway was jammed with cars, and more were parked on both sides of the street for a half-block in either direction. She could see, silhouetted in the windows, the figures of the first arrivals as they milled around an hors d'oeuvre table.

It was intimidating. Most of the guests, associate professors or higher, were going to outrank a mere instructor, and probably they'd make sure she felt the professional gulf between them.

She made her way up to the front porch and rang the doorbell. There was no response—probably the party noise was too loud—so Jill leaned on it again. Finally Maureen came to the door. She wore green and smelled of shampoo and too much perfume. Lines of anxiety had scored themselves across her face, giving her the look of the typical overstressed hostess.

"Jill," she said hurriedly, taking the bottle of Dry Sack sherry that Jill offered. "Glad you could come. This looks great. Is it all right if I tell people they can use your driveway to park in? If you don't mind, that is. I thought more of them would walk, but I guess people are lazy nowadays."

Jill was about to say yes when she spotted Bonner coming through the archway, a large grin plastered on his face. It was his superjovial mode, she saw. She thought he was about to greet her, but instead he kept walking on past her into the other room, the smile apparently meant for someone else.

She tightened her lips. "I'm sorry, but my aunt might be staying with me tonight and I have to save her a parking space."

Maureen nodded, too stressed to make an issue of it. With a bright, false smile, she pointed Jill in the direction of the hors d'oeuvre table. "We have loads of food," she said. "Tell me what you think of this caterer. Do you think he's too exotic?"

She was gone, vanished into the flurry of another arrival.

Jill wandered through the party, greeting the other members of the history department and several staffers, including the admissions secretary, who'd been friendly to her. Already the constant buzz of background noise was affecting her hearing.

"So the old buzzard finally made dean," said Cary Mead, a bearded associate professor who had once made a halfhearted pass at Jill after a faculty party. He was gripping a plastic glass filled with bourbon and soda. "I thought he was going to bust a gut playing politics, but I guess it all pays off, huh?"

"Plays off?" said Jill, leaning toward him.

"Pays off," Mead said loudly.

"Yes, well, what goes around comes around," Jill managed, looking longingly toward the bar. She decided she would only stay here for a short while, just long enough to give her official congratulations. Assuming anyone really wanted them.

The rest area was almost deserted when Vivian pulled in, parking as close as she could to the rest room building.

She got out of her car and walked into the building, passing a bank of telephones. Maybe she should call Dani from here, tell her she was on her way.

But then she thought better of it. The party by now would surely be in full swing. Besides, what if Bonner or Maureen intercepted the call and told her not to come? Then she'd have to stay away. This was hardly regular working hours and, Vivian belatedly remembered, she was no longer the official case-worker for Dani.

She walked into the women's rest room. Two stalls were occupied, one by a mother who had her little girl in the stall with her. The mother was impatiently telling the child to "hurry it up, Shelby; Daddy's waiting and we've got a long way to drive."

"No," came the toddler's piping refusal.

"Shelby, I said hurry up and pee-pee."

"No."

"Shelby. . . ." Then Vivian heard a loud, cracking sound as the mother's palm hit the child. Shelby began squalling, her yells turning to shrieks as the mother slapped her again. Vivian saw the small legs being jerked up as the mother yanked on the child.

Vivian felt a wave of nausea, followed by a fury so intense that she was dizzied. She stomped over to the stall and rapped on the door sharply. "Don't you know that's child abuse?" she shouted. "Don't you know you could be reported for hitting your child?"

"Buzz off, lady. Who do you think you are?" came the mother's voice from behind the stall, the snarl so full of virulent anger that Vivian took a shocked step backward.

My God, what was she doing, interfering like that? The mother would only take out her anger on the child, and unless Vivian wanted to call the police right now, there was little, if anything, that could be done. She was losing it, losing her cool.

Despising herself for her cowardice, Vivian used the toilet, then hurried out of the room.

She walked back to her car again and sat for a few seconds before starting her motor. A new conviction filled her. Dani was being abused, too. Suddenly she felt certain this was true. And it was all her own fault for being so idealistic. Why had she fallen in love with the Lockwoods, in love with their damned beautiful Victorian house? It was like thinking a Hallmark card was reality. She never should have approved them as parents.

Her fault.

She started the car and drove back onto the freeway. Merging with the traffic, she pressed down hard on her accelerator.

Fay McVie drove past the Lockwoods' again, noting the caterers' van parked in the driveway. She had just snorted two lines of coke—nearly her last—and her pulse was still racing as her body assimilated the drug.

A party! That was good. It meant there'd be lots of excitement, lots of people going in and out.

Plenty of opportunity to snatch little bitch Dani.

Although they had the air-conditioning running full blast, the kitchen temperature was well over eighty-five degrees. The caterers had to keep both ovens and the microwave running steadily in order to maintain a constant supply of cheese and shrimp puffs, mini-quiches, stuffed mushrooms, and lobster *de jonghe.*

The two bartenders that Maureen had gotten from the college employment agency kept returning for more olives, more onions, more mix. To add to the confusion, crowds of guests kept wandering in, wanting to chat. People loved kitchens; they felt an overpowering need to be underfoot.

"Hurry it up with that ice," Maureen said anx-

iously to Brent, one of the bartenders. She wasn't
enjoying the party at all. She'd never entertained on
this large a scale before, and she felt she was being
judged. "There's more ice in the utility room in
freezer chests, and in the basement freezer there are
six more bags of it. That had better be enough."

Dani sidled into the kitchen carrying an empty
snack tray. Dressed in the blue dress with its lace
collar, wearing matching blue flats, her nimbus of
hair pulled back from her face with tortoiseshell
clips, she looked ravishingly pretty.

"Dani . . . you do look pretty. Fill that tray right
away," Maureen ordered. "And don't let Rydell
Gramme monopolize all of those cheese puffs—the
man is a regular glutton, and we don't have enough
food to indulge him. I don't understand where he
puts it all."

But instead of refilling the tray, Dani set it on the
counter. "Maureen. Please. You *gotta* listen."

Maureen felt a flood of impatience mingled with
fear. "Dani . . ."

The door swung open and the second bartender
came brushing in, heading toward the utility room.
"Sorry," he mumbled.

Maureen felt a wave of intense relief at the interruption. "And I'm sorry, too," she said, stepping
back. "Dani, you can see what a zoo it is around
here. I have two hundred people out there, and I've
got Bonner wandering around like he's been sent
down from Mount Olympus. Can I please talk to you
later? After things settle down?"

"It's Bonner," Dani kept persisting.

"Just go out and pass your cheese puffs, *please.*"

* * *

People were packed into the room, body to body, everyone clutching a drink glass, napkin, fork, and a small plate of hors d'oeuvres. Balancing her tray, Dani could barely squeeze her way through the press. The noise was deafening. The notorious Rydell Gramme, a professor of computer science, tall and very thin, took eight more cheese puffs from her tray, carefully wrapping them in a napkin. Dani gave him one more. He was probably going to eat them at home, she thought.

She spotted Jill standing in a row against the wall with three men.

"Jill, I gotta talk to you; I've just *gotta,*" Dani said urgently, tugging at Jill's arm.

"What is it, Dani?" Jill, who was wearing a too-long gray dress and low heels, looked uncomfortable and bored.

"I can't talk here," Dani said, continuing to pull on Jill's arm.

"The little lady seems anxious," remarked one of the men. "Where'd you get that pretty red hair, honey? You're a knockout redhead."

"Please," begged Dani, dragging Jill away.

"Dani . . . this is a party. What's wrong?"

Bonner was standing only a few feet away, guffawing jovially, the center of a large group. Obviously he was basking in his new status. Panicking, Dani dragged Jill around behind them, out of Bonner's line of sight.

"We have to talk privately. Alone. Please."

"What?" asked Jill.

Dani leaned closer, practically shouting. "Alone! Please. Let's go outside."

"Oh, all right." Jill looked relieved. "Why don't we just go across the lawn to my house then? I have to take an aspirin anyway. I can't stand big parties; they give me a headache. The background noise level is so high I can't hear anything."

They left by a side door, stepping out onto the lawn. Jill led the way across the wet grass, a tall, awkward young woman in a silvery dress, the moonlight catching the dangling earrings she wore.

"What is it, Dani?" Jill asked.

Dani hesitated. She had to say this exactly right— or Jill would not believe her.

"I'm *not* lying this time," she blurted. "I know I made up lots of stories, 'cause I wanted things to be true, but *this* isn't a lie!"

They had reached Jill's side porch. Jill pulled open the door with a clutchy, nervous yank. It still seemed strange to Dani that in Madisonia people sometimes did not lock their doors. In the part of Detroit where she'd lived, even if you did lock your doors you were likely to be robbed.

Jill asked suspiciously, "What isn't a lie?"

"You know. What I told you before, about Bonner. He did things to Whitney. Awful things. He put his dick in her mouth."

Jill recoiled, backing against the side of an old dresser piled with untidy stacks of books. Her face was twisted with genuine shock and horror.

Dani cried, "He did! He did! I saw him! And he put his white stuff all over her stomach. I saw it! We have to stop him. We have to, because he's fucking on her—"

"Dani . . . Jesus. . . ."

"It's true!" cried Dani. "It is! It is!"

Jill's arms went around herself, hugging her torso. She kept backing up, into the kitchen, as if by distancing herself from Dani she could get rid of this unwelcome news.

"I don't know," she muttered. "I mean I just don't know, Dani. I . . . how can I believe you? You have no proof."

"But you have to believe me, because it happened. And he did more. He put a TV camera in my bathroom and he took pictures of me while I was on the toilet. He watched me on his TV set; I saw him. And he . . . I think he touched Tessa and Tracey."

"Oh," breathed Jill, shaking her head.

"And . . . and there are things in the attic," Dani plowed on, her voice thin. "I found some girls' clothes, underwear and things, and a whole bunch of Barbie dolls and pictures and stuff . . ."

"Barbie dolls? Dani, hear yourself. Please, don't do this to me. Dani, you're talking crazy. That man is a college dean! There are several hundred people over there in that house; everyone is there to honor him. Do you realize what you're accusing him of? *Do you realize?*"

Dani stared at Jill.

"Do you have any idea?"

"A *baby*," Dani said furiously. "He did it to a *baby*, Jill. I don't know how to talk good. I'm just a kid, and I'm a lying kid, aren't I? And I come from Detroit and my mom's a whore—oh, yeah, I heard Maureen talking about it; I heard what they think of me." Her voice broke into a sob. *"But I'm not lying about this. I'm not lying now."*

She ran out of the kitchen, pushing the door open and rushing down the side steps.

9

D*ANI RAN TO* the back of the Lockwoods' yard, plunging in among a tangle of forsythia and lilac bushes. Small branches whipped at her skin as she snapped them aside.

She reached the center of the bushes and sat down on the ground, wrapping her arms around herself. The earth was damp and smelled woody, and she could hear the party from here, ribbons of laughter drifting across the lawn. She stared through the branches at the lighted windows of the Lockwood house. People moved back and forth, carrying their drinks, laughing, talking, totally unaware of the baby sleeping upstairs or of Dani out here on the grass.

Nobody cared about her. Not really.

Bonner only wanted to do things to her, and to his own baby. Maureen hated her. And Jill Rudgate was a wimp, a poor, scared excuse for a woman who didn't dare listen to the truth for fear of what Bonner might do to *her*. Dani trembled with disgust. She really hated these people. . . . She wished she had never come here.

A breeze rippled the branches, tossing and sough-
ing in the trees.

*Barbie dolls? Dani, hear yourself. . . . How can I
believe you? . . . You have no proof.*

Angrily Dani looked to her left, where Jill's kitchen
light was still on. Dani could imagine Jill standing at
the counter, opening her refrigerator door. Taking
out a beer, as if nothing had happened. Jill drank too
much, Dani thought furiously.

She blinked away another flood of tears, and then
she froze, one of Jill's words reverberating in her
head. *Proof.*

But she did have proof. . . . She'd just told Jill she
did. *It was in the attic.*

Dani sneaked into the house through the back door.
In the kitchen hubbub, no one noticed as she darted
up the servants' stairs to the second floor. In her
room, hidden in a shoe, she located the keys she and
Ryan had copied from Bonner's key ring.

Jingling them in her hand, she remembered the
day she and Ryan had explored the attic. A wave of
sadness swept over her. Now Ry was so far away—in
the Smokies, at a place with the strange name of
Chilhowee Military Academy. But even though she'd
never called him there, she knew he still cared about
her.

She reentered the upstairs hall. A woman was
waiting to use the bathroom. Dani waited until she
went inside, then hurried toward Bonner's attic
staircase door. She used the key and in a minute was
inside the staircase enclosure. It was like diving into
black paint. She didn't dare switch on the light, for
fear it might be seen underneath the door. She

tripped, falling forward, catching herself with her hands on the rough-feeling carpet.

She reached the attic level and entered the foyer area. The rooms were hot, all the heat of the house having risen upward. But some light filtered through the shades from the streetlamp outside, making it possible to see dimly.

Dani hesitated, her heart pounding. She didn't have much time. What if Maureen started looking for her or, far worse, Bonner himself?

She moved into the TV room, where a couch and several easy chairs faced a TV set with two VCRs hooked up to it. A shelf held the collection of video movies. Dani browsed among them, puzzling out the titles. These were just regular dirty movies, she realized. Movies anyone could have in their house.

Where was the video she'd seen Bonner watching, the one that had herself in it?

Knowing where she had to go, Dani crossed the room, going toward the back, where the small, waist-high door gave access to the unfinished part of the attic.

The attic space was pitch-black, its darkness so profound that it seemed an actual, solid object. Heat jumped out at her, its breath redolent with the smells of spiderwebs, mildew, dust, old wood, and insulation. Dani could feel it catching in her lungs. Penetrating through the joists from two floors below were muffled bursts of party laughter.

Nervously she fumbled for the dangling light bulb string. She was going to have to risk it, and hope that no one downstairs would realize a light was on. Light sprang into being, casting a dim yellow that faded into uneasy shadows.

Dani started down the access plank, balancing gingerly, afraid she might stumble and make some noise that could be heard downstairs. But after she had gone a few feet she realized that this was unlikely. Down there, no one was thinking about her; she was safe, as long as no one came up here.

The storage boxes were exactly as they had been before. She edged farther along the plank to the point where the other board angled off to the right. Looking downward, she saw that the coat of dust on the boards wasn't evenly distributed but was marked with footprints. In fact, one of the boards seemed polished almost clean.

Bonner used these boards—a lot. But why? What did he do here?

Suddenly the light bulb flickered, as if about to burn out. For a half-second, the attic plunged into darkness. Dani let out a small, terrified cry. But then the light steadied, and she made her way along the second board, finally reaching the six-by-six, oddly makeshift platform made of three sheets of unevenly sized fiberboard laid across the floor joists.

Why, Dani wondered, would a grown-up man, a man like Bonner, a *dean,* keep coming out here in the attic to nothing but a place of laid-down boards? It looked like a construction made by a bum, or some kids in an abandoned house.

Moving to investigate a tuft of pink insulation that seemed to have come loose, she heard a section of the wood creak beneath her. As her weight shifted, one end lifted up slightly.

Dani caught her breath, realizing the boards had no nails.

Squatting down, she lifted up the end of the sheet next to the one she stood on. It came away with a skreek, disturbing a puff of mildew smell.

Dani stared downward. Stuffed into the spaces between the floor joists were stacks of photo albums. There were dozens, a treasure trove of them, some of the albums large, others small, each one apparently bulging with pictures.

Reluctantly Dani reached down and lifted up one of the albums, a thick one in dark maroon, with gold leaf letters that said: "Photo Memories." It was heavy and she had to hold it with two hands. She opened a page at random and saw that the pages were pasted with Polaroid photos, crammed so close together that their edges touched. More photos had been thrust loosely between the pages. All of them were of young girls, some posing in bikinis, shorts, or panties, others totally naked.

A photo fell out. It depicted a girl of about ten, standing naked in what looked like the back of a van. The girl's face was puckered with crying.

The evilness of the picture caught Dani like a blow in the stomach. She tasted sourness, her own acid.

"You little brat, I told you to sit on Mr. Wadermeil's lap. He likes you, Dani; he just wants to be friendly. Will you stop your crying and blubbering? Why do you have to be such a—"

Suddenly she couldn't hold back the nausea any longer. She lunged forward, bending over the edge of the board to vomit onto the pink insulation. Her retches were violent, ripping at her stomach. She sobbed, tears mixing with mucus and vomit, until all that was left were dry heaves that ripped the lining of her throat like sandpaper.

Finally she was finished. She felt drained, exhausted.

Crying, she reached down and grabbed thick, scratchy handfuls of insulation, using them to cover the pool of vomit. As she did so, she saw something dark glint underneath the insulation. She yanked out more pink stuff, and then felt it beneath her fingers—the slick, solid plastic.

It was a videotape.

Dani sneaked down the staircase, the videotape tucked into the waistband of her panties, underneath her dress, where no one would see it, the photo of the crying girl beside it. She thought what was on the tape *must* be bad . . . very bad. . . . Otherwise why would Bonner have hidden it?

She stood on the other side of the staircase door, listening until she felt sure the hallway was empty before slipping out. Carefully she relocked the door behind her.

Instinctively she turned toward the baby's room. She would check on Whitney again, she decided, before figuring out what to do next.

"Well, where did *you* disappear to, young lady? I wanted to introduce you to Dean Rabaul and I couldn't find you anywhere."

She looked up. Bonner was standing in front of her, blocking her way.

"Well?" Bonner demanded, glaring at Dani. He smelled of liquor and the heavy, meaty odor of food, mingled with a sharp body sweat. "Where have you been, Dani?" He took a menacing step toward her, his eyes traveling downward. "And what's all that dirt on your dress?"

Dani looked down, surprised. The blue dress was dotted with spots of vomit and smudged with attic dust and more dirt and bits of leaves from where she had sat in the garden.

"I . . . I got dirty when I took out the garbage," Dani improvised, backing away a step. The weight of the videotape stuffed inside her panties seemed enormous, and she felt sure that its outline was plainly visible through the fabric.

"Come, come," snapped Bonner. "You look like you dragged the garbage bag across yourself."

"It's nothing."

"Don't lie to me, Dani; you're as filthy as a little pig. And you smell, too."

Tears of fear sprang to Dani's eyes, and it didn't take much effort to blink, sending fat trickles rolling down her cheeks. "I felt so sick," she whispered desperately. "I got sick to my stomach and I . . . threw up in the bushes; that's why I . . ."

Bonner stared at her suspiciously. "Why would *you* be sick?"

"Because you hurt Whitney."

Immediately she knew she should not have said it.

"Oh? I hurt her, did I? *I* hurt a tiny baby? My own daughter? Who's going to believe that, Dani?" Bonner slid one arm familiarly around Dani's shoulders, pulling her close.

"And you touched Tessa . . . and you touched Tracey, I know you did, and you touched *me*, molested me, and you took videos of me—"

"Dani. Come here."

Dani shuddered, attempting to pull away, but Bonner dug his fingers into her flesh, forcing her down the hallway toward her room. He outweighed her by more than 120 pounds, and beneath his middle-aged flabbiness was iron strength.

"You and I, young lady, we have some talking to do. I'm very disappointed. You have an ugly little imagination, don't you? Why do you choose to malign me?"

Yanking open Dani's bedroom door, Bonner pushed her inside. Dani stumbled, then caught herself, hurrying ahead of him. Her right hand cupped her side, to prevent the videotape from falling out of her panties, onto the floor.

She raced to the bathroom and locked the door.

Bonner pounded on the door, rattling it. "Come out of there, you little bitch! I said right now! We're going to talk!"

Terror stole the breath from Dani's lungs. Once she'd seen Fay's pimp, Harley, kick down a door to get to her mother, and she knew the puny bathroom lock would not last long if Bonner really wanted to get in. He must not find the video. She reached underneath her dress for the cassette and quickly thrust it into the bathtub behind the shower curtain.

"Come out right now, Dani, or I'm going to take this door off by the pins; do you want that?"

"No."

Dani cowered on the other side of the door, her body shaking violently. She knew she could jump out of the bathroom window, but it was on the second floor.

His voice was crooning, vicious. "You're my little girl, Dani . . . and Whitney is my little girl, too. Do you understand?"

"Please," Dani whispered faintly.

"Both of you, you're mine. My wards. And you're not going to destroy that, Dani; you're not going to destroy me. I've worked too hard; my life is too valuable. That party going on down there is proof. I'm an important man."

Dani clenched her fists. "No," she snapped. "You're not important at all."

She heard a choked sound from the other side of the door.

And then . . . the wail of a baby.

In the middle of a conversation group, Maureen heard her daughter's cry.

"I think it's diaper time," she said, smiling brightly as she excused herself from the three history profs who were arguing about Michigan gubernatorial politics.

She made her way through her guests, whose ranks had begun to thin out. With any kind of luck at all, the bulk of the guests would be gone in an hour or so, and only a few diehards would remain past midnight. She'd be glad when they were all gone. She hadn't wanted to give the party anyway, and she didn't want to be here in Madisonia. She hated her life. When would she admit it?

She went upstairs to the baby's room and picked up her crying daughter out of her crib. Perspiration dampened the baby's hair, turning it into adorable whorls of silk. Maureen felt a burst of motherly feeling as she cradled the infant, lulling her sobs. Why couldn't women have babies without the interference of a man? It would be so much simpler, and more pleasant.

"My little girl," she murmured to the child, changing her into a fresh pair of white seersucker pajamas embroidered with small roses on the collar. "My little, feisty darling."

Already Whitney's eyes were drooping shut again. Putting her down, Maureen went out into the hall.

To her surprise, she saw Bonner emerging from Dani's room. His face was rigid with anger, his mouth tightly compressed. There were perspiration stains underneath the arms of the light summer suit he wore. And he reeked—with the sour musk of fear.

"Bonner?" she exclaimed, struck by his unusual appearance.

But he didn't seem to hear, or to see her standing there. He walked toward the main stairs and started downstairs, obviously intending to return to the party.

Had he and Dani argued? That had to be it. Maureen had sensed a growing tension between Bonner and his difficult foster daughter, and it didn't surprise her that there was conflict now. Still, her stomach had tightened, and she could not get rid of an uneasy feeling as she, too, returned to their party.

Dani waited for a long time, until she was sure that Bonner was really gone.

Out in front of the house, she heard the sound of a car motor starting up, then another one. A third car cruised slowly past the house. The party was beginning to break up, she realized; and when it did, Bonner would remember what she'd said to him, and he'd come back and try to shut her up. Dully she remembered those missing girls, especially the one who had gone to buy earrings and never returned.

And the girl in Nellis Lake, the one who'd been on the news. There was young girls' underwear in the attic, she knew; she and Ryan had seen it. Several pairs had been spotted with dark, rust-colored stains.

Blood. She hadn't wanted to believe it before, but she did now.

She had to leave here, or she would be next.

She would disappear forever just as those girls did.

But what about Whitney? How could she leave a baby to stay here, when she knew what Bonner would do to her? Bonner was crazy. He really thought he could do anything he wanted to a girl or baby who was in his house. *Bonner was evil.* Worse even than the men from her childhood, the ones who had fondled her and made her do things.

Dani began to move around the room. Hurriedly she changed into a pair of jeans and a tunic top with denim diamonds sewn on it, both gifts from Bonner. She grabbed her schoolbag and stuffed a jacket, a candy bar, and a package of Doublemint gum into it. Her little denim purse with gold studs on it contained over one hundred dollars she had managed to save from her allowance and gifts. She counted it carefully.

On her dresser was a letter she had written to Ryan on the computer, which she had not yet mailed. On the envelope was scribbled the address of the military school. She stuffed the envelope in her purse.

Regretfully, she said good-bye to the computer, remembering Mrs. Vivian. Vivian would have helped her. . . .

Dani's last act was to retrieve the stolen videotape from the shower curtain, along with the picture of the crying girl.

She knew exactly where she was going to put them.

The baby girl snuffled in her sleep, her eyelids fluttering, rosebud lips pouting briefly. Dani held her, feeling the tiny, fast heartbeat.

What she was going to do was wrong—very drastic and dangerous. But she *had* to do it. And she wasn't going to take the baby forever, only until she figured out how to tell people about Bonner and make them believe her. Dani's eyes filled. This was her own fault, because she'd told too many lies, but now everything was too important, and they *had* to believe her. She was the only one now who knew how awful Bonner really was.

The baby's car seat was sitting on a shelf, and Dani took it down, readying it for use. A box of Pampers sat beside the dresser, and she took out six or seven diapers, stuffing them in the elegant canvas diaper bag. She added a pair of Osh Kosh rompers, a tiny shirt, an empty baby bottle, and—impulsively—Whitney's favorite blue pacifier.

It was time to go.

"I'll take care of you," she whispered to Whitney, laying the baby gently in the car seat. "I will. I mean it."

The baby in the bulky seat made an armload, complicated by the other things Dani had to carry. Awkwardly Dani made her way toward the door that led to the servants' staircase. She descended the narrow stairs, worn from generations of use, and found herself in the utility room. In the adjoining kitchen, the caterers' helpers were calling to each other, playing a radio as they cleaned up.

Dani prayed they wouldn't see her, as she carried Whitney out through the back door.

The moon had slid behind a gauzy scrim of silver-frayed clouds. The air tasted of grass, leaves, and garden earth, along with the faint spice of lobster *de jonghe*. Dani heard car doors slamming in the street and realized she had to hurry. The party would be over soon.

Suddenly Whitney stiffened and began to wail.

"Please," begged Dani, putting her hand over the small, yowling mouth. Crossly the baby turned her head away, fighting Dani's touch. "Whitney, you can't cry now. You can't!"

Dani wanted to sob herself, from fright. Any minute someone would hear, and they'd come to investigate. She'd never be able to explain why she was taking the baby outdoors at nearly midnight.

Shushing the baby as best she could, Dani contemplated what to do next. It all depended on whether Jill had locked her side door yet. One of Jill's small habits was to leave her car keys on her dryer, and Dani prayed she had left them there tonight.

A door slammed, and there were more voices in front of the Lockwood house as another group of guests took their leave. She didn't have much time.

There was a clump of overgrown forsythia bushes near the back stoop of Jill's back porch. Reluctantly Dani knelt down, lowering the baby in her car seat to the ground. She fumbled in the bag for the pacifier and slid it into Whitney's mouth.

Instantly the wailing stopped. "Wait here for me,

and *don't* drop it," Dani begged, as the baby began vigorously to suck.

A minute later she was in Jill's laundry room, fumbling on the top of the dryer until she felt the telltale jingle of metal.

10

JILL'S GARAGE WAS a dilapidated one-car structure located behind her house, separated from the house by a gravel driveway. Its door rose only under creaking protest. Dani winced at the amount of noise it made. A pincer of fear clawed her stomach. What if Jill heard her and came outside to investigate?

The four-year-old Ford Tempo seemed nicely familiar, a faculty parking lot sticker affixed to the lower right corner of the front windshield. Dani had ridden in it with Jill several times when they had gone out for ice cream, and she thought she could remember just what Jill had done to drive it.

She placed Whitney in her car seat in the backseat, strapping her in as Maureen usually did. Mercifully, the baby was quiet.

Another car door slammed.

Remembering Ryan's instructions, Dani grabbed her jacket out of her book bag and folded it into a pillow, thrusting it underneath her small rump. She hoped she would look taller.

Anyway, she had to hurry. There wasn't time to worry about who saw her or what they saw—she just had to *do* it.

Dani inserted the key in the ignition, turning it. As the engine switched on, a blast of a cappella female voices exploded into the car. Dani jumped violently, but then she realized it was only the campus AM station to which Jill had tuned her radio. Her pulse hammering in her ears, she flicked off the radio.

"We're goin'," she muttered to the baby in the backseat. "But you can't cry, okay?"

In response, Whitney babbled something in baby talk.

Dani backed out of the garage, making erratic progress, and when she felt the left wheels suddenly bump and roll, she realized she'd driven two tires partly onto the grass. But at last she was in the street, and she was reaching for the gearshift lever to put the car in drive when the driver's door was suddenly jerked open.

"Where do you think *you're* goin'?" The voice was terrifyingly familiar, and so was the sickening gust of drugstore perfume and salty female odor.

Dani could only goggle at the sight of her mother.

"You're comin' with me," said Fay, bending over. With her massive blond wig, Fay looked like a thin and angry Barbie doll. She wore a yellow spandex minidress and long, glittering yellow earrings. "You're going back to Detroit with me, kid."

"No." Desperately Dani grabbed for the door handle and attempted to shut the door, but Fay blocked her, inserting her thin body inside the swing of the door. "Don't give me any trouble, you little bitch, because *I'm* your mother; *I'm* the one who has the legal rights to you."

As Fay reached down, attempting to drag Dani out

of the front seat, Dani stiffened her body, using the emergency brake as a grab bar.

"Come *on,*" Fay panted.

"No."

"You little *bitch!*" Fay slapped Dani, rocking her head forward.

"I'm *not* goin'!"

"You're coming with me, you little piece of dog shit." The long, thin, strong arms of Dani's mother reached into the car to pluck her out. Dani rolled and twisted, managing to land a good kick on her mother's bare right thigh.

"Bitch! Ugly little bitch!"

"*You're* the bitch!" cried Dani, her old, fiery language coming back to her with instantaneous recall. "You're nothing but a sleazy whore! A stupid coke-head! Shitface! Ugly! Ugly!"

Fay spat with fury and grabbed a handful of Dani's hair, pulling her sideways. Needles of pain shot through Dani's skull, and her eyes watered with the intense agony. But she gritted her teeth against the pain, kicking and clawing, sinking her teeth into the smooth flesh of Fay's wrist. Fay jerked her arm away, then backhanded Dani across the mouth.

Their struggles had caused the horn to beep.

Just as Dani was realizing, to her terror, that the horn would attract attention, they heard a new group of people leaving the Lockwood house, laughing as they spilled onto the side lawn. Any minute one of them would look up and see the two struggling in Jill's car.

"Oh, *shit,*" snapped Fay, realizing the same thing. She shoved Dani over to the passenger side and climbed into the driver's seat. She jerked the car into gear, and within seconds they were squealing down the street.

Jolted around in the backseat, Whitney began to scream in terror.

"What the *fuck*?" Fay yelled as they slammed down to the corner and turned a sharp left. "We've got a *baby* in here? Jesus fucking Christ!"

Dani saw that blood was running down her mother's neck in red lines; Dani must have scratched her when they were fighting. She should have fought harder, she told herself ferociously. Why hadn't she clawed Fay's eyes out?

Despair settled in her stomach like a load of coal. *Fay was going to take her back to Detroit and sell her as a prostitute. And now Whitney was in the car, too. What had she done?*

They sped down Observatory Street, then turned on Henry, past rambling rooming houses, several fraternity houses, one of the fudge factories, assorted college buildings, and old houses that had been made into counseling centers. The baby's hysterical protests filled the car.

"Please," begged Dani, near tears. "You gotta stop—right now. You have to let us out."

"The last thing I need's a fucking baby. But I do need *you*, Dani girl. Otherwise Harley is going to ream me out with a knife."

Horrified, Dani gazed at her mother's face, its dead paleness made even whiter by the flashes of streetlights as they drove through several intersections. There was a crazed twist to Fay's mouth—a look Dani knew well. Fay was getting strung out. She had been tooting, but now she needed something more.

"Take us back," Dani begged. *"Please.* Take us back home. I promise, I'll come with you, I'll go anywhere, if you'll just take Whitney back."

"Oh, *ho,"* cried Fay. "Now she promises. Well, girlie girl, I bet that's a lie. I just bet it is. I bet you don't mean a word of it, do you? And I ain't falling for your shit."

"She's crying," sobbed Dani. "She's scared. You hurt her."

"I didn't hurt her. I'm not *gonna* hurt her. I'm just looking for a place now, a place we can leave her. I don't want a damn kidnapping charge."

They turned onto a side street that backed up to the playfields of Madisonia High School. Between the houses could be seen the shapes of wooden bleachers and score signs where the Madisonia Eagles racked up points against visiting teams. A Cyclone fence separated the playing field from the houses that ringed it. One of the homes, a large corner bungalow, was dark and had a deserted, abandoned look. A Century 21 real estate sign decorated its overgrown lawn.

"Here," Fay decided, pulling the Tempo into the driveway. She stopped the car with a jerk.

"Here?" Dani cried, horrified.

"Gotta leave her somewhere, right? You think I got time to fuss with a baby? Besides, it's *illegal* to take someone else's baby," Fay smirked. "It's legal for me to take you, see, because you belong to me, but not her."

Suddenly all business, Fay leaned over the gap between the front bucket seats and plucked the infant girl out of her car seat, not bothering to support her head. The baby struggled, jerking her arms and legs.

"No!" screamed Dani. "No!"

"You sit here in the car, while I dump this baby. And if you dare to move, *even one inch*, you know what I'm going to do to this kid?"

"Please," sobbed Dani.

"I'm gonna lift her high up in the air—like this— and then I'm gonna drop her on her head and see if she breaks open," declared Fay, shaking the baby as if she were a sack.

As Dani watched in horror, Fay walked up to the front bushes that had been planted around the foundation of the old house and laid Whitney down at the base of a thick evergreen shrub. The child uttered a fresh wail of protest as she was laid down, the whiteness of her seersucker pajamas disappearing to become only a blur in the darkness.

"Okay," said Fay, wiping her hands off as she got back into the car again. "Now, unless the doggies get her, or some squirrel tries to screw her, ha ha, I think she's got it made. I mean the kid does have a good set of lungs, right? Someone'll hear her, and she'll be okay."

They pulled away and drove off down the street.

Frantic with fear, Dani turned to watch as the bungalow disappeared from their view. Desperately she tried to memorize its location. The neighborhood seemed quiet and deserted. What if no one found Whitney? What if she cried for hours and no one heard? Or, worse, what if a dog did find her? Dani had heard the kids at school talking about pit bulls. . . .

She began to weep.

"What are *you* blubbering about?" Fay demanded.

"You can't just leave her there!"

"Someone's going to find her. The way she's yelling and crying, it won't take long."

"But she's a *baby*."

"Shut up, will you?" snapped Fay.

Dani's skin hurt in a dozen places from where she had been slapped, hair-pulled, jerked, and mauled. But somehow the pain didn't seem real, as if it were happening to another part of her, a part of her that didn't care. Despair washed through her. Why had she done it . . . taken the baby? Now this had happened and it was all her fault.

She realized that Fay was talking again, mumbling to herself as she sometimes did. "Okay. Okay . . . first I gotta pull aside and do a little tootin', if you know what I mean. I'm gettin' needy. *You're* gonna be good news for me, Dani, know what I mean? See, a pretty girl like you . . . well, she never has to be lonely, get it?"

Fay's hollow laugh was the most terrifying thing that Dani had ever heard.

Vivian Clavell was exhausted by the time she pulled into Madisonia. The constant succession of oncoming headlights had given her a pounding headache. The thought of a bed, sleep, was almost irresistible. She was still recuperating from a major illness and she knew she'd been a fool to risk her still-precarious health in this manner.

She nearly decided to go directly to the College Inn and register, and visit the Lockwoods first thing in the morning. After all, it was after midnight and she certainly would not be welcomed there tonight. But then something, some probing, uncomfortable instinct, stopped her.

It wouldn't hurt just to drive by the house, she decided. It would only be five or ten minutes out of her way, not that much of an effort really. And it would help her to sleep better.

She drove down College Street.

Flashing blue and red lights in the distance strobed the night. Vivian's breath caught in her throat with an awful click. A horrible apprehension had begun to hum in her head.

As she drove closer she saw that two police cars were pulled up at odd angles onto the lawn in front of the Lockwood home, their dome lights still flashing. Crowds of people had gathered in front of the house, some in party dress, others wearing bathrobes or blue jeans.

Vivian managed to pull her car to the side of the street and park. Her mind was vibrating with terror.

Dani.

Somehow, even in Rochester she'd sensed this, she'd felt it. My God, something *had* happened. . . . She'd been right.

Jill Rudgate looked anxiously around the Lockwoods' family room, littered with party debris when the caterers had been sent home. The huge arrangement of flowers that the history department faculty had sent to Bonner had begun to emit a sweetish stench that mingled sickeningly with the leftover smells of cooked shrimp, cigarette smoke, and tomato sauce.

Jill smelled the staleness and tried not to retch.

Even from here, she could hear Maureen in the living room, still hysterically sobbing. *"Is my baby* dead? Did that girl kill her? Did that awful girl do something to my baby? Why can't you find her?"

Jill wanted to put her hands over her ears to blot it all out. That crying was so unnerving. It made her feel like cowering. And Bonner's yells were far worse. The man was furious with the police because they'd taken five minutes to respond to Maureen's 911 call. His anger lashed out at everyone, as if it were their fault that Dani had taken the baby girl. They knew she had done it because she had packed the baby's things and her own.

Jill had talked to Dani. She could have stopped all this.

"Ma'am, ma'am. Could you tell us again how you happened to notice that your car was missing?"

The police detective, his name tag reading BOB SEE-LEY, was about thirty-five, thin and wiry in build, with a black mustache and button-brown, searching eyes. He had already put out an APB on Jill's car, after some confusion when Jill could not recall her license number. The registration had also been in the glove compartment, complicating things still further.

"Ma'am?" he repeated politely.

"I don't know; I don't know!" Jill cried, bending over and putting her throbbing head in her hands. She was wearing jeans and an old T-shirt, the first things she'd found to throw on when she'd heard the police sirens.

"Now try to calm down. We'll be done here in a minute, ma'am. This is only routine, for my report."

"I . . . I went into the laundry room to get a clean shirt," Jill said after a moment.

"Did Dani seem upset about anything?"

Jill fought to think. Should she tell him? The

things Dani had said to her—the unmentionable things. But it could be dangerous to talk. She had no idea whether what Dani said was true or not. And here she was, sitting in Bonner's house—Bonner Lockwood, who had just been made dean of Madisonia College. Bonner, who authorized her paycheck, who could sue her for millions of dollars if she said one word to damage his reputation. Who could see to it that she was blackballed at every educational institution in the country.

"No," she said. "I don't think so."

"Ma'am?" said Bob Seeley, glancing down at his notebook. "Did the girl say anything about going back with her mother? Mr. Lockwood told us her mother came around here, threatening to take her back."

Jill stared at him dully. "How would I know?"

Maureen sat in a chair in the living room, alternately crying and shaking all over. The room seemed to expand and contract all around her in tiny dots of light. Five minutes ago, Vivian Clavell had arrived. Maureen didn't understand it. Why would Vivian have arrived tonight, of all nights, and after midnight?

Then her thoughts slid away from the puzzle, unable to hold onto anything for more than a few seconds. Did Fay McVie come and take Dani away, as she'd threatened? But why would she have wanted Whitney, too? But Dani had packed the baby's diaper bag, her car seat and bottle.

One minute she felt as if Whitney were already dead, and the next she knew she wasn't. How dare Dani do this? How dare she! Treating their kindness and love with such viciousness.

That police detective, that skinny one, who was treating both her and Bonner with ostentatious respect, believed Dani had taken the baby and was running back home to Detroit to find her mother.

"Foster home runaways do things like that, ma'am," he'd told Maureen. "We always look for them at home first, and usually we're right. No matter how much abuse some kids get, they still come back for the love."

"Love, bullshit!" Maureen had cried, out of control. *"Why did she take my baby?"*

"That's what we're trying to find out, ma'am."

"Then find out! Find her! Find my baby!"

Now Maureen sat shaking, her fingers plucking at the folds of the dress she'd worn tonight, the green silk that she was going to tear off her body and never wear again. Her baby. Her beautiful little girl.

Bonner stalked through the house, fear giving him strength to endure the people who politely questioned and probed and questioned again. They were giving him the red-carpet treatment, of course, deferring to him as the dean of the college, an important position in a college-centered town. That pleased him, but he'd decided it wouldn't hurt to bluster a little, accuse them of incompetence, keep them on the defensive.

Still, he was on the line. His whole damn life. And it had spun away from him . . . shit, shit, shit!

"Her case record was as fat as a telephone book," he told Seeley. "She was a disturbed girl—you can ask her caseworker about that—and we heard plenty of lies around here, too. I can give you lots of verification for that. In fact, her caseworker is here. God knows why she picked tonight. She was in the area, I guess."

It was to his advantage to have Vivian verify Dani's lies.

The collection, he thought with a fresh burst of terror. Jesus Christ, it was all upstairs in the attic, everything, his innermost fantasy life, and hadn't that been dust on Dani's dress? Attic dust.

Oh, Lord. Lord. *She'd been up there.* Bonner's scrotum had crawled up close to his body, bunching itself into a tight fist. The little bitch had poked and pried in his things. What had she seen?

This was awful. This was terrible. The stress was killing him. But he didn't dare have a heart attack, not now. He had to think of a way to get rid of the collection, hide it, just in case they decided to search the house. He tried to calm himself. They had to have a warrant to search, and how could they get a judge to sign one when they had no facts, no real allegations?

Carefully he told Seeley about Dani's prostitute mother, painting as bleak a picture as he could of the girl's history. If they did pick her up, he wanted her accusations to seem like vicious, spiteful lies.

"Also, she wasn't getting along with my wife," he said in his authoritative educator's voice that had intimidated a generation of students. "Maureen is— well, she can be picky sometimes. They would fight over the baby. Dani was fairly possessive. I think she really wanted a little baby doll of her own. And there was a lot of stress with planning this big party . . ." He let his voice trail off. He'd implied enough. And they could see for themselves Maureen's hysteria. Yes, it rang true.

God, he prayed, as he talked and talked. *I didn't*

mean it. I won't do it again. I'll throw all of the stuff out. I swear I will. I'll never look at it again, if you'll only help me this one, one time. It's all I ask. One time. I'm the dean now. I worked damn hard to get here. I can't be caught now.

The detective seemed surprised to see Vivian, who had introduced herself as Dani's caseworker.

"Ma'am, would you mind stepping into the kitchen? I want to ask you a few questions."

Vivian nodded and did as she was requested. She was still stunned by the events of tonight. God, what urgency had driven Dani to do a thing as reckless as take someone else's baby?

"Mrs. Clavell, I have to ask you," said Bob Seeley, fixing her with brown eyes that looked tired, as if they had seen everything ugly already. "Why did you show up here tonight, of all nights? Isn't it a little unusual for a social worker to pay midnight calls?"

Vivian hesitated. "I had reason to believe that Dani had been trying to call me all week, leaving hang-ups on my answering machine. Then there was a rather frantic message today. I became worried. I'm responsible for her placement, and I'd been ill, and I felt I'd neglected Dani, so I just impulsively drove over here."

"Tell me, Mrs. Clavell, what kind of girl is she? I gather you have a lengthy case record about Dani McVie."

Vivian began to fill Seeley in on Dani's background, while he took detailed notes. Much of it was a matter of court record, but she wanted him to see Dani as a person, not a statistic.

"Pretty hard-core, huh?" Seeley commented. "We don't get many cases like that here in Madisonia."

"Dani isn't a *case*," snapped Vivian. She went on, "Yes, the girl has had problems. But it isn't so simple. She has . . . a capacity for love. Pure, selfless love. And that's the one thing that isn't written in her case record. Frankly, I don't think she's going to hurt that baby at all. She loves Whitney. I think she'd do anything for her."

"Do you think her mother might have come over here to get her? Mr. Lockwood told me the woman came here, demanding her daughter."

"Fay McVie tried to sell Dani's body to an undercover cop. Dani never would have gone with her willingly."

Still, beginning to shake, Vivian wondered if Dani *had* been abducted by Fay McVie, kidnapped back to a life as a juvenile prostitute and possibly AIDS.

When Seeley indicated he was finished with her, she gathered up her purse, deciding to go back to the motel. Both the Lockwoods were exhausted, and there was nothing she herself could do here tonight.

She and Jill Rudgate left the house at the same time.

Vivian watched as Dani's tutor stumbled out of the front door, obviously extremely shaken. There was a panicky quality to her movements.

"Jill, this must have all been terribly difficult for you," something made Vivian say.

"Oh, yes."

"I imagine you were very fond of Dani," Vivian probed.

"I . . . yes. I was. Please. . . ." Jill hurried ahead, obviously not wanting to talk, her body language like that of a fleeing fugitive.

Vivian walked to her Camry and got in, turning to watch as Jill practically ran to her house and let herself in. A light switched on, revealing Jill's profile as she rushed into her kitchen. Stopping suddenly, Jill put her face in her hands.

Thoughtfully Vivian started her engine. Why should Jill Rudgate be so panicky? Admittedly, her car had been stolen, but it would probably turn up, or she could replace it with the insurance money. Did she feel guilty somehow about Dani's disappearance? Was there something she had not told the police?

11

IT WAS 3:30 A.M. At last the police went away, leaving Bonner and Maureen to their private demons.

Maureen had wept and raged, and now a dreadful chilliness had taken possession of her stomach. She paced the kitchen, erratically putting away cooking pans, barely realizing what she was doing. This couldn't be . . . *her* fault in any way? *No.* She might have flaws, but she had loved her baby.

"Will you stop your damn pacing? You're acting insane," snapped Bonner. The long evening had taken a toll on him. Somewhere he had shed his suit jacket and his tie. His shirt collar looked wrinkled and untidy, and huge blots of perspiration stained each underarm.

He went on, "She wanted a baby so she stole one. Then she went back to her whore mother; it's as simple as that. She's a liar and a juvenile delinquent and we got taken in."

"*You* got taken in, you mean!" Maureen cried. "Bonner, you know all this was your idea from the beginning. You begged me to take her in; you insisted we needed a full family; you insisted we could do so much for her. You were so persuasive you convinced me, too."

"And we could have," her husband snapped. "If you hadn't driven her away."

Maureen sagged against the kitchen counter, astonished and horrified. "Me? *I* drove her away?"

"You were a shrew and a nag, you hounded her, and you rejected her. Now we're paying the price," Bonner added viciously. "We've lost our little girl, our baby daughter, and I don't think the bitch is going to bring her back."

For a brief moment she wanted to rush forward and dig her hands into the saggy places on Bonner's neck, squeezing him until he choked for air.

"You were a rotten father," she snapped. "Bonner, you pampered her and you spoiled her. You spent hundreds of—"

"Shut up," her husband said in such a savage tone of voice that Maureen's words died in her throat. "I'm a prominent citizen in this town. In case you hadn't noticed, tonight's party was for me, and I am an educator and an exemplary father in every respect." He lowered his voice spitefully. "But her. She's a runaway . . . the lowest, most vicious and ungrateful kind. A teenage runaway. There are thousands of them in this country, Maureen. They're on every milk carton."

The picture that flashed into Maureen's head was not of Dani on the carton, but of her own three-and-a-half-month-old baby. She began to cry again.

"Yes, milk carton," snapped Bonner. "Anything could happen to her and the baby, Maureen. Anything."

* * *

Bonner left his wife weeping in the kitchen and walked upstairs to his attic haven. He needed a few minutes to himself desperately.

Maureen's crying and blubbering disgusted him. Why had he chosen her anyway, a woman like that? She had seemed pretty to him once, with her slim, childish body, but now her face had taken on accusatory wrinkles and her eyes looked past him and her tongue was far too sharp. She *was* a nag; she *had* driven Dani to do this.

He reached his study and flicked on the lights.

He slumped down in his swivel chair, staring at the blank screen on which he was writing his Korea book that everyone predicted was going to win national awards, if he could just finish it. The screen stared back at him, gray and faceless, accusing him.

Not my fault, he thought.

Why did they make young girls so beautiful, so soft and feminine, so seductive, and not expect a man to notice them, to try to touch them and love them? He had only loved them, and then they had cried and betrayed him and so he had done what anyone would do under the circumstances. . . .

He realized that he had begun to punch the screen lightly with his fist, bruising his knuckles against the opaque glass. If Dani was caught . . .

If the authorities believed her accusations . . .

He would be reviled.

And that wasn't all the authorities could find out. Bonner felt the sweat pour down his sides, soaking his shirt. If they ever found the deed to his three-acre piece of land near Hastings . . . if they were to *dig* there . . .

Bonner's shudder shook his entire body, becoming a fist-punch of dread. He had to stop Dani; he simply could not let her unravel his life like this; he could not let her destroy him.

"Please," said Dani, her body throbbing from the blows Fay had landed. "This is crazy."

The car sped down the side streets.

"I told you, sit there in that front seat and don't you move a fucking muscle," Fay ordered, making another erratic turn. "Because if you try any funny business, Dani, I'm going to turn this car around and drive back to that house. I'll put that cute little baby in the road and I'll run the car wheels over her."

"No," Dani choked, her blood turning to ice.

"Hey, I can be a mean mama."

Dani sank back in the passenger seat, her icy fingers clutching the door handle. It took all her strength to hold back her sobs. They'd been driving around for what seemed like hours. Fay wanted to wait until the police left so she could return to pick up her Toyota, still parked within a half-block of the Lockwoods'.

Dani fought to think clearly. Fay was strung out; there had to be a way to use that. Dani knew that if she was going to make any kind of move, it had to be now, while they were still in Madisonia. Once they were on the expressway, the car would be going too fast, and she would be trapped.

"Do you—I mean does Harley still keep you supplied?" she asked desperately.

"With what?"

"You know. . . ."

"Yeah, and I really do need something," Fay said twitchily. "I was trying to make it last, but what the hell. Harley keeps me so short, he never gives me enough. He's such an asshole. I hate assholes. I'm gonna get rid of all the assholes in my life someday, and he's gonna be the first one."

A red-and-blue neon sign materialized ahead of them, the sign advertising a party store called the Campus Quik-Party. Dani had been here before, with Bonner, to buy ice cream.

"I want a Pepsi," Dani suddenly said.

"Well, you aren't getting one."

"Look," Dani said, pointing to the party store. "Look, there's a good place where we can get some pop and you can, you know. There's plenty of place to park, and it's nice and dark behind the store, see? The police wouldn't see us there."

"Okay." Fay pulled the Tempo into the lot. "But only because I can't make no trip back to Detroit without it. And you ain't getting no Pepsi. Let me tell you, girl, one funny move out of you and I'll go back and I'll kill that little baby. I *will*. Do you believe me? I *will*. I'll drive this car right over her ugly little head; I'll smash it like a worm."

Fay drove around the side of the building, where a brick wall concealed an overflowing Dumpster. Sandwich wrappers and drink cups blew around the pavement.

"I'm so-o-o *thirsty*," Dani complained. "Please, just one Pepsi."

"Tough shit. Just shut up, will you?" Already Fay was fumbling in her purse for the mirror.

"I *need* a Pepsi. I'm thirsty. And I've got two dollars." Dani shoved open the passenger door and jumped out, starting toward the store entrance.

"You—come back here!" Fay screeched, getting out. Her legs flashed white, her impossibly high hem riding up to reveal a dark shadow at her crotch.

"And a candy bar!" Dani called over her shoulder.

"You mouthy little bitch!" Fay teetered after her, running awkwardly on her three-inch high heels. Her wig glowed orange in the garish light of the store floodlights.

Dani danced ahead of Fay, expertly judging the distance. Suddenly, like the ghetto rat she had once been, she darted around her mother, raced back to the Tempo, and jumped in, pushing down the electronic door lock as she had seen Jill do. She restarted the engine with a satisfying roar and drove out of the parking lot.

Fay shrieked something after her, but the words were blown away.

Dani drove back the way they had come, realizing when a car honked at her that she was driving nearly in the middle of the street. Hastily she veered right. *I have to drive like a grown-up,* she told herself nervously. The Tempo still reeked of Fay's cheap perfume.

Her driving skill increasing with each block, she finally found Observatory Street, which ran parallel to College. She didn't encounter any police cars or even much other traffic. It wasn't like Detroit, where the action never stopped. Madisonia didn't have a very big police department, and she figured they were probably looking for her by the expressway.

In minutes she was driving past the sprawling two-story brick building where she herself would have attended high school if she had stayed in Madisonia. Now, she didn't know where she would ever go to school again, and she didn't care. She had only two things on her mind: getting Whitney and driving down to Tennessee to see Ryan.

Ryan would help her. He had to! They'd find a good place to keep Whitney, maybe a tiny little motel, and when they had her safe, where no one could get her, then she'd call Michigan. She'd call Mrs. Vivian, she'd tell her everything, and Mrs. Vivian would help them.

If Mrs. Vivian still cared about her. Maybe she didn't. Maybe that's why she hadn't answered her phone . . . because she didn't want Dani's calls anymore.

Pushing back her doubts, Dani drove on past the circular school driveway where the buses pulled up, then the football field that stretched out behind the building, the backyards of houses visible beyond the Cyclone fencing. One of those houses was where Whitney was—but which one? Dismayed, Dani realized that the field was much bigger than she'd thought. There might be as many as a hundred houses, on several streets, that backed up to the field.

The moon was entirely obscured by clouds now, and the sky overhead, massed with pearl-colored clouds, seemed low and smothering. Dani could only see a few dots of stars, and even as she watched, a section of cloud drifted over and snuffed them out.

She turned on a side street and drove its entire length before she realized that none of the houses backed up to the school. Anxiously she turned onto another street and repeated the process. More than three-quarters of the homes were dark, giving the streets a deserted, abandoned, midnight look that chilled Dani.

For the first time it occurred to her that she might really have done something terrible.

If Whitney dies . . . I'll die, too, Dani thought, her throat closing as tears gushed out of her eyes, burning down her cheeks.

Then on her left she saw the FOR SALE sign. Beyond it was the empty bungalow, swathed in shadows. Dani slammed on her brakes. Squinting, she stared into the darkness. There was no spot of white seersucker baby pajamas visible in the shadows underneath the bushes. She couldn't hear any crying.

Where was Whitney?

Bonner knew he had to take emergency measures. He opened the crawl space door, pulling on the hanging light bulb string. Thin light reflected the familiar setting, the planks laid over the joists, his various storage boxes, the fiberboard covering for his collection.

He had worked years, literally twenty or more years, to build his collection; it was his pride, his joy, his solace, his curse. He couldn't destroy his collection; it would be like killing part of himself. He needed the collection.

But what was he going to do with it? Maybe, he thought feverishly, he could move it out tomorrow morning and take it to the ministorage place on Van Buren Avenue, north of town. He could rent the smallest-sized bay. There, at least, it would be safe, as long as he continued to pay the storage fees, and he could come and look at it occasionally, often enough to keep him sane.

He had to stay ahead of everything; that was it—he had to play this exactly right, and he would be okay.

He walked, crouching slightly to avoid hitting his head on the slanted ceiling, until he came to the fiberboards. Gazing down, he could see the disturbance in the nearby insulation, the coagulating pool of vomit.

Chill fingers of ice clutched at his stomach. Dani *had* been here—she'd seen this. He felt a sensation of violation. How dare she gaze at his private fantasy life? He wanted to kill her. He wanted to hold the barrel of his .38 Smith & Wesson up to her mouth and gaze into her fear-shiny eyes before pulling the trigger.

Tears filled his eyes as he began readjusting the insulation materials that covered his homemade videos. What could he do with them until morning? Then he remembered the hole under the eaves that he'd repaired when the squirrels got in.

He could easily break the hole open again, drop some of the most incriminating items down inside, then repair it. *Yes*, he thought feverishly. It wasn't perfect, but it would do for now, and when he had time he would move the videos out, along with the albums and other things.

Fifteen minutes later, his work was finished and he descended the stairs toward the bedroom level, carefully locking the stairwell door behind him.

Bonner walked down the hallway to Dani's room. It had already been searched by the police, but he felt sure he could find something they had overlooked. He knew in his gut she hadn't gone to see that mother of hers; she'd been terrified of Fay. The fear Dani had shown had been genuine. Nor did he think that cunt Fay had kidnapped Dani *and* his daughter.

Not when Dani had carefully packed both her things and the baby's.

He began going through the piles of her clothes, the glitzy T-shirts, hair ornaments, new lavender Reeboks, a locket that had appealed to him, all of it purchased for but one reason: to break down her defenses. What a fool he'd been. She'd broken *his* defenses.

Becoming anxious, he tossed papers aside, flipped open books. A crumpled note, in scrawly boy's handwriting, said: "Tonight O.K." There were tubes of lipstick, sample packs of eye shadow in pinks and greens, stacks of Sweet Valley High romances. But nothing that made any sense, nothing that told him where she had gone.

But the note intrigued him. He remembered the boy who had lived across the street, Bing Sokol's son. The little asshole had been shipped off somewhere by his parents to a military school, if Bonner's memory for college gossip proved him right.

The IBM-clone computer that Vivian had given Dani still sat on its table. On impulse, Bonner went over to it and flipped the ON button on the surge plate, quickly pulling up WordPerfect on the screen. Frowning, he fussed with the menus—his own computer was a Mac—but finally he was able to summon up a menu that contained a list of various documents.

Beginning to feel better now, he moved the cursor down the list until he came to the document that had been named "Ryan." A second later, he had pulled the letter to the screen.

Dear Ryan I wish you hadn't gone. I don't know if you got to the mountains yet are the Smokeys nice.

I always wanted to see Mountains but I never been outside Mich. I was going to put dickhead on your dads garage but

Bonner gazed at the screen, breathing rapidly. The Smokies . . . Ryan Sokol was in the Smokies. Yes, it was coming back to him; now he remembered that Bing Sokol had sent his son to Chilhowee Military Academy, a small school located just outside Knoxville near the Great Smoky Mountains National Park.

Would she really go that far to see the little asshole? A thirteen-year-old girl who could barely drive a car? Then Bonner wanted to laugh at himself for his naïveté, his stupidity. Dani might be thirteen in age, but she was thirty in behavior. She was a tough little ghetto kid. She'd been brought up by a whore, for God's sake; she was streetwise. She had stolen a car and kidnapped a baby. She was dangerous. . . . She'd stop at nothing.

He flipped off the computer and left Dani's room. Weariness overwhelmed him. He decided to try to grab a few hours of sleep.

He would sleep upstairs on the couch in his study, he decided. Walking down the hall, he didn't even bother to glance inside Whitney's room to see the empty crib, the soft night-light that Maureen had left burning there as a matter of habit. Whitney had become a blank in his head. It was Dani he was thinking about.

Dani was his enemy. Dani was dangerous.

The group of high school boys who had picked Fay up outside the party store were raucously drunk, the kind of sniggering yet naive kids that Fay occasionally serviced when business got slow. They argued loudly about which bar to go to next. They wanted Fay to come with them.

"Hey, come on—it's a cool place. They have dancing; we can really boogie," urged the driver, a weedy youth named Kyle.

"No, man," insisted Fay. Despite Dani's fleeing, Fay had managed to snort two lines of coke, and her pulse rate was over 150, hammering in her veins. "I just want to go to this house on College Street. I left my car there, you know? Me and my boyfriend, we had a fight. Now I got to go back and get to my car."

The boys suspected what Fay did for a living—her wig, the scratches on her neck, her minidress, and her three-inch heels were good clues. A hand fell on Fay's bare thigh. "Hey, do you have to pick it up right away? We could party. Come on, you wanna party, don't you?"

Fay knew she could turn tricks for them, but why should she? All she wanted was her car. As far as she knew, it was still parked on the street near the Lockwoods'. This was Podunkville. Maybe the police hadn't written down the plate number yet. Maybe no one would be there now and she could safely drive away in it.

When she got home, Harley was going to kill her, she realized with an icy, twisting sensation in the bottom of her stomach. *Jesus.* . . .

"Hey . . . hey-y-y-y-y-y," a boy was crooning as he snaked his hand across Fay's lap and into her crotch.

"Stop that, you little shit," she snapped, slapping his hand away.

The next street was College. Fay could tell by the sign that flashed green in the car headlights.

"Let me out here," she said.

"Aw. . . ."

Fay shoved open the car door before it had rolled to a complete stop and jumped out. She started off down the street, her gold-plastic high heels wobbling disastrously. The driver, Kyle, blasted his horn and made a U-turn, squealing his tires. Wolf calls hooted at her, trailing away as the car accelerated.

Viciously Fay bent over and snatched off the shoes, tossing them across someone's lawn. She had a pair of LA Gears in her trunk—if her car was still there. If some shitass cops weren't waiting for her.

She continued in her stockinged feet, her fury gradually pumping higher. *Dani.* That little bitch! Dani was the cause of all this, and Fay knew she could never go back to Detroit without her, not unless she wanted a knife blade up her nose.

She hoped Dani got picked up by the police for kidnapping. She hoped Dani got taken to jail and raped by the guards—she hoped Dani fucking got AIDS and died. Dully Fay realized that tears were running down her cheeks, but they were for herself, not Dani.

Dani ran up over the curb, her feet sinking into the grass as she raced toward the spot where Fay had left the baby. "Whitney . . . Whitney . . ." she sobbed.

The row of evergreen shrubs formed a long mound of blackness silhouetted against the slightly lighter siding of the house. Wind rustled their branches, releasing a crisp piney odor mixed with the scent of damp earth. Throwing herself to her knees, Dani bent and began feeling underneath the bush where she thought Fay had placed the baby.

There was nothing now but wet earth and handfuls of moist leaves. A few houses away a big dog began to bark, its voice deep, ferocious. A German shepherd? A Doberman? Dani's mind began conjuring up terrible pictures . . . torn-apart skin . . . a baby's tiny fingers bitten off and bloody . . .

"*Whitney!*" she screamed. She clawed deeper under the bush, frantic now, her hands digging up more dead leaves. Pine needles scratched her face. Was this the right bush? Maybe Fay had put the baby down a few feet away. Frantically Dani crawled over a few feet, repeating her search.

"*Whitney! Whitne-e-e-e-e!*" Her cries cut across the night, causing the dog to increase the rhythm of its barking, but Dani was too distraught to care.

Finally she sagged back on her heels, too numbed to cry. Her hands were filthy and sticky; blood was running out of her finger from where she had cut it on a piece of broken glass. Whitney was really gone. What should she do next? Now she *had* to call the police; she had no other choice.

Awkwardly Dani lunged to her feet, and that was when she heard the tiny mewing sound.

"Whitney?"

The mew became a baby's cranky grizzle.

"*Whitney!*"

Dani knelt down again, trying to follow the sound. The bushes fought her with their sharp, spiny branch ends. She could still hear the cries, but she couldn't see the baby.

Finally she lay down on her stomach, peering underneath the first bush, the one where she had originally started looking. The shadows were inky, the bush blending in with the dark foundation of the house. Yet . . . wasn't there a tiny *lightness* plugged into that shadow?

Something scrabbled; was it a small animal? Dani crawled forward, reaching out her hands ahead of her, feeling the mucky dankness of dirt and the wetness of more rotting leaf matter. Suddenly her hand touched something soft.

She wriggled forward, wedging herself between gnarly trunks, and carefully clasped both hands around the roly-poly infant stomach.

The baby had rolled. Dani wanted to laugh, then cry. Whitney had rolled over!

"Oh, baby," Dani wept.

She pulled Whitney out and looked down at the three-and-a-half-month-old. Whitney's hair was matted with leaf mold and dead pine needles, dirt encrusted on her rose-embroidered pajamas. But the baby uttered a coo, tiny beads of spittle glistening at the corners of her mouth. Her dark eyes seemed pools of intelligence.

"You're very, very, *very* brave," Dani crooned joyously, cradling Whitney to her. She started for the car again.

The all-night Sunoco station, lit by garish floodlights, was located near a ministorage place that contained row after row of garage doors, some big, some skinny. Dani slowed the Tempo, spotting an outdoor phone booth situated at the edge of the station lot. At nearly 3:30 A.M., the gas station was practically deserted, except for a man inside, reading a magazine as he stood at the counter.

Trying to make up her mind, Dani drove another block down the road, but her bladder was too full, her throat too dry. She awkwardly turned the car around, making a wide U-turn and heading back the way she had come.

She drove up beside the phone booth, managing to place the car so that it shielded her from the view of the man inside the station.

Fumbling in her purse, she located a quarter. As the phone began to ring, a huge truck roared past on the road, its tires rumbling.

Dani held onto the phone as Vivian's phone rang. *Mrs. Vivian,* she thought, sagging against the dirty metal of the open booth. *Where are you? I need you! Please . . . please be home. You have to be home this time.*

But again she got only the message. She slowly replaced the receiver, glancing back at the Tempo. Through the side window she could see Whitney in the backseat, her infant face peaceful in sleep, trusting Dani totally.

Dani broke. She leaned against the phone that was dirtied with years of greasy pencil, lipstick marks, and old, hardened wads of gum, and she began to sob. The cries racked her, shaking her shoulders violently.

The baby could have died if Dani hadn't come back to find her. She had rolled herself so far under the bushes that no one would have ever seen her. She should take Whitney back—now. But how could she, when she knew what awaited her? Bonner was evil and disgusting. Bonner didn't *care* about Whitney; he only wanted to use her tiny body . . . exactly as Dani herself had been used, and would be used again in the future if Fay ever got hold of her.

And if she did try to tell the truth, Bonner would tell everyone what a liar she was. And they would believe him, because she *had* told lies. Lots of them. Dani bit down on her lower lip, loathing every boast, every exaggeration, every inflated wish that had ever come out of her mouth.

Gradually a shivering calmness took possession of her. She stood there breathing deeply. *I'm okay*, she told herself. *I can do it. I can. I HAVE to.*

She left the car parked where it was and walked around to the back of the station where she saw two doors marked MEN and WOMEN. When she tried the handle of the women's room it was locked, so she walked a few feet farther, until she saw a water spigot sticking out from the wall.

Using her cupped hand, Dani drank thirstily from the faucet. When she had finished, she washed her hands and face and brushed the worst of the leaves and dirt out of her hair. She glanced longingly toward the station, where she'd seen a candy machine. But there was a candy bar in her bag, and it would have to do. Luckily, she had a bottle to use for Whitney, but she would have to stop along the way to buy milk to fill it. Farther away from Madisonia, she sensed, they wouldn't be looking for her, and it would be okay to go into a store.

Her bladder seemed painfully ready to burst. She walked toward the inky shadows that loomed at the back of the station. Two wreckers were parked here, along with a row of old clunkers that the auto mechanics were working on, one car up on blocks, another with a crushed fender.

Dani found a shadow, pulled down her jeans, and squatted. Her urine made a trickling noise as it hit the tarred pavement. As she urinated, she stared at the rear bumper of one of the cars, an old green Chevrolet with rusted-out fenders. Its license plate said DNI 862, almost her name. It seemed to call to her.

When she had finished, Dani reached in her purse for the Swiss army knife that Ryan had given her before he left. Quickly she figured out how to take off the license plate, struggling a little with the rusty screws. The plate would fit perfectly on Jill's Tempo.

A minute later she was back on Van Buren Avenue, driving slowly into the night.

12

A DOG WAS barking insistently, the sound drifting in through the opened bedroom window. Maureen awoke slowly. Her eyelids burned from crying, feeling scratchy as she forced them open. She glanced toward Bonner's twin bed, expecting to see her husband's sleeping body, but his bed had not been slept in.

She blinked her gummy eyes fully open. The night came flooding back to her, Whitney's disappearance, and she uttered a low moan.

She sat up, throwing away the tangle of sheets, and got out of bed. Her nightgown rustled as she walked in the darkness to the hallway.

She'd forgotten to turn on the hall night-light, but the small light in Whitney's room cast a dim glow, enough to see by.

"Bonner?" she called, her voice sounding hollow under the high Victorian ceiling. For the first time she realized that she and Bonner were the only people in the house now.

"Bonner?"

Her husband did not respond, and Maureen swiveled her head from side to side, a hard anger pushing up inside her. Her daughter was missing, and he was holed up in the attic as usual, wanting to get away from her, unwilling to face her or support her when this tragedy was driving her insane.

She walked to the door that led to the attic stairs. There was a thin crack of light beneath it. "Bonner, damn you! Damn you!" She tried the lock, then began beating on the door with her fist. "You asshole, how dare you treat me like this! Come down here. . . . Come down!"

There was no sound, not even the creak of a floorboard overhead to indicate any movement.

"I need you!" Maureen cried, banging on the wood.

The silence of the house was totally hollow. He'd fallen asleep with the light on, she thought. He was sleeping while his baby girl could be anywhere, could be in any kind of trouble, or even dead.

"You shit!" screamed Maureen, hammering now with the side of her fist. But the door, built of solid oak, withstood her punishment, and after a moment Maureen slumped against it, burying her face in her aching hands. Bonner wasn't acting right, the thought came to her. He was too angry, too defensive, and he'd projected the blame for this onto her. *There was something wrong with him.*

She made it back to the bedroom and collapsed on the bed, sleep overtaking her like a freight train, sweeping her up helplessly.

After checking into her room at the Campus Inn, Vivian was so exhausted she thought she would drop right off to sleep. But when she closed her eyes, her thoughts kept jumping around. Dani . . . her eagerness, her exaggerations. That boy she liked so much. What was his name? Ryan? Yes, Ryan Sokol.

Finally she sat up, switched on the bedside lamp, and began trying to find a channel on the TV set that wasn't showing a Western or a slasher movie.

Why? Why had Dani done this? What motives would drive a thirteen-year-old to take away someone else's infant? Did Dani actually want the baby for herself as some sort of live doll? But try as Vivian might, she could not understand just what Dani thought she was going to do, on a permanent basis, with an infant. How did she think she was going to rear it? Dani had seemed much more grounded in reality than that. Didn't she realize that police in four states would be searching for her?

A grimmer thought occurred to her. Dani might have done this as a means of punishing the Lockwoods, taking away their baby because they hadn't loved her enough or had paid, in her mind, too much attention to the baby girl. But this sort of jealousy didn't seem like Dani. If anything, Vivian thought, Dani was too warmly generous.

There was another possibility, much more sinister. Was Dani somehow trying to *protect* Whitney?

Vivian stiffened, as the idea sank in. More than ever, she regretted not having talked more thoroughly to Jill Rudgate. Jill was hiding something. Vivian had sensed this earlier tonight, and now the conviction was growing stronger. The woman had seemed shaken, panicky, and her body language in the kitchen, the way she'd put her face in her hands, had seemed to confirm this.

Vivian slid out of bed, reaching for the twill pants and cotton sweater she'd worn for the trip. It was about a ten-minute drive to Jill's house.

If *she* couldn't sleep, perhaps Jill Rudgate couldn't either, and Vivian was determined to have some answers.

Grayness tinged the sky to the east, but the moon had not yet set. College Street seemed deserted, a street of darkened houses with their porch lights turned on, a street where all the residents slept, unaware of any nighttime dramas.

Jill Rudgate's front porch was slightly damp from dew, the boards creaking under Vivian's feet. Standing there, she gazed across at the Lockwoods' house. It, too, was dark, its windows black, somehow forbidding. She wondered if Bonner and Maureen had been able to sleep. Apparently so.

She pressed on the doorbell again. At last she heard sounds within the house, and then Jill herself appeared at the door. She stared at Vivian with wide, startled eyes.

"It's Vivian Clavell—remember, the social worker on Dani's case. Please, I know it's late, or rather, it's awfully early, but I had a feeling you would still be up, and I really need to talk to you."

"Now?" Jill was now dressed like a college student crash-studying for exams, in jeans and a tattered T-shirt that said: "Joni Mitchell, Chalk Mark in a Rain Storm." Her lank brown hair was tangled, and Vivian could smell the strong odor of beer and corn chips.

Vivian stepped forward and took the door in her hand so Jill couldn't close it. "Please, Miss Rudgate. I wouldn't ask you if I didn't think it was terribly important."

Jill hesitated, then sighed. "Oh, all right."

Jill's house was as shabby as the Lockwoods' was beautifully restored. The flooring in the foyer was old black-and-white tile yellowed with a decade's worth of wax buildup. The wallpaper, a blue and white flock, was peeling apart at the seams. There were books everywhere, in cartons, stacked on wooden shelves, piled beside chairs, and tumbled on the floor.

"I'm still doing my shelves," Jill muttered.

They went into the living room. Here a TV set was playing *Lord Jim.* A coffee table held a row of four or five beer cans, along with a nearly empty bag of Fritos corn chips and an empty Häagen-Dazs container.

"I don't know what you're here for," Jill said, throwing herself on the couch. She was still sober enough to speak clearly. "I mean it *is* practically morning."

Without being invited, Vivian lowered herself into a nearby overstuffed chair.

For a while she attempted to draw Jill into small talk as she asked questions about some of the books she'd seen stacked around. There were thick history tomes mixed with an eclectic collection of novels, everything from Stephen King and Clive Barker to Proust, as well as a number of books on Hollywood, apparently an obsession with Jill.

"I speed-read," Jill told her. One hand unconsciously went to the ear that held the hearing aid. "I don't really read a book, I 'consume' it, as I think of it."

Vivian was patient, asking Jill how she had found a class to teach herself this skill and whether she had taught any of this to Dani. The woman was shy, skittish, she realized, a very vulnerable person. Even her voice was pitched too low, and seemed hesitant.

"How did you come to be Dani's tutor?" Vivian finally asked.

Jill shrugged, her mouth tightening. "Bonner knew I'd worked for a few years as a reading disabilities teacher before I got my master's, and basically I was his employee. When Bonner Lockwood wants you to do something for him and he happens to be your employer—well, you do it. He paid me $6.00 an hour. It should have been double that."

Vivian nodded, sensing the hidden anger of one who had been bullied into saying yes.

"Were you able to spend some time with Dani—besides tutoring, I mean?"

Jill studied a beer can, picking it up and rolling it between her palms. "Well, yes, I took her out for ice cream a couple of times, and we baked cookies together once or twice. She kind of got excited about the books sometimes; I liked that. It wasn't her fault that Bonner was trying to push her so hard."

"Jill . . . I understand she's confided some things in you."

Jill looked away. "Yes, well, she's a kid. You know kids."

"I can understand how you might be reluctant to betray her confidences," probed Vivian, studying Jill's face intently. "Perhaps she said things that were upsetting."

"I guess she did. I don't know." Jill began crumpling the Coors can.

"It must be difficult, hearing confidences from Dani when her father is your employer," Vivian suggested.

"You can say that again."

"You might think, well, that anything you said

about her might possibly get back to him and cause repercussions."

Jill suddenly thrust the can back on the table with the others. "Mrs. Clavell, I really—"

"Jill, I realize this is difficult and upsetting, but there are two children at stake here, one of them an infant. Whatever Dani told you, no matter how serious, will just stay between you and me. I'll do my best to promise you that."

"Oh, sure," Jill said bitterly. Her eyes slid toward the window that overlooked the darkened Lockwood home. "Tell that to *him*. He's the one. . . . Do you realize how hard it was to get this job here at Madisonia? I used pull; my father is a professor emeritus here. But I can't even hope for tenure until I get my Ph.D." Red spots had appeared in the woman's cheeks. "Bonner Lockwood makes damn sure I know how ephemeral my job is, that I'm the lowest one on the totem pole."

Vivian heard the fear in Jill's voice. "You must be very afraid of him," she said quietly.

"Of course I am. I just told you. He controls my whole damn career. Have you ever heard of slander? Well, I can't slander him. I can't do that—I can't afford a big lawsuit. You see how I live. I can't even afford bookshelves, or decent wallpaper."

So there *was* something. Vivian's heart rate had begun to increase, and she could feel a fine patina of sweat beginning to pop out across her forehead and upper lip. "Anything you say will be kept in strictest confidence."

"Yes, well, I'm not saying anything."

"But you have to. Dani—"

"Dani is a little liar. Everyone knows that. Bonner himself told me that a thousand times. So how can I act as if something she told me is the truth when it might not be? I'd be hanging myself! I'm not a fool, Mrs. Clavell."

"I know how hard this is," Vivian said, taking the risk of reaching out and touching Jill's hand. At first the young woman seemed to resist her touch; then Jill shuddered, and her shoulders slumped.

"She said such terrible things," Jill muttered. "So ugly. I wish I hadn't heard them. I wish I hadn't drunk so much beer."

"You must tell me. Even if there is only a 20 percent chance that Dani was telling the truth, we still need the information in order to investigate the truth of it. A thirteen-year-old girl and a baby, Jill. They're out there somewhere, and you know how rough it could be for them." Vivian didn't have to fake the anxious tone of her voice.

"But if it turns out to be a lie . . ."

"Just tell me what *lies* Dani told. Bonner won't be damaged if you preface your explanation with the fact that you believe Dani's statements may be untruths." As Jill hesitated, Vivian urged, "Please. Please do this for the girl's sake."

There was a long frightened silence. Finally Jill raised her eyes and looked at Vivian. "She said that Bonner was . . . that he was . . ."

Another long, vibrating silence.

"Yes?" questioned Vivian, hardly daring to breathe.

"She said . . . that Bonner . . ." Jill rubbed her hands across her mouth.

"Yes?"

"That he . . . abused the baby. Sexually. She was very graphic. I can't give you the details. It's too . . . horrible."

As Vivian recoiled, Jill went on dully. "And she said lots more, too. She said that Bonner put a TV camera in her bathroom and watched her. That he touched her. I don't know; it had to be a lie, didn't it? He's a college dean, and the girl came from Detroit; she came from such . . . such . . ."

Jill had begun to cry.

Awash in her own feelings of shock and horror, Vivian shook her head. She stared at this young woman who had held back such important information from the police.

Jill muttered, "She came from a terrible life. I mean prostitution and worse. And she'd told stories before. To me. I thought—I mean how could I trust her?"

Vivian nodded, feeling sick. Suppose everything Dani said about Bonner Lockwood was absolutely true. If it was true, then that meant that Bonner Lockwood was a reprehensible monster, a man who had sexually abused a three-and-a-half-month-old infant, his own child, and probably Dani, too. Maybe other girls as well. Child molesters often abused dozens, even hundreds in a lifetime. A sharp nausea pressed its way up from Vivian's stomach. *Dani,* she thought. *Oh, Dani.*

Vivian slowly rose to her feet, feeling as if she had aged twenty years in the space of a few minutes.

She fled outside, onto the porch, and stood looking around. Dawn was now in the first, tentative stages of bird twitter and pearlized light. A few cars had begun to move on the streets again.

Vivian descended the porch steps, her hand to her mouth.

She had done this.

This was her fault, her responsibility.

She had become enamored with the Lockwoods, removing Dani from the temporary foster home where she'd been happy, where she had been treated kindly, and placing the girl in the middle of a nightmare.

God, forgive me, Vivian whispered. She walked toward her car, realizing that she had already accepted what Dani said as truth. Poor brave, quixotic Dani, facing the world with only the limited resources of a girl who was thirteen, trying to save the baby she had grown to love.

Vivian opened the door of her Camry and slid inside, her exhaustion gone now, every muscle in her body tensed wire tight.

Where had Dani gone?

Then, gazing across the street at the Sokol house, Vivian had her answer.

"Please, I've been on hold for *ten* minutes. I need to talk to Detective Seeley . . . I think that's his name . . . the one who's handling the Lockwood case," said Vivian into the telephone. "This is very, very urgent."

She'd driven back to her motel room to collect her things and check out.

"Ma'am, Detective Seeley is . . . wait, he's coming in right now—yeah, here he is."

"Seeley." The detective's voice sounded tired, impatient. There were hurried institutional sounds in the background, voices and telephones ringing.

"Detective Seeley, this is Vivian Clavell again, Dani McVie's social worker. I really need to give you some information. I went back and talked again with Jill Rudgate, the woman who was tutoring Dani, and she told me something I think you should act on right away."

Jill's worries about slander were probably unfounded—after all, this was a police investigation. Lie or truth, what Dani *believed* to be true had caused her to act. If Bonner was innocent, let him prove it, she thought angrily.

"Yes, well, what did she say? Ma'am, this is a busy night."

"It's about Bonner Lockwood," Vivian said quickly. "Jill says that Dani told her he was sexually abusing the baby and probably Dani herself as well."

"What proof does she have?"

The impatient comeback startled Vivian. "Why—none except Dani's statement."

"Are there any witnesses? Any other victims? Anyone who has any information that can corroborate this? You yourself told me the girl comes from a troubled background and has a history of lying. Whereas Bonner Lockwood is a good citizen with a clean record and not even a misdemeanor."

"Bonner Lockwood may have molested a *little baby.*" She realized that she was shaking.

"Mrs. Clavell, I'll go over to talk to Jill Rudgate again," the detective said wearily. "But we've already questioned the Lockwoods thoroughly. Believe me, we consider angles like that, that's our job, but at this time, we have found nothing to—"

Vivian cried, "But aren't you going to *do* something? Put out a search warrant or something, search his house? There's got to be some evidence!"

"Mrs. Clavell, I wish people didn't watch so many cop shows on TV; it confuses everything for everybody. A search warrant isn't a casual thing that I just decide to serve on someone and then hope some-

thing turns up. I have to prepare a statement to take
to a judge, a statement that authorizes a police officer to go in and search for whatever is described in
the warrant and bring it to court. I have to list all the
pertinent details of my case, including a summary of
the testimony of the victim or victims. I have to list
the specific evidence we expect to find. No guesses. I
have to *know* what I'm looking for."

"But—" began Vivian.

"Mrs. Clavell, this case isn't at that stage yet. I
need corroborating names, dates, places, facts. *I
need at least one victim.* I have nothing like that right
now, except what you've just told me, and that's secondhand. It doesn't come from the girl herself, and
we can't find Dani. Until we do talk to her directly,
until we have more to go on, our hands are tied."

"You mean you can't *do* anything?" Vivian said,
her voice rising in disbelief.

"We are doing plenty. For starters, we picked up
Dani's mother here in Madisonia. Her car was
parked near the Lockwoods' house. She told us that
she did try to kidnap Dani, but the girl drove off in
Jill's car."

"Oh," said Vivian.

"The baby—well, she said they abandoned the
baby here in town. We're looking for it now. We've
put out an APB on Jill Rudgate's blue Ford Tempo."

"She may have driven down to Knoxville," said
Vivian. "She has a friend, Ryan Sokol, who goes to a
military school there."

"Okay. We'll alert the Knoxville police. But I don't
believe she'll get that far. How far can a thirteen-
year-old get driving a stolen car? Now, Mrs. Clavell,
you sound exhausted. Why don't you just relax, go

back to Detroit, but leave us your number in case we need to get in touch with you again."

"Fine," snapped Vivian, rattling off the numbers of her office and her home. As she slammed down the phone, tears sprang to her eyes.

She pictured Dani driving south on I-75, a fugitive. The state police would be on the lookout for her, but suppose she was wily enough to elude them somehow, or to take side roads?

Dani was a bright girl, and streetwise. Despite Seeley's opinion, there was a possibility she might actually reach Knoxville. What then? Would the police arrest her? Throw her in some juvenile hall, frightened and alone? Treat her as a criminal instead of the rescuer she really was?

Vivian realized that tears were rolling down her cheeks. The girl had to have someone there for her, someone who cared. Someone who would stand up for her and provide some sort of emotional support. Obviously neither of the Lockwoods was going to do that.

She stood up, closing her overnight bag. Quickly she dialed her sister's phone number.

"You're going *where*?" Judy mumbled sleepily.

Vivian explained what had happened. Then she hung up and carried her bag out to her car.

Dani, I love you, she thought, realizing she had just crossed some sort of line.

Dawn light penetrated through the attic shades, suffusing the attic with glowing pink. Bonner had just finished carrying his albums and videotapes out to his van, sealed in boxes. His precious things were now reposing in the van, with an old blanket thrown over them, waiting for their trip to the storage place.

It was going to hurt, not having the collection immediately accessible to his needs, but he'd had no choice. He would use his false driver's license to rent the space. Three years previously, while attending a meeting in Ann Arbor, he'd found a stolen wallet gutted of money, but with its license and ID intact. He'd used it on several occasions and had even ordered a Visa card in the man's name, giving the address of a postal drop.

Now he moved swiftly around the attic, collecting the other things he would need. The .38 Smith & Wesson Model 36 Chief's Special he'd found among the things in his father's estate, untraceable to him. A plastic bottle filled with gasoline. And, of course, the small bottle of chloroform he'd bought several years ago at a drug supply house in Mexico City. The heavy, colorless liquid, eight times as potent as ether, and able to be applied by medicine dropper to a handkerchief face mask, was still used in Third World countries as an anesthetic.

He lifted the bottle, gazing at its label crudely printed in Spanish. Memories swept over him.

Not just the girl in Nellis Lake, but a long line of them stretching back in time.

He shuddered. He didn't need those kinds of memories. . . . Why did his loves always end so sadly, so irrevocably? Why couldn't his pretty babies love him as he loved them? Why did they always betray him?

Somewhere beside the road, Dani pulled over and threw Jill's old license plate into a ditch filled with stagnant water. The splash it made sounded lonely in the silent vastness of dawn.

It was getting lighter out, the sky suffused with great swatches of pink. The air smelled grassy and fragrant. Dani saw a farmer walk out to his barn, sighing and yawning.

She'd been lost for several hours, driving farther and farther into flat, endless farm country. Farmhouses, isolated on huge plots of land, looked like wooden toys. The fields were covered with a low-lying wispy mist. There had been a village called Lyons, but all the houses were dark, even the gas station.

Dani was worried about Whitney. Her first bottle usually was at 7:00 A.M., but the night had been disruptive, and already the baby had begun to squirm and mutter. Why hadn't she brought some milk with her? Why had she been so dumb?

Tears threatened to fill her eyes, and angrily Dani blinked them back. Worse, the gas gauge on the car indicated less than a quarter of a tank. She would have to stop somewhere, soon, and spend some of her precious stash of money.

Whitney's cries had deepened. Dani turned and gazed into the backseat. Despite Dani's makeshift efforts to clean her, there was still dirt matted in Whitney's silky hair and sticking to the seersucker pajamas. The rich, ammoniac smell of baby urine permeated the entire car.

She pulled over to the side of the road near a tumbledown roadside stand. It was shuttered up, a sign advertising FRESH MICHIGAN STRAWBERRIES OR U PICK.

She located a clean Pampers and crawled into the backseat. Lifting the infant out of her car seat, Dani stripped off the soiled pajamas and saggy, wet diaper, managing to wipe the worst of the dirt away with one of the clean diapers. As she worked, Whitney stopped crying and gazed at her reproachfully.

"Whitney? I'm sorry. I'm gonna get you a bottle . . . in a little while." Dani hoped it wasn't a lie.

The baby puckered her lips, suddenly grinning as if she understood.

Dani pawed in the diaper bag, pulling out the trendy little pair of Osh Kosh jeans. The denim hung on the baby; Maureen must have been saving them for when she grew bigger. But they were Whitney's last article of clean clothing, so it would have to do.

"Now don't wet," she ordered the baby. She kissed and nuzzled her, making a game of it, for a second or two forgetting where they were, and where they were going. "Mmmm!" she cried, kissing the curled-up, miniature fingers. "I love you!"

But the body contact had activated the infant's hunger impulse, and she began to cry again, this time in earnest. Her legs kicked angrily, her arms pinwheeling.

On impulse Dani pulled the key out of the ignition and walked around to the rear of the car, opening the trunk. Jill's trunk was a jumble of old blankets, snow scrapers, and winter deicer, even a bag of secondhand books. To Dani's delight, there was a tattered *Rand McNally Road Atlas*. As she was getting ready to close the trunk, Dani spotted the red and blue of an unopened Pepsi can.

"Food," she said to Whitney, getting into the backseat. "Well, almost."

The baby made a horrid face as she first tasted the warm, carbonated fluid. She made a retching noise and pushed the bottle away.

Dani stared at her. "You don't like Pepsi?"

Whitney began to sob, her wide-open mouth revealing pink gums.

Dani sighed and returned to the front seat, where

she opened the road atlas and began leafing through it. Why hadn't she looked in the trunk earlier? She was dumb—so dumb! It was Whitney who was going to have to pay the price for her stupidity.

The maps were intimidating, with their confusing networks of lines and tiny print, but Bonner had shown her how to read a map once, while they were looking for a place to snowmobile. She bent over the atlas, scowling at the closely printed pages, until she figured out the route she would have to take.

Maureen walked into Whitney's bedroom and stood staring down at the empty crib. Although the police had forced Fay McVie to take them to the place where she had abandoned the baby, Whitney had not been found. Dani's tortoiseshell hair clip had been lying underneath a bush, however, and now the police speculated that Dani had returned and taken the baby away with her again.

Since 6:30 A.M., the phone had been ringing off the hook—friends, faculty, Dean Rabaul, someone from TV-2 in Detroit, a woman from the *Detroit Free Press*. Maureen had hung up on her, slamming the phone into the cradle. Everyone wanted to know why Dani had done it.

The lingering odor of talcum powder and Baby Wipes stabbed at her heart. Tiny crumples in the crib sheet marked where her daughter had lain. Maybe if she had been a better mother this wouldn't have happened. Now she was being punished.

Dully she went downstairs to the kitchen and made herself a cup of instant coffee. But the smell made her feel sick, and finally she just sat staring at the cup.

Bonner banged in from the garage, a smudge of dust across the front of his shirt. It was the same shirt he had worn the night before. His eyes slid past her guiltily.

"I couldn't sleep," he explained.

She looked at her husband, feeling an unexpected stab of pity. Bonner looked terrible. His appearance was haggard, his face crumpled into networks of sagging wrinkles. There were bluish-black circles under his eyes, which looked hollow and haunted.

"I wish you would spend some time with me," she said, less sharply than she'd intended. "I looked out the window and saw you carrying boxes. Are you moving things?"

"Just some of my old notes. I'm throwing them out. It's very frightening, Maureen. This. All this. I had to deal with the stress some way; it was just a little housecleaning to take my mind off things, that's all."

Bonner went to the pantry and found a package of strawberry Pop Tarts, favorites of Dani's. He unwrapped two and began stuffing them in his mouth, washing them down with a swallow of orange juice straight from the carton.

"Maureen," he said, his voice muffled as he chewed and swallowed. "I can't just stay around here today when our baby is missing. You know what the police are like in this town. They're going to be very, very ineffective in dealing with this." He went on, "I'm going to be gone for a day or so—I'm going to search for Dani myself."

She stared at him, roused out of her lethargy. "Detroit? But, Bonner, the police said she might—"

"The police are worth crap. I'm going to Detroit. I'm going to look around a little, ask questions, maybe stop at the school she used to attend; she told me about some of the kids there. I'll talk to people, see what I can find out."

"But what if the police come back and want to talk to you again? What if we have to . . . do anything?" She meant identify the corpse of their daughter.

"Tell them I went to Detroit to look for my child. That's hardly a crime, is it? I'm Whitney's father; I have a right. Tell them anything you want, Maureen. But I'd prefer you didn't mention it unless you have to."

"All right," she reluctantly agreed. What did she care? Maybe it would actually be easier if Bonner wasn't here.

The phone was ringing again.

Bonner drove away from the house, his heart lightening as he turned the Dodge van in the direction of the storage facility. The thick, clogged feeling in the center of his chest had begun to dissipate, now that he was about to do something instead of waiting around helplessly.

The girl *had* gone to Knoxville, he felt increasingly certain. Like any rebellious kid, she'd disobeyed him and continued to see Ryan Sokol, and the boy had been her only real friend here. She hadn't had any girlfriends. She couldn't go to her mother, so where else was left?

As soon as he had dropped off the boxes at the storage depot, he planned to drive out to a small private airport on the outskirts of East Lansing and charter a plane.

He would get there fast, do what he had to do, and return.

With any luck, no one would know where he had really gone.

13

IN HER CAR seat, Whitney slept, surfeited from the bottle of whole milk that Dani had purchased from a 7-Eleven in Ionia. Dani had splurged and bought a small Styrofoam cooler and some ice, putting a half-gallon of milk in the cooler and some jars of Gerber baby food, along with some Pepsi and a ham and cheese sandwich. She bought a package of Hostess chocolate cakes and ripped open the package, tearing hungrily at one.

There was a small display of baby things, so she bought some talcum powder, another box of Pampers, and an ugly rubber pacifier.

"This, too?" asked the middle-aged woman clerk, pointing to the green cotton sun hat with garish pink flowers on it.

"Yeah. . . ."

The clerk didn't seem the slightest bit interested in why Dani was buying these things, or who she was. Thoughtfully Dani purchased a big bag of M&M's, adding it to the pile.

In the car, she stuffed all of her red hair up underneath the hat. It made her look different, more grown-up, she thought. She decided to foster this image by smearing her lips with some dark red lipstick she found in her purse. She remembered to put her folded-up jacket under her rear, so she'd appear taller.

Before leaving, Dani tried again to reach Vivian, and this time a woman answered the phone.

"It's Dani McVie. . . . Could I speak to Mrs. Vivian?"

"My sister isn't here right now; she's gone to Madisonia on some wild-goose chase. I just came over to her condo to clean up a little for her."

Dani clung to the phone. "She's in *Madisonia?*"

"Yes, you'll just have to try to reach her when she gets back. May I have your name?"

"Dani. Tell her Dani called."

Dani hung up, fighting another rush of despair. Vivian really *did* care. But it was too late. She had already stolen Whitney and the car; she was on her way to Ryan; what could Vivian do now? She swallowed down a lump of the Hostess cake, which threatened to come up.

She fumbled in her purse for the letter she'd written to Ryan, staring again at the address. The Chilhowee Military Academy, Maryville, Tennessee. Ryan had said it was near Knoxville. Should she try to call Ryan, too?

But she was afraid to. What if someone at the school listened in on his conversation and then called the police? No, she decided reluctantly, she'd try to call Ryan later, after she arrived.

The expressway sign loomed ahead of her, beyond it a terrifying four-lane spectacle of zooming cars, huge trucks, and green signs. Dani instinctively touched her foot on the brake, unnerved by the sight. She and Ryan had never driven on an expressway.

But she *had* to drive on it.

Desperately, she followed a Mayflower moving truck onto the ramp, driving at the same speed it did. Like mother duck and baby, they curved down the long entrance ramp. A car honked at her, but Dani managed to insert the Tempo into heavy morning traffic without having an accident.

Her underarms and crotch were damp with perspiration. But she'd done it. An absurd rush of joy filled her. She had driven on the expressway! What would those other drivers say if they knew she was only thirteen and had no license, or even a learner's permit?

She drove twenty more miles, doing exactly what the Mayflower truck did. When he sped up, she sped up. When he slowed for construction, she did, too. A sign fastened to the back door of the semi said: CAUTION: TRUCK MAKES WIDE TURNS. Dani had no idea what that meant. But the semi was her only companion, her guide, her lifeline, and she hoped it would get her to Knoxville.

It turned into a hot day. Sun glared on the shimmering blacktop, bouncing off the cars and trucks. Once a police car passed her. The driver stared briefly at the blue Tempo, but Dani sat tall, and turned her head, so that mostly all he could see was her hat. Anyway, she had a different license plate now, and she'd begun to realize that Tempos, especially blue ones, were among the most common cars on the road.

The land was farming country, soft green vistas and pretty farmhouses. Charlotte, Brookfield, Olivet, Battle Creek, Marshall, Tekonsha. The towns didn't seem real to her. Just green signs, whizzing past.

She grew tired, first her hands, then her shoulders, aching from gripping the wheel so hard. She taught herself to hold the wheel with one hand, then the other, to rest herself. Periodically she took her right foot off the accelerator and flexed her toes.

Finally the truck pulled off at a rest area, so Dani did, too. Gazing at a big freestanding map, she realized she had crossed into Ohio. She grinned at the map, doing an awkward hopping, twirling dance. *She was doing it.* Maybe by tomorrow they'd be with Ryan.

A news program on Vivian's car radio briefly mentioned a missing thirteen-year-old Michigan girl and baby but said the police were searching for her in Detroit. The female broadcaster then went on to give a story about a naked, bound, and mutilated sixteen-year-old girl who had been found dead in a culvert near Creek Parkway in Indianapolis.

"Police are still searching for information that may lead to her identity," said the woman in an unemotional voice.

Vivian shuddered. But she knew it couldn't be Dani. Dani was only thirteen and looked younger. Vivian realized that she was going to have to get a grip on her fears, or she'd never make it to Knoxville.

She flicked to another station and settled back to a run of bland easy-listening music. But Melissa Manchester, Barry Manilow, and Nat "King" Cole seemed to grate on her, making her nerves edgy. The world *wasn't* lazy-hazy-crazy days and I-made-it-through-the-rain. Didn't her own twenty-two years

of social work teach her that? There were fathers
who hurt and raped, mothers who allowed it. Stepfa-
thers who got drunk and put out lighted cigarettes
on little girls.

What chance did Dani have, an unwanted baby
born to a woman who sold herself to get cocaine, who
had introduced her own child to sex at the innocent
age of six? It was a miracle that there was such love
in Dani, love that burst past all the ugliness like a
flower growing out of a crack in the pavement.

A sign for a rest area flashed past, but Vivian decided not to take it—she had an instinct that she
should hurry, that everything depended on her at
this point.

Indianapolis was clogged with traffic, and she took
I-465 around its perimeter, connecting with I-74.

What had Bonner done to Dani? Or to that baby?
Vivian shuddered violently, her head giving a re-
newed throb. It wasn't unusual for men like Bonner
to molest an appalling number of victims, some as
many as three or four hundred children in a lifetime.
These men were permitted to operate because people
didn't want to admit the unspeakable into their
minds. They rationalized; they persuaded themselves that someone *couldn't* have done it, because
he didn't look like a molester. He was a good citizen,
a pillar of the community. He was devoted to children; look at all he had done for them. Even in the
face of hard evidence, the testimony of dozens of victims, some still had excuses for the perpetrator.

Vivian realized that her anger was curdling, sharp
and hot, against the lining of her stomach. She made
a split-second decision. When she found Dani, when
she cleared up the mess, when the agency took over
Dani's case again and was charged with finding her

a new home, that new home was going to be her own.

I want her, she told herself, gripping the steering wheel as she passed a flatbed truck carrying electrical equipment. *Why didn't I decide that earlier? Dear God, please, don't let it be too late.*

The flight to Knoxville was heavy with turbulence. Bonner fastened his seat belt tightly and gripped his armrests with both hands as the small twin-engine plane bounced underneath him.

Maybe the plane would get caught in one of those downdrafts Bonner had read about and he would plunge to the ground, smashed to oblivion against some farmer's cow pasture, and all of his problems would be solved forever.

Arriving at McGhee Tyson Municipal Airport in Knoxville, he rented an Aerostar van and drove immediately to a Kmart where he purchased shaving gear and bought a clean shirt. In the men's room, to the nasal sound of the PA system advertising blue light specials, he shaved, staring anxiously at his face in the glass.

Shit, he looked bad. He looked like any little girl's idea of the boogeyman. When had the circles under his eyes become so baggy? He prodded the loose flesh with his forefinger, angry at this change in himself, furious at the aging process, at the way everything was turning out.

He could hardly wait to find Dani and kill her.

Of course, once he had her in his grip, safe, he might allow himself to relax a little, have a little pleasure with her before doing what had to be done. That was why he'd leased the van using his fake ID. Later he'd turn it back in to the rental agency and it could never be traced to him.

As he drove toward the sprawl of Knoxville, he saw the long blue-folded line of mountains. A map the rental company had given him included a guide to the national park. The Appalachian Mountains formed its jagged spine, its southern edge ringed with the fjords of Fontana Lake. There were landmarks called Look Rock, Grotto Falls, Rainbow Falls, and Clingmans Dome.

A gas station attendant told him that the Chilhowee Academy was located about thirteen miles outside Knoxville near a little town called Maryville. But Bonner decided to drive into Knoxville and find a motel, grab a few hours of sleep. He was already exhausted, and it would be hours before Dani arrived, if in fact she did at all. He was gambling that she would. He did know kids, he assured himself. A lifetime of being attuned to young girls was going to serve him now.

He drove fast along the hilly roads, his mind too revved up to be careful. All of his fantasies were bonging in his brain—images of immature girls, their soft, sweet thighs, their hairless, clefted labia. He remembered one of the girls out of his past, Ashley. She had wept and sobbed, huge tears running down her cheeks as she knelt before him. *Pretty*, he thought raggedly. *So pretty.*

He didn't think about Whitney. His mind had already blanked his baby daughter out, pushing her into grayness.

This wasn't about his daughter anymore. It was about his own survival. And he intended to survive.

* * *

The sun had set over the mountains in a splash of fuchsia and salmon, dropping behind the hills almost too quickly, so that the world seemed suddenly quenched. When Vivian drove into Knoxville it was nearly midnight.

Wearily she pulled into a Days Inn, dizzied when she finally stood up after being trapped in her car for so long. Had Dani reached Knoxville yet? Or had she already been picked up by the police? And if so, in what town along the way?

Not for the first time, it occurred to her that she might have driven these long miles for nothing. What was she doing? What middle-aged craziness had come over her, veering her out of her usual daily routine?

She walked to the motel office, the ground rising and falling under her feet as if she'd been riding on a ship, rather than in a car. But she forced herself to look at a local map that had been framed on the wall and ask directions to the Chilhowee Military Academy.

"An excellent school," said the desk clerk. "My sister's boy goes there."

The woman produced a glossy catalog, full of photographs of fresh-faced teenage boys wearing military uniforms, in a setting of green trees and rustic harmony. Vivian glanced through it. "Chilhowee has been designated an 'Honor Unit' by the Department of the Army since the inception of that rating in 1922."

Vivian put the catalog in her purse and went to her room. She dialed Detective Seeley in Madisonia, only to be told he was off duty until tomorrow morning.

After a hesitation, she dialed the Lockwoods' num-

ber. Maureen answered, her voice hoarse with tiredness. "Yes?"

"Mrs. Lockwood, this is Vivian Clavell. I'm calling
from—well, I just wanted to know what news there is
about Dani. Has she been picked up yet?"

"No."

"She's still on the loose, then?"

The woman's words came out in a long sigh. "I
can't believe she could make it for this long. She's
only thirteen. At thirteen I was still making dresses
for my sister's dolls. I can't believe she would just
take my daughter."

"Did you wonder *why* she took her?" Vivian said.

"I . . . of course I wondered why! It's without explanation." There was panic in Maureen's voice. "I just
can't . . ."

At the University of Michigan, Vivian had heard
one of her instructors say, "Incest always involves
three people." She asked, "Is there anything else
going on?"

A hesitation. "I don't know what you mean."

"All right, sorry," said Vivian, realizing that Bonner had not been charged yet, and perhaps would
not be. She hung up without asking to speak to him.
She was afraid that something in her voice would
betray the revulsion she felt.

The room she had been given had two queen-sized
beds and cable TV. Vivian threw herself on one of the
beds without bothering to turn down the covers, and
within a few seconds was asleep.

Driving mile upon mile, trapped alone in the car except for the baby, who wasn't much company, Dani
began to feel powerful waves of loneliness. Cars sped

past her, hundreds of them, and no one looked at her. She saw two or three police cars, but the policemen were busy giving tickets to other drivers. The blue Tempo might have been invisible.

Her body hurt from Fay's blows, and from being cramped behind the wheel for so long, and she began to feel as if she didn't quite exist, as if no one in the world cared about her.

At a rest area near La Follette, Tennessee, Dani left Whitney in the car for a minute or two and went inside to try to telephone Ryan. She needed to hear his voice, to connect herself to *someone,* to some real person who would care.

She dialed the operator, and a recording gave her the number of the school.

"Chilhowee Military Academy," came the bored, clipped voice of an operator.

Dani hunched over the phone, pushing her hair, which kept falling down, back up into her hat. Her lipstick had worn off, and she would have to replace it. She was so tired she thought she would be sick to her stomach, and her hands ached from clenching the steering wheel. "I . . . can I speak to Ryan Sokol?"

"This is an answering service; the academy's switchboard will be open tomorrow morning at 7:30 A.M."

"I *have* to talk to Ryan!"

"Is this an emergency, ma'am?"

"Yes, it's—" Then Dani cut off her words, panic filling her. What was she thinking about? She couldn't leave a message. What if the police intercepted it? She would have to wait until morning, when Ryan himself could come to the phone. They'd arrange to meet somewhere, and they would run away together. Ryan had probably already been to

the Smokies and knew where to go. Maybe there
would even be a cave. Dani felt sure that in the
mountains they'd be safe, until they could decide
what to do about Whitney.

"Ma'am?" said the operator.

Dani hung up.

A couple was walking beside her, back to the parking lot. The fat wife caught sight of Dani in her odd
hat and nudged her husband. Dani caught a few of
her words: ". . . all by herself at this hour."

Flushing, she hurried back to her car, unlocking it
and jumping inside before the woman could follow
and see the baby in the backseat.

She got lucky and found another truck, this one
carrying furniture, to follow onto the ramp. Carefully
she adjusted her speed. The moon now hung overhead, looking as if it had been pinned directly over
I-75, a gleaming silver plate marked with shadowy
mottles that could be a face. Her eyes watering with
tiredness, Dani wondered if the man in the moon
was watching her. Was he was trying to help her?
She doubted it.

Whitney began to cry again; she had been
strapped in the infant seat for twenty-four hours.

"Oh, all right," sighed Dani. "I'll sing for you
again." She began singing the lyrics from Madonna's
"Express Yourself," and then went into "Justify My
Love," reedily trying to imitate Madonna's funky
tones.

But the baby's protest rose, becoming even more
high-pitched. Another green exit sign was looming
up ahead. Dani swerved off the expressway, following the exit ramp around. There were two gas stations, one with a convenience store attached.

Beyond these structures, a two-lane blacktop road stretched into yawning darkness.

Dani drove for a mile, the only car on the road as she passed an auto junkyard, then a trailer park. The land was hilly, cut with rocky bluffs, thickly massed with trees. Near a hilly escarpment, dark and dense with pine trees, she found a small track that led off the road.

She pulled in, wearily switching off the car's motor. As the engine died, she could hear tiny pops and snaps under the hood. There were cricket sounds and bird noises, along with the rustling of branches and, coming from far away, the distant roar of trucks along I-75.

She crawled into the backseat and picked up the squalling infant. Whitney's Osh Kosh jeans were soaked with urine, and chilly. Dani took off the jeans and put another Pamper on Whitney, fastening its tabs around the baby's stomach. She hung the Osh Koshes to dry over the seat back, and left Whitney to wear only the Pampers, putting her own jacket over her.

"Bottle? You want a bottle?" She rummaged in the cooler for the remainder of the cold milk.

Whitney's cries ceased with almost comic rapidity when Dani put the nipple in her mouth. Despite her exhaustion, Dani couldn't help grinning. She cradled the suckling baby, a soft, sweet, warm ball that snuggled into her arms, trusting her.

Was this what it was like to be a mother? The sweet ache in your chest, the feeling that the baby was part of you? Her spirits lifted a little. Tomorrow she'd see Ryan. He'd help her, and they would both be safe.

* * *

Maureen's nightmare was of hands reaching for her. Gnarly, hard-bitten hands that were covered with calluses and dark whorls of hair, hands that reminded her of her grandfather. Hands that were trying to take *her* small hands and put them around something that she didn't want to touch.

She uttered a strangled cry and snapped awake. She struggled to sit up, realizing that it was the alarm clock that had awakened her, coming on at its usual time; she had forgotten to switch it to the off position.

What a strangely disturbing dream. And it wasn't the first time she'd had it. Actually, the dream had bothered her several times a year, from her teen years on. Had she been molested as a little girl? She had no conscious memory of it, though. She thought her childhood had been happier than most, even though she and her mother and sister had gone to live with her mother's parents.

God. she thought, feeling her heart pound. She lay still, listening to the silence of the house, without even a creak or a door slam or a baby whimper to echo among the high Victorian ceilings.

Where is my baby girl? I'm tired of waiting. I want her back now.

Bonner wasn't in the bed. He hadn't come home last night. Was he in Detroit someplace, driving aimlessly around, asking futile questions? Or she supposed he could be drunk somewhere, guzzling down whiskey to assuage his pain. He had a drinking problem, Maureen believed, that he tried to keep hidden. But she'd seen the occasional Jack Daniel's bottle in the backseat of the van.

Where in the hell was he? Why hadn't he called her?

The asshole, she thought. So selfish, never letting her know. And what was she supposed to say to that detective, Seeley or whatever his name was, when he called this morning? He'd already called once, and she'd made some thin excuse, saying that Bonner was attending a college deans' conference in East Lansing.

After Whitney was found, she was going to divorce Bonner, she decided, getting up. The marriage had been dead for years, if it had been alive at all. She could feel the hatred curdling in her. She never wanted him in her bed again. She never even wanted to look at him again. There'd be some financial settlement of course; she didn't care what. She didn't want anything from the man. *Just let me get away,* she thought.

Not bothering to put on a robe, she walked into the adjoining bathroom, rummaging through the vanity drawers in search of a bottle of Extra Strength Tylenol to assuage her pounding head. But the bottle was empty, so she walked out of the bedroom and down the hall to her writing room, where she always kept a second bottle of Tylenol in her desk.

She yanked open her right top desk drawer, but instead of her hand closing on the familiar rounded shape of the Tylenol bottle, it fastened around something rectangular and hard.

Maureen looked down. Someone had put a videotape in her desk drawer, a plain one, still in its original, packaged slipcase.

She picked up the video, not really curious as to what it contained, but not wanting it in her space. That was when she saw the Polaroid photograph underneath. Her eyes widened as she saw the weeping

young girl, her nakedness as sparse and pathetic as
that of a plucked chicken.

No, Maureen thought.

Jesus, no.

She grabbed up the videotape and walked downstairs to the family room. The house smelled empty,
stale from the party, and her antique furniture, so
carefully chosen, now looked unused, like the stage
set of some melodrama set in 1890. Her mouth
tasted sour and frowsty, and she could feel a sticky
coating on her teeth.

She picked up the remote and switched on the TV
and VCR.

First there was dancing white fuzz, electronic
static, and then a child's face filled the screen. She
was about eleven or twelve, with long, untidy blond
hair—just beginning to grow out of the awkward,
big-toothed stage into a tremulous prettiness. She
wore a ruffled blouse and a pair of navy blue shorts.
The backdrop of the video appeared to be the navy
blue interior of a van, the Ford van they'd had before
they got their current one. Maureen could even see
something that looked like an issue of *Atlantic*,
which she subscribed to, protruding from a seat
pocket.

"No," said the girl, putting both hands up to her
mouth and splaying her fingers. "No, I . . . I can't."

"All the other girls do," came a soft, half-whispered
voice that Maureen instantly recognized as belong-
ing to her husband. "All of them have posed for me,
and they were very happy with the pictures and with
the ten dollars I gave them. Each a nice, crisp, new
ten-dollar bill, *and* a signed picture of New Kids on
the Block, *and* a Funtime Barbie."

Maureen felt a thick chill that froze her throat to a

column of ice. She clenched the remote in her hands with such force that her fingers accidentally pressed fast-forward. She watched as the picture frogged ahead. The girl's figure became cartoonish as she began to strip off her T-shirt and shorts, for an instant jutting out her hips. It reminded Maureen of jerky Nazi movies she had seen of Holocaust victims.

She wanted to know what was on the tape but was afraid of seeing the details. Choking, she pushed fast-forward again. The girl jerkily pulled back. Hands reached for her, pushing something toward her—a square of white. As a hand pressed the square to her mouth, the child collapsed, her knees sagging. She looked puppetlike. The images jerked and jumped. Bonner lying on the girl. Forcing her arms back behind her head. Putting his . . . And then . . .

The remote fell from Maureen's hands, tumbling to the carpet. Dizziness attacked her. She collapsed forward, her head meeting her knees. She fought an ugly blackness that tried to suck her into its maw.

Everything that Dani had told her was true. It was all here on tape—the hideous proof. Bonner was a . . .

He had . . .

She couldn't say it, couldn't think it.

Oh, God! Oh, Jesus!

She quivered and shook, grabbing handfuls of her hair, gripping her own scalp, her fingernails pressing into her temples. Her grandfather's hands in the dream melded with Bonner's hands, the curly brown hair growing on Bonner's fingers. She had begun to sob, the sound low and tormented.

What had Bonner done? What had he destroyed? Their lives, their daughter . . . Dani, too. . . .

And she . . . she had not wanted to know.

She couldn't sit still any longer. She leaped to her feet and began wildly pacing the family room, her surroundings now seeming so evil, so hideous, that she wanted to throw up at the sight of the chair where Bonner sometimes sat to watch TV. What, exactly, had he done to Whitney? He couldn't have . . . could he? It was physically impossible.

For a quick second, she had a flash of herself as a young bride, slim and tiny in her long white dress, gazing toward the sanctuary where Bonner stood with a grim face, his eyes avoiding hers. She should have run away then. But she hadn't. She'd continued her walk down the aisle because everyone expected it.

She'd made a horrible mistake . . . horrible . . .

Maybe this was all just a nightmare. Maybe she would wake up in a couple of minutes and find it was all just another dream.

She found herself in front of the telephone.

She stared down at it. Then her hand reached out.

14

*T*HE CHILHOWEE MILITARY Academy campus looked like the campus of a small southern college. Tucked among the green folds of hills, with the bulky foothill of Chilhowee Mountain as its backdrop, the school's mellowed brick buildings were covered with ivy and tradition. Uniformed cadets marched in rigid formation on a quadrangle.

The sight appealed to Bonner. The beauty, the precision, everything proper and as it should be. Nothing out of place or left to chance. *Immutable.*

As he drove onto the grounds, Bonner kept away from the main buildings, two huge three-story structures that probably contained classrooms and barracks. To his left, boys were practicing football on a big playfield. They were supervised by a man wearing military fatigues.

Bonner narrowed his eyes, staring at the boys. He thought he recognized the tall, knobby stringiness of Ryan Sokol, but as the boys were wearing full equipment and shoulder pads, he could not be sure.

As he continued along the winding two-lane blacktop that had been surfaced recently, he heard shots coming from an outdoor rifle range. There were several clay tennis courts, two in use, and an outdoor basketball court, currently vacant. He saw a maintenance building, a surprisingly beautiful English-style garden, the Jacob Husom Memorial Library, and then the campus petered out to a series of fields that ran into a woods that butted up to a bluff.

A huge oak tree, probably at least two hundred years old, dominated the edge of the woods, its bark scarred with so many generations of cadets' initials that it looked cancerous. This had to be a school rendezvous, Bonner realized, remembering his own unhappy three years in a New York state prep school.

He nodded with satisfaction. It was as he had thought. The more oppressive the school, the more ingenious became the boys' escapes. He would bet that the woods were riddled with boys' paths, possibly homemade tents or shelters, their stashes of liquor or beer, perhaps even drugs.

He turned, driving back toward the playfield again, and this time saw that the game had broken up. Some of the cadets were in a huddle with the coach, and others were walking across the grass toward the barracks. Ryan Sokol was among these. The boy had slung his football pads over his shoulder and carried his helmet. Perspiration ran down his neck, soaking his Chilhowee Athletic Department gym shirt. He did not glance at Bonner in the van but kept on walking.

Bonner made sure he kept the van behind Ryan, out of his line of sight. He debated what to do now.

Obviously, Dani hadn't yet arrived, but he believed she would do so soon. In fact, if Bonner was any judge of teenagers, she and Ryan would probably slip away from school and go into the woods. Bonner figured that their meeting place would probably be that huge oak tree with the initials. Kids were all the same, he thought.

He turned back toward the wooded area. Near the tree was a four-wheel-drive track. The van rocked, its suspension bouncing, as he drove into the green-swarded beauty of the trees. The track was rutted but passable, scattered with garbage tossed by the cadets—a beer can, a soft-drink cup. He wondered where it went; was it a road built by rangers as a firebreak? Or did it have some destination, such as a small lake, campsite, or quarry?

The track leveled off. He spotted a grassy area clear of trees and pulled in, parking the van behind a stand of trees so that it would not be visible from the trail. As he came to a stop, tree branches batted against the windshield of the van, slapping the glass. A green bug fluttered toward the windshield and began to crawl across it.

Bonner switched off the motor. Silence rushed into the cab, along with a blast of sunshine. Then in the distance he began to hear the rifle shots from the firing range, staccato and irregular. He chuckled to himself. Any shots he fired would be masked. But he didn't think he would have to fire his .38. He had a much better plan, one that fit the circumstances. If they arrived, of course. That was the one weakness.

He forced back his doubt, convincing himself that he was right to be here. They *were* coming here. Every one of his instincts, honed over the years, told him this was the place and sooner or later Jill Rudgate's Ford Tempo was going to be driving down this track.

Thoughtfully he got out of the van and smeared dirt along its license plate, just in case any little asshole cadet, sneaking into the woods, was smart enough to look at it.

Footsteps and voices echoed and reechoed, combining with the thick, soupy blast of multiple TV sets and boys yelling. A door slammed, the sound reverberating against 120-year-old plaster.

Still wearing his soggy football clothes, Ryan Sokol bent over the hall telephone, hunching his body around the receiver so that no one passing up and down the loud, noisy hallway would be able to hear his words. He had been surprised to get a call, even more surprised when he realized the caller was not his parents.

One of the juniors was having visitors, a set of middle-aged parents. The mother looked nervous at being on an upper hall in a boys' barracks.

"Dani?" Ryan said into the phone. "Dani, is that you?"

"Yes, I . . . it's awful, Ry. I have to see you; I'm coming to see you."

"Speak louder. It's so noisy here, I can barely hear you."

"I said . . . Whitney . . . I took her. I've gotta . . . He did bad things. . . ." The words came out garbled.

He thought she was calling from Madisonia. "Dani, do they know you're calling? Can't you speak any louder?"

"I'm at a *phone booth.*" Suddenly the line cleared and her words came in clearer. "I'm, I don't know where I am, somewhere on the freeway, I think. I'm close to Knoxville; I think I'm right outside it. There's these gas stations and a trailer park; we slept all night here—"

"Knoxville?" Ryan nearly shouted it. *"You're outside Knoxville?"* He hung onto the phone, fighting a wild urge to toss the phone up in the air and hoot loudly.

"Yeah, I've got Whitney with me. Ryan, you've gotta help me. I ran away with her. I took her; they don't know where I am."

Amazed, he struggled to make sense of it. *"You took her?"*

"—and we've gotta run away or something before *he* does something really awful to her."

"He?"

"Bonner."

"Bonner Lockwood?"

"Yeah." Dani's voice was desperate. "Ry, I told you all this. I told you."

"Okay, okay," he said, as he tried to remember directions to the academy. His own car trip to the school had been spent in a sullen fog of silence. "Now just where are you? You've gotta drive here to the school."

Haltingly he gave her directions.

"And, Dani, when you come into the school, see, there's this winding road that goes around and around, past the barracks and the football field and stuff. Well, you've got to follow it all the way, right to the back. There's this cool rifle range, you'll hear the rifles going off, and then off to the side, yeah, to the right, there's this big old tree. I don't know what kind of a tree it is, but it's humongous, and you can drive your car right up this little track, see, up past the tree."

"A tree, okay," Dani said.

"It's got initials all over it. How long do you think it'll take you to get there?" Ryan glanced at the clock hanging on the corridor wall that had told fifty years' worth of cadets when to go to drill. It was nearly time for lunch formation.

"I don't know."

He said, "Hey, I'll meet you there, okay? Right by that big old tree."

Vivian parked in a visitors' area in front of a long ivy-covered structure with several wings, set on a curving driveway overhung with lush, flowering trees. In the square between the two main buildings, a squadron of cadets was quick-marching, their left arms swinging in unison as a boy shouted out army-type marching commands. All the youths were carrying rifles locked over their right shoulders at a precision angle.

Appalled, Vivian stared at this sight. The boys looked so young, but their faces had that grim, intent expression typical of West Point cadets. Everything regimented, she thought. Did their firm army discipline include push-ups, sit-ups, enforced marching? A boot camp mentality?

Troubled, she got out and walked toward a sign that said ADMINISTRATION OFFICES.

"Yes?" A middle-aged woman secretary, dressed in the type of interlock knit dress sold in mail-order catalogs, looked up as Vivian entered the office. She was busily typing at an IBM computer.

"My name is Vivian Clavell." She gave the name and location of the agency she represented. "I need to talk to one of your students, a boy named Ryan Sokol. It's a very pressing matter, really quite urgent."

"You would have to talk to Colonel Diggs then; he's

the deputy commandant of cadets. Colonel Diggs is on the telephone but should be finished in a few minutes. Would you like to wait? There's a coffeepot on the table near the window, if you'd like to help yourself."

Vivian nodded. The waiting room, curiously gloomy, was carpeted with threadbare Wilton rugs, its walls covered with dark, aged paneling that wasn't veneer but the real thing. Dozens of framed photographs lined the walls, including several of men who appeared to be Confederate officers. She studied a class photo taken in 1929, depicting twenty young men wearing high-collared old-fashioned military uniforms. Those in the first row sat with their legs crossed at identical angles, their shoes and socks matching.

Suddenly a door opened and a tall gray-haired man emerged, his well-cut army uniform fitting his body as if it had been tailored for him. He was about fifty, military retirement age, and possessed a chest full of ribbons and a firm, thin-lipped mouth.

"Mrs. . . . ah, Clavell? Did I get the name right?"

"Yes." She shook his hand. "I need to talk with one of your students; it's a matter of great urgency."

"One of our cadets?"

"It's Ryan Sokol; he's a new student here. It will only take a minute," she pleaded. "I can talk to him here, in your office, if you'd like."

Colonel Diggs frowned. "Our school schedule is quite regimented, Mrs. Clavell. Even on Sundays the cadets have somewhere to be just about every hour. And I'm afraid I'll have to ask for some identification."

Today was Sunday? She'd been driving so long she'd lost track of the days. Vivian shook herself, fighting a feeling of disorientation. She pulled out her agency ID card with her photograph.

"Ah. Ah," Colonel Diggs said, staring at the card so long that Vivian wondered if he even knew what a senior placement worker was. "Mrs. Wease will have to look up Sokol's schedule. I'll leave this to her; I have a trustees' luncheon to attend."

He was gone, leaving her to the attentions of the secretary, who seemed visibly to relax once he had left.

"It's a big weekend with all the trustees coming in," the woman explained. "That's why we're open today. They are all alumni, and they expect everything to be shipshape . . . I'm sure you know how that is. Oh, yes, what did you say the cadet's name was?"

"Ryan Sokol."

"Well, he's been given demerits already for fighting. He's a very hostile boy; so many of them are at first. But we build character here. We accomplish miracles sometimes."

Vivian nodded, impatiently waiting until Ryan's schedule was produced.

"Lunch has just finished. He's supposed to be in study hall right now," said the secretary. "On Sundays, the study hall is shortened to only one hour."

"Could I just go to the study hall and talk to him there? I promise to keep it short." Vivian stretched the truth. "The colonel didn't seem to object."

"I'll phone over there first."

Vivian waited while the secretary dialed. After a few seconds, she hung up, frowning. "Sokol isn't there. He never showed up for study hall. Or lunch formation either."

*   *   *

Vivian left the office, more alarmed than she had dared to show to the secretary, who had made another call to the barracks and found that Ryan was not in his room either. Ryan was AWOL . . . but why? Was it that he disliked the military-style discipline, or had Dani shown up?

Anxiously Vivian walked out onto the quadrangle walk, noticing a cadet in dress uniform, accompanied by his parents, exiting from what had to be the cadets' barracks. As the three came down the walk, the woman nodded shyly at Vivian. She was wearing a light summer dress.

"Do you have a boy here, too?" she asked.

"Yes, I do," said Vivian, impulsively turning and going into the barracks through the same door they had exited from.

She stepped into a long corridor paved with tile squares that looked as if they had been laid down in the sixties. The hall was lit at intervals with forty-watt bulbs encased in wire cages, and reverberated with layers of noise—voices, TV sets, doors banging. Her own tapping footsteps added to the cacophony. The corridor was lined with doors, each one neatly labeled with two last names.

She spotted two boys headed toward her. "Do you know where Ryan Sokol's room is? I'm his mother," she lied.

"Is he new?"

"Yes."

"Then he's on the top floor, I think toward the end. Names are on all the doors."

Vivian met more boys as she progressed deeper into the maw of the barracks, which, despite what had to be heavy foot traffic of active young men, was immaculately clean, the floor waxed to a glow.

At the end of the top floor, near a window that overlooked the quadrangle, she found the door that said R. SOKOL and P. VAN GILDER.

Just as Vivian was lifting her hand to knock, a boy burst out, still buttoning his khaki shirt. His hair was cut short on the sides, and he was chewing on a Snickers bar. The odor of chocolate surrounded him in a cloud.

"Are you Ryan's roommate?"

"Yeah."

"Is he inside? Could I speak with him? I'm his mother."

"Ryan isn't here. He didn't show up for lunch."

The boy seemed about to skid down the corridor, off to some cadet activity, and once he was gone, Vivian knew she'd never find him again. "Please," she begged. "Please, this is so important. Where would Ryan go, assuming he wanted to go somewhere off by himself for a while and didn't want anyone here to know where he was?"

The boy stared at her.

"Please." Vivian pleaded, watching as he popped the last of the Snickers into his mouth. "I have something I have to give to Ryan—some money he needs— and I'll pay you a fee, too, a finder's fee, if you'll tell me where he might have gone. I assume there are stores around here, places where you can spend your money?"

The youth hesitated. "The Cadet Store."

"Here," said Vivian, opening her purse. She took out her billfold and grabbed handfuls of bills—ones, fives, a ten. She thrust all of them into the roommate's hands. "Here. This is so important; I *need* to find Ryan. I promise I won't tell that horrible colonel where he is. I swear it. If you have any idea . . . any clue at all—"

"Probably the quarry," said the boy, pocketing the bills. "There's an old road that goes back along the bluff; we go there sometimes and swim. We aren't supposed to, but we do."

Dani reached the tree later than she'd thought. She had gotten lost, taking the wrong exit on the expressway, and had to drive a long way in the other direction before managing to pull off the highway and follow the signs to get back on. She'd nearly been in tears by the time she accomplished this feat.

What if Ryan didn't wait for her? What if he thought she'd stood him up?

Now, anxiously, her eyes traveling across the woods, she pulled Jill's Tempo off the blacktop road. The car jounced as it met the unevenness of Tennessee earth. She could see the big old tree ahead, the one scarred with the initials, but there was no Ryan.

Fear prickled her. She'd driven all this way. Where was he? Her heart hammering in her throat, she drove the car off onto the track, parking as close to the tree as she could.

Whitney was awake and alert, making bubbly baby sounds and waving her fists. Dani made sure she was all right in her car seat, then got out of the car. Immediately the rich woodsiness surrounded her, a smell of sunbaked grass, and leaf humus, insects humming and flying and swooping around her, their wings lit by sun. In the distance she heard the staccato popping of rifles.

As she approached the old tree, she realized how big it was. The trunk was so gigantic that it would have taken two of her to stretch her arms around it. Dani narrowed her eyes at the ancient letters scraped in with boys' penknives. She saw a date scratched in: 1923. Some of the boys who wrote their names here had to be old now, or maybe even dead.

Despite the hot sun, she shivered. The tree was too big—they didn't have trees that big in Madisonia. And behind it the woods seemed almost oppressive, the trees in places too thick to walk through. The ground was covered with loose rocks and mats of dead leaves mixed with pine needles that formed a soft, spongy carpet.

She paced back and forth, her Reeboks scuffing the alien softness. She didn't even like the woods, she told herself. She would never speak to Ryan again if he left her here all alone with Whitney.

She walked around some more, plagued with the uneasy sense that someone was in the woods, staring at her through the trees. But when she turned, she saw nothing except a flash of bird wings.

I don't like birds either, she thought, slapping at a gnat.

The minutes ticked slowly by. Dani glanced at the sky, then at her watch, then walked back to the car to see if Whitney was all right. The baby had fallen asleep, her fine hair curled back from her forehead in damp, sweaty tendrils.

What would she do with her if Ryan didn't come?

The enormity of what she had done swept over Dani. A baby couldn't live in a car forever. It needed a house, a crib to sleep in. It needed diapers, many boxes of them, and it needed pajamas and blankets and pacifiers and Gerber applesauce and baby toys and teddy bears.

Dani leaned her forehead against the roof of the

Tempo, the sun-heated metal burning against her skin. For a long time, on the drive down here, she'd felt like a hero. She'd felt as if she were doing a brave and wonderful thing, but now she didn't feel brave anymore at all. She felt little, small, and helpless.

Without Ryan, this wasn't an adventure anymore.

It was just an awful mistake, one she didn't know how to correct. Now that she was far away from Bonner Lockwood, now that she was standing here in the middle of these woods, even he had faded, and she couldn't remember the full horror of what he had done. *Had* she made a mistake? Not seen him correctly? Maybe she had been wrong.

She heard a crunching noise behind her. Dani jumped, whirling around. A boy wearing a pair of gym shorts and a T-shirt was limping across the field, waving at her.

"Ryan? Ryan!" Dani waved back, jumping up and down. She rushed across the grass, dodging around a clump of bushes, nearly tripping on a cairn of rocks. "Ry! Ry! Ry!"

Bonner sagged back in the front bucket seat of the van, perspiring in the heat that blasted through the windshield.

Something had awakened him. Some high-pitched sound.

He'd been dreaming of the girls again, the girls outside the movie theater. Their faces like beautiful flowers, which began to wilt and melt and change, their skin peeling back from their cheekbones, their eyeballs hardening, drying in their skulls.

He jerked upright, blinking to remove the terrible sight from his retinas. What had he heard? Just a

birdcall? Or perhaps voices, carrying from the football field?

He glanced around, trying to orient himself. According to the dashboard clock, he'd slept more than
an hour. The sun had moved slightly, and fluffy
white clouds were drifting over from the mountain.
On the dashboard sat his "things," encased in a
plastic bag. The little chloroform bottle was slightly
dusty, its clear liquid as innocuous as water. Underneath the driver's seat of the van was a bottle of
whiskey that Bonner had brought with him from
Madisonia, and he reached down, opened it, and
took a long, burning swallow.

Where was the little bitch?

This all could be blamed on Dani, laid squarely at
her door. She had driven him to this, and she would
be punished thoroughly for her part in it. He would
kill both of the kids, he decided. Dani was already a
missing runaway, and Ryan . . . well, military
schools got runaways all the time. No one would be
surprised if he turned up missing. There might be
holes, but basically his reasoning was sound and he
knew he could make it work. Anyway, who would
dare to question him? Wasn't he the dean now—a
college dean? A person of respect and authority.

Some small gnats had entered the car and were
whirling frantically, flicking their bodies at Bonner's
head. He fanned the air, trying to push them away.
His heart had begun to pound sickly. He waited,
monitoring the swift beats. Was he having any extra
systoles? If he had a heart attack, that would be her
fault, too. It had all gone too far, he realized.

He couldn't fuck up his entire life because of a
thirteen-year-old kid. Who would ask him to do that?

After several more swallows of whiskey, Bonner

felt a pressure on his bladder. He pushed open the door of the van and stepped down, urinating copiously against a nearby bush, watching the yellow, bipartite stream as it splashed on green leaves before seeping to the ground. He pictured Dani naked, lying down, passively awaiting his command.

As he was zipping himself, he heard the sound of a car.

He straightened, his body freezing, his hand still on his fly. Yes, it was the sound of a car engine. . . . It had to be her. Who else, down here on a Sunday? Dani McVie and Ryan Sokol. . . .

Welcome, he thought, pulling his lips back from his teeth.

Dani felt an attack of violent shyness. Ryan looked taller than she remembered, his skin far tanner, his eyes much bluer. He actually looked handsome, a *babe*, as the girls at school said. His hair was short and neatly trimmed. He was wearing an unfamiliar pair of blue gym shorts and a shirt that said CHIL-HOWEE ATHLETIC DEPARTMENT. He smelled pungently of sweat, like a grown man, not a kid.

Dani swallowed back her outburst of joy. Suddenly she was angry. "Why were you so late? I thought you were never coming!"

"Geez, I couldn't help it. I twisted my ankle when I was jumping across the ditch back there by the barracks. I had to go back in and get an Ace bandage."

"Oh. . . ."

"Why are you here?" said Ryan. "This is crazy, Dani. Is that Jill Rudgate's car? Did she loan you her car?" He shook his head, scowling. "You drove this far? Dani, this is hundreds of miles away."

"I told you; I had to. It was—I told you; Bonner did awful things to Whitney," Dani blurted, looking at Ryan's high-topped Adidas instead of at him.

There was a silence, and she saw the Adidas step back a pace or two. He didn't believe her. Dani felt it with a crunch to the center of her stomach.

"Are you sure?" Ryan asked.

"Yes, I'm sure, dammit! Yes, I'm sure! I saw it! Ry, don't you believe me? I wouldn't lie to you. I'd never lie to you. Oh, God—" Tears sprang to Dani's eyes as she realized the horrible unfairness of it, the terrible irony. She'd driven all this way to Ryan because he was the one person who believed her, and now he didn't believe.

"Hey," he said uncomfortably.

"Shit on you!" she cried. "Hey . . . just shit on you! You jerk, Ryan! You are such a dweeb, I can't stand it. Did I ever tell you a lie? Did I tell you *one lie?* Why would I drive all this way if I wasn't telling the truth? The man is a monster; he did things to a little baby; he put his white stuff all over her stomach; *do you know what I'm talking about?*"

"I, uh . . ." began Ryan.

"You *know* what I mean. Why would I tell you that—it's embarrassing—unless it was true? Ryan, I have her in the car. I have Whitney in a damn car seat. She's been sitting in that car seat for two days, I don't even know how long; it's been forever. I'm running out of milk, I spent most of my money, and she's getting this red rash on her bottom, and I don't have anything to give her for it, and she needs a bed, Ryan, and she needs a b-bath . . ." Dani had begun to shake.

"Hey."

"But *you* think I'm lying! *You* think I'd do this just for fun, don't you?"

"No, I . . . I don't. But you did drive—"

Dani stared at Ryan, seeing the youngness to his mouth. He was jealous, she realized, because she'd driven hundreds of miles alone, something he wanted to do himself. *"Driving!* Is that all you think about? You and your dad's damn 'Vette. Hey, *you* taught me to drive, Ryan, so I drove. Anything wrong with that? Now you gotta help me figure out what to do about Whitney. We gotta take her someplace where nobody's gonna make me take her back to Bonner."

There was a silence long enough for six or seven rounds of rifle shots to penetrate through the trees, followed by the faint carry of yells coming from the football field, drifting toward them on the wind.

"Well?" snapped Dani. "Are you going to just stand there?"

"Okay," Ryan said reluctantly. "I'll help you, Dani. I don't like this school anyway. I hate it here. They made me do push-ups, and they stand over you while you do your homework; you have to have some asshole in a military uniform telling you what to do. I hate my dad for sending me here. I have to have some friend, even if it's you."

To her shock Dani saw the sheen of tears glittering in Ryan's eyes. Violently he turned away, hiding his face from her.

"Ry," she said, reaching out to touch his arm.

They stood leaning together for a few minutes, and then his hand crept out to clench hers. There was only the sound of his choked sobs as he wrung her fingers, sending pain through her knuckles all the way up to her wrist.

Dani felt a rush of strength . . . a return of her confidence.

"I'm gonna get you *and* Whitney out of here," she declared, pulling him, limping, toward the car. "All you gotta do is tell me where to go and we'll go there. Where's that little road lead to, anyways?"

Ryan spoke hoarsely. "There's a quarry; the guys go swimming there sometimes. I think the Civil War soldiers used to dig their stone there, something like that. I haven't been there yet, but they say the water is so cold it'll give you stomach cramps and you'll drown."

Dani nodded. "Well, we're gonna leave here and go to a McDonald's somewhere and buy some milk for Whitney—and some hamburgers for us. And we need some Pampers, too."

Bonner heard the motor again, chuffing a little and then fading as it drove away. On foot, he hurried through the trees, peering between the trunks, belatedly trying to get a glimpse of the vehicle.

It was gone.

He stood in the middle of the tire ruts, cursing. It was her. He knew it. It had to be; that was who he'd heard yelling in the woods, waking him up. And now she was probably laughing at him for being such a fool, such an idiotic and criminal fool. He should be put away in prison, for a lifetime. And he probably would be, now, his whole life destroyed, because he had been stupid enough to miscalculate.

Bitterly he walked back to the van and got in, fishing around until he'd located the whiskey bottle again. He uncapped it and tilted it to his mouth.

He followed that swallow with another, then another. He didn't know what to do next. Those two kids, a thirteen- and a fourteen-year-old, had truly beaten him. Dani had seen him, Dani knew, and now she was sure to talk. Even if he had discredited her as a chronic and compulsive liar, that bitch social worker, Vivian Clavell, was pretty sharp, and she might catch on to what he had done. Once Dani told about the videos, the police would probably get a search warrant.

But, he assured himself, he *was* clean there. He'd stored away the collection, and now, as long as he paid his storage fees, it was safe. His land was under a secret name, too, the burial place where the bodies were.

Then, with a icicle stab to his gut, he remembered the hole in the light fixture in Dani's bathroom. Jesus, he'd forgotten to patch and repair it. If she told the police he'd been spying on her, they could go into the bathroom and look up in the ceiling fixture and the evidence would be right there to see.

But he thought he could weasel out of that. Yes, he would lie; he would tell them that a previous owner of the house had put that hole there. But if he could get to Dani first, if he could silence her, then he would have time to go home and close up the ceiling hole, repair it. Once that hole was repaired, who would ever guess he had had a video camera in there? That was it—he needed time. Killing Dani would buy him time to return home and cover all of his traces.

No, no, he begged some unseen god, tears rolling down his cheeks. *Don't let it end this way, please. I'm sorry; I won't do this again. This is positively the last time; I swear it. Just let me get out of this. One more time.*

*   *   *

Dani drove the Tempo into the parking lot of a small market in Maryville that catered to students from nearby Maryville College. Ryan sat in the front seat beside her, cradling Whitney in his arms. On the seat between them was the carryout sack of hamburgers from McDonald's, their fragrance filling the car. A second bag held two large chocolate shakes, two containers of Pepsi, and a carton of milk for Whitney.

"We look like a regular mama, papa, and baby," Dani said, giggling. "Ready to have our dinner."

Ryan blushed scarlet.

"I'll run in and buy the Pampers," Dani declared, shutting off the motor. Carelessly she stuffed her hair back up under the silly sun hat.

"No, maybe I should. They might be on the lookout for you, Dani. The police might ask questions about a girl buying stuff for babies."

"Well, *you* certainly can't buy it. Guys don't buy baby things," Dani said, staring to slip out of the car.

"Wait!" Ryan's arm stopped her. "Let's park around the corner, just in case."

Dani moved the car to a leafy side street lined with small clapboard homes, then walked over to the market. She picked up a small basket and roved around, going from rack to rack, mentally adding up the prices of things in her head. More Pampers . . . would one box be enough? There were some flimsy, sleazy-looking baby T-shirts hanging in the drug aisle, and some terrycloth shorts that Dani thought might fit Whitney. Then she decided they couldn't afford them. She put three cans of Gerber's in the basket, choosing banana, Whitney's favorite. She added a half-gallon of milk. The items began to weight down the basket, pulling at her arm.

Did she have enough money to pay for it all? Anxiously she rechecked the money in her billfold. She had thirty dollars now. After she paid, she calculated, she would have less than eight dollars.

As she started toward the checkout counter, a police officer walked into the market. He was about thirty, thickset, with blond hair, a blond mustache, and a pleasantly bland face. He was the type of officer that Fay called "just a dumb baby-faced pig." But Dani didn't think he looked dumb. She thought he looked very smart indeed as he walked up to the counter and began talking to the clerk. Light glinted on the grip of his revolver, the heavy nightstick that hung from his belt.

She edged behind the candy display case, hiding herself.

". . . a girl," she heard the patrolman say. "Only thirteen. We're putting pictures up. . . . She's kidnapped a baby up in Michigan. And she may be with one of the cadets from the Chilhowee Academy. They faxed us her picture; isn't that something?"

Her picture!

Dani jerked in alarm, causing the baby food jars in her basket to rattle. A sick, hot feeling began choking up from her gullet. Nervously she edged toward the soft-drink case, praying that Ryan wouldn't get restless in the car and come in to find her, that Whitney wouldn't decide to start crying.

The policeman lingered, gossiping with the store clerk. Dani stayed hidden until she heard the front door of the market slam, a bell tinkling. Quietly she removed the half-gallon of milk from the basket and put the rest of the items down in a corner, behind a wine cooler display. She waited until the clerk was occupied with ringing up another sale before sidling out the door.

The patrol car was gone. She skidded across the cement, the stolen milk sloshing in its cardboard container as she dashed for the car.

"There was a policeman!" she gasped to Ryan. "And they're giving out pictures of me—my picture! And they're looking for you, too!"

His face looked white, pinched with anxiety. "What did I tell you? I saw him; I saw him go in. We've got to leave, Dani. Let me drive, will you? It would look a lot better, and we won't attract as much attention."

Wordlessly Dani climbed in, taking Whitney onto her own lap. The infant stirred, smacking her lips open, balling up her fist, and thrusting it into her own pink mouth.

"At least I got milk," Dani said. "More milk, for later."

"Did you pay for it?"

"Well, no."

Ryan turned right, driving through a peaceful residential area. "Now we *have* to go back to the quarry," he told her. "They'll be watching all the freeway entrances, but I can take side roads where they don't patrol. We'll wait until night, when we won't be so visible; then we'll leave. We'll go . . . oh, further into the mountains; they won't find us there. We'll find an old cabin or maybe a summer place; we'll break in and live there for a while."

Dani thought of the huge old oak scarred with initials of dead cadets. The dark woods, the ranks of trees that marched over all the hillsides and foothills, broken by craggy outcrops of rock. She remembered the feeling she'd had before, the feeling of being watched.

"No. I don't like woods. I don't like all that woodsy stuff."

"Dani, they have *pictures* of you."

"Okay," she said dully. As Ryan drove, she held on tightly to the baby. With only thirty dollars, how long could she and Ryan manage on their own? How would they buy gas or food? She'd have to think about trying to call Mrs. Vivian again. But she knew once she did that, it would be out of her hands.

A tear squeezed out of Dani's eye, and savagely she swiped at it, pulverizing it under her fingers. If they refused to listen to her again, if they didn't believe her, then Whitney would go right back to Bonner. She would be helpless against his abuse. How could a baby fight back? A little baby not even four months old yet?

No, Dani thought fiercely. No, she wasn't going to give Whitney up until she was sure.

Ryan was right. They were going to have to go back to the quarry and hide until dark.

Vivian didn't know what to do. She drove her car down toward the wooded area behind the school property, as Ryan's roommate had suggested. She parked, staring toward the woods, which seemed to present a green wall. Beyond stretched the bulk of the Chilhowee Mountain for which the school was named, its huge shape vaguely threatening.

She knew it was entirely possible that Ryan being missing and Dani being missing were not connected and that Dani had been stopped somewhere farther north on I-75, and even now could be in police custody.

Yes, but the girl and boy had been friends, both of them rebels, the kind of friends driven together by adversity.

Vivian shaded her eyes, beginning to make out a rutted track that extended up a slight rise and wound to the left, disappearing behind a grove of trees. That had to be the path that led to the quarry, she thought.

She parked at the edge of the road and began walking back toward the track, sweating in the noonday sun. The ruts were marked by tire tracks, one set of which seemed to veer off the trail into the trees. The sight caused her to feel a rumble of unease. But surely the tires were too wide for a Tempo. Besides, she couldn't tell how old they were. They could be days old, she thought. She was no police officer, no tire expert who could trail a car by tread marks alone.

She trudged on, stepping around an occasional beer can, feeling more and more as if she were on some foolish, Don Quixote errand. She hadn't been in a woods in years. Her shoes with their one-and-a-half-inch heels made walking difficult, and she slipped and slid on loose stones.

A chipmunk broke from cover, scurrying across the trail in front of her. Vivian watched it disappear into a thicket of low creepers, feeling defeat sag over her.

She'd tried . . . but she had come as far as she could.

Nobody was in these woods.

She turned and started back the way she had come, tears of frustration blurring her vision. She felt overwhelmed by a sense of failure. She herself was pathetic, wasn't she? Getting feelings of love for a waif of a girl, driving across half the country on a wild-goose chase.

What should she do now? She guessed she should go to the police station in Maryville, assuming there was one, and tell them what she knew. As she reached her car, a sudden sense of urgency took over her, causing her hand to shake as she inserted her key in the ignition.

15

A VOLLEY OF rifle shots popped in the hot, close air, disturbing a bird that fluttered away from a branch. Bonner could hear the distant buzz of some off-road vehicle, but he figured it had to be a mile or more away, too distant to be a threat. And if there were any cadets in the woods, he hadn't seen any. Fortunately, it was too hot yet, and also it was broad daylight; he imagined the kids would not come to the woods until dusk.

Bonner was about to start the engine and drive out the trail when he heard the car entering the woods. He jumped, nearly dropping the bottle. Could it possibly be?

He sat stunned, then shut off his engine and pushed open the door of the van. To avoid making any noise, he didn't close it. His heart pounding, he hurried over the hillside, and in a few seconds he saw it—a flash of medium-metallic blue metal. The Tempo!

He backed away a little, sheltering himself behind the spiny branches of a large pine tree.

The car passed by his vantage point. He stood as

delicately poised as a deer, feeling himself blend with the pine tree, his heartbeat slamming with elation. He had them. . . . He had them now. The trail wound ahead, rising at a low but steady grade toward a bluff that loomed in the distance. It was barely passable for one vehicle, let alone two abreast. Bonner doubted very much if there was another exit to the trail.

Which meant that once they penetrated up the track, he could block their exit with his much bigger van. This was the perfect place to dispose of two kids, Bonner thought gleefully. And an idea was coming into his mind . . . a glimmer of just how he might do it and still come off looking innocent.

The Tempo was now passing him at its closest point, so close that Bonner could have burst out of the underbrush yelling and reached the car in less than ten seconds.

That was when he heard the noise.

The sound of a baby crying.

He stiffened rigidly. His heart pinwheeled, banging against his chest wall. *A baby. Whitney! She had the baby girl!*

Bonner gasped for air, staggering backward into the needly prickles of a pine branch, revulsion flooding him like vomit. My God, it was the one most horrible thing he had ever done, the thing he had not been able to *stop* himself from doing. His curse, his hell. He had lusted after an infant, his own flesh and blood. Ever since, he'd blanked it out of his mind. Now here was this crying, reminding him, pointing a bony finger of guilt at him.

The baby's cries gradually faded as the Tempo rumbled on past, disappearing around a curve behind a weedy stand of small maples.

But he was guilty only if someone caught him, the thought came to him like a healing spray of light.

If the baby never came back, no one would know what he had done—that is, if it died along with Dani and Ryan. Which of course it would have to, since he could hardly rescue it and come trekking home carrying it wrapped up in a blanket. "Oh, look what *I* found," he would have to say, and they would arrest him and send him to prison. He'd read about what happened to child molesters in prison. No way. Not for him. Prison life was impossible for men like him.

He took another step, then another, walking so unsteadily that he listed from side to side, more drunk from fear than he was from whiskey. He was terrified by the abyss in which he now found himself.

He was not—not the way it seemed.

No. He *was* a good person. He had only tried to love his pretty babies. Things had turned out badly, but it was not his fault; it was theirs for being seductresses, for being too sexual.

He heard one last trailing baby squall, and a sudden murderous wave of hatred swept over him. He hated the baby for tempting him. Females were *born* with their wicked sexuality; they put it into use almost from birth. Whitney had taught him that. . . .

They were *never* innocent, were they? Not even for a few weeks, not even at the beginning. They were not the same species as men. They were evil and blandishing, seductive and coy and wicked and sensuous. It was built into them, born into them, even the infants, yes, even them.

The car motor noise had faded away. Somewhere close an insect whirred its chitinous wings. Bonner was sweating, rivulets of moisture pouring down his body, soaking his shirt. He could smell his own sour, curdling stench.

He *had* to do it.

He had no choice.

Why wouldn't they see that? He was a man who had never had a choice. He hadn't asked to be this way, had he? He had been born a clean male. He was pure in all of his parts, and God was with him. God knew, and would understand and save him.

He went back to the van and started it up.

In the distance they heard the mosquitolike whine of an off-road motorcycle, but the sound seemed to come from the opposite side of the track.

"Is this trail big enough? It's so bumpy! Aren't we going to get stuck?" Dani kept saying as Ryan drove the Tempo farther and farther up the winding track. They passed scraps of garbage, beer cans, and then something round, rubbery, and disgusting that Dani recognized as a used Trojan.

Ryan seemed to love being behind the wheel. "My dad drives his van through stuff a lot worse than this. This is nothing. Me and my brother and my dad drove up north one time and were out in the woods for two days."

Up north meant northern Michigan, Dani realized. Michigan seemed impossibly far away, part of a life she didn't belong to anymore. What would she do when this was over, she wondered. She knew she could never go back and live with Maureen. Where would she go?

The track turned again, two hundred yards later emerging at the top of a hill that overlooked a quarry dug out of limestone. Its walls were perpendicular in places, tumbled and decaying in others. At the bottom, cupped in the stone, was a small lake, its color electric blue, as if strange metals in the rock had leached into it, turning it poisonous.

"Oh," said Dani, looking down.

"I don't know how you get down to the lake," Ryan was saying. "I guess you have to climb."

The trail had petered out, the tire tracks abruptly fading to nothing but scattered gravel, bare rock, and flattened grass. Ryan stopped the car, turning off the ignition. The shots from the rifle range were now tiny, insectile poppings. Dani had never been so far away from civilization before. It gave her an eerie, vulnerable feeling.

"Well, I guess we're here. I guess this is it."

As if sensing their arrival, Whitney had stopped crying. She fastened one of her fists in Dani's hair, tugging firmly on red frizz.

Dani laughed, untangling her grip. They sat still for a minute, looking down at the blue shimmer of the lake, which didn't look very inviting at all, but dangerous. Dani, who had progressed only to intermediate swimmer, wondered what it would be like to struggle across the lake only to meet a steep rock wall with no handholds. Again she had the chilling feeling of being watched . . . a sensation of someone waiting.

"We'd better eat our hamburgers," said Ryan after a long minute.

"Yeah."

They unwrapped the bag and attacked their Big Macs, slurping down drafts of chocolate milk shake, which had begun to melt from being carried in the bag for so long. The Pepsis were equally runny, the ice melted, but Dani gulped hers down thirstily.

Whitney began to smack her lips, so Dani poured milk into a bottle and continued to feed the baby, while finishing her own soft drink.

It was then that they heard the car engine, rumbling steadily up the track.

"Somebody's coming." Dani turned her head to peer out of the back windshield.

"Oh, maybe it's four-wheelers," Ryan said uneasily. "They use this place; that's what the guys say."

Dani's pulse beat had quickened. Somehow she knew it wasn't. No, there was something too steady about the sound of that motor, approaching them with almost stalking intensity.

"Maybe we should get out of here," she suggested nervously.

"Where? It's going to take me a while to turn around—this track is pretty narrow."

"I don't know. I don't like this. Ry . . ." Twisting around, she narrowed her eyes as the van appeared around the bend in the trail. Sun glittered on its windshield, obscuring the driver's face. *But a van,* something whispered in Dani's mind. Bonner had a van . . . Bonner liked vans.

"Just sit still and they'll see us and turn around," Ryan instructed her, sipping on his milk shake. "There isn't room for two cars here."

"I don't know," Dani muttered. She stared at the blaze where sun met glass. Then the van passed under the shadow cast by a large oak. The sun glare vanished, revealing the face of Bonner Lockwood.

"Ryan!" Dani grabbed Ryan's arm, her fingernails cutting into his bare skin. "It's him! It's Bonner!"

Her heartbeat was drumming, shock nearly bursting through her chest wall. *He had followed her here! He had followed her!*

"Bonner? Aw, Dani, how could it be? How could he even know we're here?"

"He does; he does; it's him! Ry . . . we've gotta get out of the car right now. He's got us blocked in here; we can't let him catch us. Oh, God! We've got the baby! Ry, this is serious. Ryan . . ."

In a panic, Dani picked up Whitney, gathering her softness into her arms. The act seemed to take forever; it felt as if she were moving through jelly. To make matters worse, the baby suddenly grabbed at her hair, gripping her bangs so tightly that Dani's eyes watered.

"He's parking," Ryan reported anxiously. "He's getting out of the van. He's got us trapped. We can't turn around."

Holding onto the baby, Dani shoved open the passenger door, while Ryan jumped out of the driver's side. Awkwardly Dani started across the rocky scree, her balance off because of the baby in her arms. Bonner stood near the van, pointing something at them.

"Stop! Stop, bitch!"

A chip of stone went flying near Dani's foot. At the same time she heard an amazingly loud explosion.

"Put that baby back in the car!" Bonner yelled. "Or I'll shoot her!"

Dani dropped to the ground, protecting the infant's soft head with both of her hands, as she tried to twist farther toward the quarry. Ryan had thrown himself down, too, and was crawling for safety underneath the car.

"Dani!" the boy yelled at her. "Get under here!"

"Get back in the car, both of you!" called Bonner in his deep, commanding, dean's voice. Yet he didn't look like a college dean anymore. His rumpled clothing was soaked in sweat, his lips moving like an old alky from the Cass Corridor in Detroit. His face had an odd look, as if he was listening to voices they couldn't hear.

Hugging the ground, shielding Whitney with her body, Dani stared at the man who had put a video camera in her bathroom, who had touched and fondled her, who had molested a little baby and probably even killed. Oh, yes, she believed that now. The blood on those panties in the attic had come from dead young girls.

Another shot ricocheted past them, exploding the fallen baby bottle into flying shards of milky glass. Dani cried out, clenching Whitney to her. The infant, crushed and uncomfortable, began to scream.

"Hush, hush," Dani said automatically.

"We've gotta get out of here!" Ryan cried. "Jesus, he's gonna shoot, Dani! And they'll never hear him because of the rifle range!"

"You're right," said Bonner, approaching the Tempo. His shoes scrunched on loose rock.

"Put the baby back in the car," Bonner ordered, licking his lips. To her horror, Dani saw a distended bulge in the front of his pants. *"Now,* Dani." He motioned the gun at her.

Terror splashed through her like acid, yet still Dani hesitated.

"I said now!" Bonner snapped. "Do it, girl—you follow my orders now. You do everything I say, or that baby goes in the quarry with a bullet in her."

Sobbing, Dani got to her feet and walked the few steps to the Tempo, pulling open the door and depositing Whitney in the front passenger seat. The infant resisted, twisting her body in a roll. Dani knew the baby was probably going to roll onto the floor of the car and hastily tried to prop her with her purse.

"Now!" called Bonner. "Dani, I want you to come here and get this piece of cloth."

As Dani stared at him, startled and terrified, he began fumbling with something he had taken out of a small plastic bag, a medicine bottle and a white square of bandage cloth. Unscrewing the bottle top, he removed an eyedropper and began saturating the cloth. Dani smelled a sweet, almost ethereal odor, mingling with the more familiar smell of whiskey.

"No," she said, instinctively realizing that the cloth meant something horrible. She darted a sideways glance at Ryan. The boy, flattened under the car, was gradually squirming away. Hope filled her. In a few seconds he'd jump up and burst through the woods, running away. Maybe he could escape. He could run to the school and bring back help.

"You, boy!" shouted Bonner, seeing the movement. "Stay where you are or I'll shoot your head off."

Ryan froze as if already shot, digging his face into the dusty earth.

The man's voice became a croon, saccharine with evil. "Now, you, Dani, come here. Yes, you, I want you here, and don't give me any trouble, darling, because you're too pretty to disobey me. I'm not going to hurt you. Oh, no, no, Bonner doesn't hurt anyone. I never hurt my pretties; I wouldn't dream of it."

Dani's terror had evaporated, to be replaced by a computerlike clicking of her mind. She flashed back to the apartment she'd shared with Fay. An old drunk used to hang out in the neighborhood with his bottle of Thunderbird. Old alkies got mugged all the time in Detroit. They were stupid, slow, and weak. Right now, Bonner was like a smarter, meaner version of one of them. She had to use that. But how?

Bonner fired another shot. She saw a stone jump into the air. *"Come on, come on,* I haven't got all day; just hurry, will you?"

Dani knew she had no choice. As slowly as she could, she walked toward her foster father.

"Now," he told her, his voice high. "This isn't going to be very hard for you, pretty Dani, not at all. I want two things. First, I want that juvenile delinquent boyfriend of yours to get in the backseat of the car. Yes—*Now! Jump! Jump!"*

He sounded so crazy and waved the gun so wildly that Ryan obeyed, sliding his awkward arms and legs into the backseat.

"Now, you, Dani. You can follow my simple command, can't you? Your job will be extremely easy. I just want you to get in the backseat with your friend Ryan and then put this piece of cloth over his nose and hold it there."

"I . . . what's on the cloth?" Dani said, stalling for time.

"Just a little chloroform. Nothing harmful. A mild anesthetic. Just press it on his nose and mouth, and he'll go to sleep; he'll take a nice, nice nap. *Do it,* Dani girl—unless you want to see that baby spattered there at the bottom of the quarry."

That baby. He was speaking of his own daughter. Dani listened in horror as Bonner laughed. "Do you think she'd be able to swim across that lake? Ha ha."

Dani quietly wept as she walked to the car and got into the backseat, gingerly carrying the folded square of gauze that Bonner had pushed into her hand with its sickening, sweetish smell. After she put Ryan unconscious, she had no doubt that Bonner was going to do terrible things to herself and Whitney.

Ryan backed away from her as far as he could get; he knew what was coming. His terrified eyes were fastened on the cloth. "Dani . . . that's got . . . Dani. *Don't.*"

"Ry," she said despairingly, holding up the cloth. *"Don't!"*

Bonner watched as Dani got in the car, her face drained white. She was going to do everything he said, and so was the boy. He no longer felt drunk. He *wasn't* drunk. He was on a power trip, in control of every action at the quarry, supreme ruler of all he surveyed, from Dani and Ryan to every leaf blade, piece of gravel, and hunk of granite.

His plan was simple, and he knew it would work. The news broadcast he'd seen months ago on Channel 7, the two Utica teenagers found dead in their car, had given him the idea. He would knock both kids unconscious with the chloroform and then set their car on fire. They'd die of smoke inhalation— together—with the baby in the front seat perishing, too.

It would all look so innocent.

Two runaway kids hiding out at the quarry, falling asleep, one of them smoking. The cigarette sets the car on fire. Boom. Another tragedy for the media to hash over.

He saw Ryan was still moving. Why was Dani delaying following his orders?

"Hurry up," he snapped. "Put the cloth on the kid's face . . . go on; do it!"

"I won't."

"Do it!" Furious at being thwarted, Bonner approached the Tempo and thrust the nose of the revolver in through the opened passenger window. He aimed it at the baby, who had rolled onto the floor mat and now lay on her back, crying loudly. He had already ceased to think of Whitney as his daughter or as anything really except an object, something he had to use.

"Put him unconscious, girl, just do it. If he fights you, push the cloth on his face and keep it there. He'll have to breathe in."

Ryan felt as if he were trapped in a nightmare from which he couldn't wake. He was almost wetting his pants from fright. The stuff on the cloth smelled awful, and somehow he knew it was poisonous, not nearly as "mild" as Bonner said.

"Ry! Pretend you're sleeping," Dani whispered, under the baby's yell. *"Just go limp."*

But he couldn't. He stiffened, fighting away the cloth. Hitting at her. He felt a burst of nausea, a writhing mass in his stomach.

"Go limp, dammit!" Dani snapped.

Ryan felt like bursting into tears, but finally he forced himself to slump over, letting his arms and legs go loose. The position made him feel unmasculine, painfully vulnerable, and weak. He lay there, helpless, his terror so intense that he thought he would pee, or even really pass out.

Bonner's voice was sweet, wheedling, with an undercurrent of violence. "Dani, have you done what I said? Is he out?"

"Yes."

"Kick him. See if he moves."

Ryan felt a stinging pain in his left calf but managed not to cry out. He felt the seat cushion lift as Dani got out of the backseat, slamming the car door to enclose him safely inside. He dared to open one eye, and caught a brief glimpse of Bonner Lockwood, standing outside the car. He was smiling.

"Now come here," Bonner said to Dani.

The creep, the creep, Ryan thought, and knew with a deep wash of shame exactly what Bonner Lockwood wanted to do to Dani. Ryan began to cry quietly. He wondered if he would see his mom and dad again, or his brother, Brandon. Would his dad be sorry when he was found dead? Grief washed over him, so painful that he wanted to sob. He was too young to die. You weren't supposed to die at fourteen.

"Okay, okay, take off your clothes," Bonner said to Dani.

Ryan listened, shuddering.

"I will," came Dani's reply, soft, fainter, and trembling. "I will, but . . . first I want to kiss you. Can I kiss you, Bonner? Just one time, just because, well, because you are my foster daddy, and I love you."

There was a silence. Bonner had to be shocked at the request. Even Ryan froze, amazed at the words. Did Dani mean it? Had she gone crazy? Nausea flooded his throat. *What was going on?*

"Please," begged Dani in a tone so seductive that it chilled Ryan to the core. "Please, Bonner, can I kiss you?"

* * *

Vivian followed the two police cars back to the school, speeding dangerously in order to keep up with them as they swerved around curves and exited at the Chilhowee Military Academy. Their overhead dome lights were flashing, but the sirens were off.

The social worker's hands were covered with sweat as she gripped the steering wheel. Her head gonged with the most vicious headache she'd ever encountered. Her temples seemed almost ready to burst. The minute she'd stepped into the police station and told them what she knew, matters seemed to have skidded onward, out of her control. Bonner Lockwood had disappeared from Madisonia, and his wife had found an incriminating videotape and photo.

Was Bonner here, in Tennessee? At the Chilhowee Academy?

But where else could he be?

Vivian knew that if Dani was his only witness, he had to silence her, or his entire life would crack apart like a highway bridge in an earthquake. *The baby,* Vivian thought nervously. *The poor little baby, what will happen to her? And Dani, my Dani.*

The police seemed to know right where the track was; probably they had been here a thousand times to break up cadet beer blasts and hassle necking couples. The two cars sped down the blacktop road past the two big quadrangles where cadets and their visitors were walking, past the ivy-covered library and the big gymnasium building. Vivian heard gravel skid under her tires as she raced to keep up.

They reached the woods. The rifle range was still going, gunshots popping like popcorn. The first squad car didn't bother to stop; he just plowed across the grass and aimed his vehicle up the track. The second car was right behind. There were still no sirens, just the blue, flashing lights.

Vivian hesitated, but only for a moment. She drove her car right behind theirs.

When Dani was six, Fay had pushed her forward, ordering her to kiss "Mr. Watermelon" on his crepey, bristled neck.

"Now it won't hurt you to be nice and friendly. Come closer to Bob; climb on his lap, baby. Hug him; put your arms around him. He likes little girls. He likes to kiss them. . . ."

"Please, can I kiss you?"

Dani couldn't believe she had really said that. It all seemed to be happening to another girl, not her. Her throat closed up, her mouth painfully dry of saliva, as she battled the nightmarish memories she usually kept suppressed.

"Dani," said Bonner, slurring her name, making it sound long and sexual. He seemed shaken but delighted at her change in attitude. "Dani, I always wanted you. . . ."

"Yeah, I always wanted you," parroted Dani, putting her arms at her sides and palming the chloroform-soaked piece of cloth so that it wasn't visible to Bonner.

"You're so pretty," he breathed. "You're beautiful."

They faced each other. Dani trembled with the effort of maintaining the smile she'd pasted on her face—the seductive smile. The smile that was going to save her, and Ryan, and Whitney, if she could just keep it on her lips for a few minutes longer.

"Closer," he told her. He had lowered the gun.

She crossed the gravel-covered ground, sauntering her hips as she had seen Fay do. She added a few grinds of her buttocks. She was sweating.

There were only a few steps to take, just a few, and then she was standing in his aura, breathing his smell. She wanted to sob with horror. It was like Mr. Watermelon again. But she couldn't allow herself to show her emotions, or he would kill her.

She waited as his arms slid familiarly around her, running down her sides and along her hips, his fingers cupping inward at her buttocks where the crease was. She forced herself not to shudder.

Over Bonner's shoulder she thought she saw lights flashing but decided it was only her terror, playing tricks on her.

"Kiss me," she repeated.

Bonner bent over toward her, his face nearing hers. He looked grizzled, saggy, old. His silvery hair was rumpled, and every wrinkle showed, every whisker follicle. But Dani was looking at his breathing, the way he sucked in air and then released it in short, choppy breaths.

He had just exhaled, was about to inhale. Timing it as best she could, Dani lifted her right hand, the one with the saturated cloth in it, and placed it over Bonner's opened mouth and nose. She pressed down hard, just as he had instructed.

Bonner stiffened in surprise, trying to pull away.

But Dani cried and screamed as she fought him, clinging to him. He pushed at her, but she refused to be dislodged, shoving the cloth practically into his mouth. Under the cloth she could feel the terrible heaving suck as Bonner tried to breathe in, and received only the chloroform.

He cried out something unintelligible, and then

she felt him sink. It happened in sections, knees sagging, kneecaps meeting the ground, then his torso folding. When he lay on the ground he looked old and used, his mouth slack, spittle wetting his lips. His mottled face was covered in sweat. He looked exactly like one of the old drunks that the kids rolled, back in Detroit, off Woodward Avenue near Eight Mile, back in the ghetto she had come from.

When she looked behind him she saw the police cars.

And behind them, Vivian.

Vivian drove her Camry down College Street, where leafy tree branches met overhead, rustling graciously in the June breezes. Lawn mowers buzzed, and somewhere children screamed and shouted as they kicked a ball. It was the sunny Madisonia of her imagination, the little college town she'd fantasized for Dani and, she supposed, for herself.

But today, hanging from the street sign at the corner of College and Lurie, was a hand-lettered sign that said LOCKWOOD IS A MONSTER. The bodies of twelve young girls had been found buried on property Bonner Lockwood had secretly owned under another name. The owner of the ministorage place had also recognized his picture and come forward. More than sixty videocassettes and thirty-five photo albums, obtained in a search, were grisly evidence in what was becoming Michigan's biggest mass murder case in years. Bonner Lockwood was going to spend the rest of his life in prison, the lowest of the low in the general prison population.

Dani sat in the front seat cradling Whitney in her lap, wearing a brand-new tunic and shorts that

Vivian had bought her in Toledo. The baby girl wore a little yellow dress trimmed in white eyelet that Dani had picked out.

As they drove past, Dani gazed wide-eyed at the hate sign.

"They know about him, then, huh? Everyone. The whole town. All the people. It's probably been on TV, huh?"

"I'm afraid so, darling," said Vivian.

"They know what *I* did?"

Vivian pulled her car over to the curb and parked in front of a big frame house with petunias in pots on the front steps.

"Not all of it, honey. No one knows how brave you really were, how tough it was, and I, for one, will never tell them."

Dani nodded. "I . . . I don't want them ever to know."

"Of course I'll keep your confidence, Dani." Then Vivian hesitated. The entire trip home, north on I-75 through Tennessee, Kentucky, and Ohio, this question had been burning at her. But she'd been nervously putting off asking, and now they were back in Madisonia. Decisions had to be made, and she had to ask now.

"Dani . . . we need to find another placement for you."

"Yes," said the girl dully.

"I was thinking," began Vivian in a measured manner, and then she saw the flare of disappointment in Dani's eyes, the hot hurt, and she blurted, fast, "I want you with me, honey. I always have. I could be an adoptive mother for you; it could be a single-parent adoption, Dani. Will you consider it?"

Dani stared at her, stunned.

Vivian felt tears running down her cheeks. "Dani, I'm fifty-six years old, I live in a condo in Rochester, by the time you're in college I'm going to be over sixty, and when you're a young mother I'll be even older. I'm far from rich. I can't—"

"Yes," cried Dani. "Yes!"

Vivian was shaking. "Are you sure?"

"Yes," said Dani, and they both looked at each other, startled.

In front of the Lockwood house, Dani suddenly didn't want to get out of the car. She clutched Whitney, burying her face in the baby's wisp of blond hair, in which Dani had tied a yellow satin ribbon.

"She smells so pretty," Dani mumbled. "I love the way babies smell. I love the way they feel. They have skin as soft as flowers, and their hair is like . . . I don't know . . . maybe dandelion fur. . . ."

Tears were running down the girl's freckled face.

"Dani," said Vivian gently. "You know Whitney belongs with her mother."

"I know."

"Someday you'll have babies of your own—a dozen of them if you want."

"I want ten."

"Ten?" said Vivian, feeling her heart contract as she thought of all those grandchildren.

She got out of the car and walked around to the other side, helping Dani, who was still clutching the baby, to get out. They walked up to the porch. Someone had scrawled the words CHILD KILLER on the beautiful gingerbreading with black spray paint.

Dani put her finger on the doorbell, but before she could ring it, Maureen pulled open the door. She looked pale, ashen, dark semicircles carved under each eye.

"Dani." Maureen's voice was barely audible. "Oh, Dani."

"Here," said Dani, choking as she held out the infant.

Maureen took the baby in her arms. She gripped the child, her body shaking as she cried, kissing the baby's forehead over and over. For several minutes she seemed totally lost in the reunion, unaware of Dani and Vivian standing there. But finally she looked up, her cheeks wet. "Dani . . . I don't know what to say. Thank you."

Dani was silent, standing rigidly.

"*Dani* . . . I wronged you. I know I did. I refused to believe you. Can you ever . . ." Maureen started to cry again.

Dani waited. Then the words burst out of her in a low, passionate plea. "Can I see Whitney again? I mean, can I ever come and visit?"

"Yes, of course. But you'll have to come and visit us in Maine; that's where we're going. You can stay as long as you want, any time you want."

Dani's face lighted up, sunlight spreading across her features as her smile became dazzling. "Maine. I've never been to Maine. Does it have any ocean? Oh, Mrs. Vivian," she said, looking at Vivian, instinctively turning to her to share this joy, this pleasure so deep.

"Dani," said Vivian, touched beyond measure as she pulled the girl to her.